ACKNOWLEDGEMENTS

I'd like to express my appreciation to my Wife Donna for her assistance in editing and reflecting upon the content of this Book. A special thanks goes out to my buddy Lou Anderson who provided insight, support, and suggestions which enhanced the final writing. I also appreciate my lifelong friend Jim Olson who wrote a book and assisted both Lou and me with content and technical support.

Thanks to the many people whom I had encountered throughout my career as a law enforcement officer, and the many martial artists who provided me with the skills that enabled me to come home at the end of my shift.

Thanks to my kids Blake and Kenna who have a special place in my heart. Thank you, Zeus, my four-legged furry companion who laid patiently in the chair beside me during the many hours of typing and revising.

Most of all, thank you God for your grace that is eternal.

THE SHADOW AT TIMBER CREEK

By Gale J. Swihart

Introduction

Imagine leaving your home and your life to start fresh. You're no longer young but you're not too old to start again. You find yourself behind the wheel of your car driving and later landing into a picturesque setting of the small country town of Timber Creek. The breath of fresh air pulls you to a pause and into a small diner that changes your life forever.

Josh Stark is a recently retired law enforcement officer come to town in search of a new life. Kim Cooper is the charming and beautiful manager of Sandy's Diner who is captivated by this kind and unique stranger.

A series of events coupled with violence and even death falls upon Timber Creek. Is this stranger bringing or simply responding to these onsets?

The writer takes the reader on a journey down roadways paved with the unexplained and romance as Josh and Kim struggle to find answers. Are visions and apparitions good, evil, or just imagination? How would you respond to such messages? Dive in to these pages and see how true love and righteousness can conquer or tame the evil in this world in which we live. Then embrace the reality that true love does exist.

TABLE OF CONTENTS

Chapter 1

"Sandy's Diner"

The hot Oklahoma sun came up over the treetops and woke the sleepy morning. The red clay banks along the shoulder appeared as friendly sculptured invitations. Dry grass along the ditch waved a gracious gesture as the wind echoed off the dirt ridges and whistled a soothing song. To add special enhanced effects the early morning dew steamed off the blacktop upward toward the heavens for a soft invitation.

Although he was in a strange and unfamiliar setting Josh felt comfortable and at ease. The disappointment he carried was lifting along with the dew dancing into the sky. He drove onward into the morning wonder.

As Josh followed the bend in the road, he caught glimpse of a restaurant up ahead with a sign, "Sandy's Diner." The thought of a warm country breakfast slowed the white 4-Runner and pulled it into the parking lot. Josh climbed out of his car, stretched, and inhaled as he smelled the fresh fragrance of an old country atmosphere. Josh opened the heavy glass door of the café and stepped into the cool air. He breathed deeply and quickly melted into a red leather booth. It was as if he had walked back into time and entered an old Hank Williams song. Old men sat at the counter wearing straw cowboy hats, checkered shirts with pearl buttons, and ironed blue coveralls. A pole across the bottom counter stools found dusty cowboy boots that had been in and out of pastures for many years. An attractive waitress approached and asked, "Coffee?"

Josh paused and answered, "Please." The smile from the waitress reminded him of his age. He thought she looked young enough to be his daughter. At 48 years old he was a lost and wondering soul looking for answers. He had gone off on a journey toward an unknown destination in search for answers to questions that he knew not. All he knew was that he needed to get away. So, he left it all. And here he was. Someplace else, somewhere new. A place other than where he had been. A place where he hoped would provide some clues. At least he felt relieved and free.

Josh had spent the last twenty plus years of his life as a law enforcement officer and had embraced both the joys and the ills of the profession. Although it was exciting, he later found that it was a young man's game. He had spent much of his entire career as a patrolman working the streets. He also became a part time SWAT team member, a training officer, and a defensive tactics instructor. Unfortunately, the politics of the department began to erode the pleasure. Once administration became more of an enemy than a friend, he lost the passion.

Josh was an honorable man and believed that ethics and morality held greater treasures than status and wealth. The measure of success was determined by the amount of value you brought to people's lives and not the number of certificates hung on an office wall. As the years passed Josh became more distraught with the inconsistencies and incompetence of the courts, the ridicule and dishonesty of the media, and the lack of support from the citizens.

When the department lost its vision and direction Josh lost his motivation and left the profession. Now here he sits in a quiet café in search of a new life.

He felt the warmth and comfort as if he was seated in a picturesque Norman Rockwell painting. The waitress smiled and comforted her guests in a unique heart filled manner. The magnificence of her physical beauty was overwhelmingly enhanced by her inner beauty. This lady appeared angelic. She was as a magnet pulling Josh away from his trouble status toward her heavenly being. He was deeply and sincerely intrigued.

The reflection and sips from the coffee brought focus and awareness to Josh as he rested his tired and troubled body. The door opened and closed as customers entered and took up residence. Smiles and greetings projected from the waitress like the bright morning sun. The sound of warm and friendly voices shared the air that contained the fragrance of fried eggs and bacon. The Danish rolls displayed in the glass container upon the counter brought back memories of the old Walgreens when Josh was a child.

The wind outside picked up dust from the cratered gravel parking lot and created curved tornado silhouettes that danced about. Josh glanced out the window occasionally and watched the performance. He couldn't resist the temptation to look over his right shoulder from time to time to catch a glance of the attractive waitress who moved gracefully and quickly around the diner dropping smiles and friendly salutations. Her attractiveness was irresistible and he felt slightly embarrassed as she would occasionally look up to catch his observations. As his eyes paned around the scenery, he caught glimpse of what appeared to be a shadow out of the corner of his eye that disappeared as quickly as it had appeared.

The door opened hard and like a flash of cold air startled the warm and comforting moment. Josh felt his body tense and his heart race as all became quiet. Then beside him he heard a voice shout, "Cliff! You get on out of here right now! The police are out looking for you!"

At the end of the counter sat a woman who looked up in fear. Her long brown hair fell back and showed a dark and swollen left eye. Josh stood up and blocked the isle. His body tensed and his eyes focused tightly upon the opponent who approached him. The waitress stepped back with wide eyes and pressed against the counter chairs. Cliff stopped and stared down Josh as he deeply mumbled, "Out of the way old man this does not concern you."

Josh smiled and calmly said, "The lady said you should leave. You're going to have a very bad day if you don't take her advice."

Cliff continued forward with tight teeth and drew back as if to punch. Josh quickly stepped forward and threw a quick punch to his throat. The impact sounded like a hammer striking a hollow tree. A bone braking elbow impacted Cliff's ribs and tilted the big man over. Josh then grabbed Cliff by the throat with his right hand, encircled Cliff's right arm with the other, dropped to his knee, and threw Cliff to the ground. The thud shook the diner. The six foot four two-hundred-and-fifty-pound man laid in silence. The cook came running around the counter and shouted, "I called 911, they'll be right here!"

The entire diner was silent as Josh reached over, took a sip of coffee, and asked, "Young lady. Can I get you to warm this up a bit?"

The waitress stood in shock but slowly answered with a grin, "Sure… old man."
Josh could hear the sirens coming from the distance as he sat back down. Cliff gasped for air and rolled to his side.

Josh looked around, bent over, and softly whispered, "You better stay down asshole or I'll rip your kneecap off and throw it out in the parking lot." Cliff slowly rolled over onto his back and glared in fear.

A thunder of dust followed the two police cars that slid into the parking lot. Two police officers rushed into the diner and quickly handcuffed Cliff. They pulled him to his feet and escorted him toward the back of a patrol car. One officer opened the rear door of the patrol car as the second, an athletic built black man, firmly pressed Cliff against the roof of the patrol car. The veins of the officer's neck were swelling along with his biceps that appeared to nearly burst out of his short-sleeved shirt.

Cliff began to speak but was quickly silenced as a strong hand forced his neck forward to the inviting warm roof. The officer aggressively shouted into Cliff's ear with wide eyes and great emotion. The black officer then pulled him back and shoved him into the back seat. The waitress had followed the officers outside and stood talking with the black distinguished and professional appearing officer who wrote on a small note pad. The officer's disposition quickly changed as a smile came across his face accompanied by friendly nods. Josh looked back and saw the waitress grin at him as she continued conversing. A few old men in the booth behind Josh snickered as they whispered and nodded in agreement.

After a few minutes the black police officer entered the diner and approached Josh. "Sir, may I see some identification?" Josh leaned over to retrieve his wallet from his back pocket and replied, "Yes sir." Josh handed over his driver's license and watched the officer walk back outside.

The waitress returned inside and approached Josh. "The owner would be pleased to offer that breakfast is on the house." Josh looked up and noticed that the young waitress was not actually as young as he had first thought. She had a youthful looking face and a slim figure but showed maturity around her smiling eyes. As Josh began to speak, she quickly interrupted him and said in a slight southern draw, "Wait. Let me just surprise you with our big breakfast." She then winked and walked away as quickly as the police officer returned.

The police officer sat down across from Josh and said, "Pleased to meet you Officer Stark, I'm Officer Lou Powell."

Josh quickly responded, "I'm retired."

Lou quickly said, "Why didn't you identify yourself?"

Josh responded, "I'm not presently armed and I am no longer on the job. I also did not feel the need to announce a position I no longer held."

Lou leaned back and said, "Well, usually we frown upon fighting in public in this town. But since everyone agrees that you were defending yourself and it was ole Cliff who got his ass beat. I guess all is well. Besides, that fool needed his noggin knocked."

Josh and Lou traded dialog back and forth and very soon appeared as if they were old friends. Josh said, "I expected to find laid back donut eating cops out here in the boonies. Not distinguished track stars."

The waitress sat down a cup of coffee in front of Lou. Lou thanked her, took a sip, and replied. "Well, you see us kind are a valued commodity out here. With diversity and all becoming popular an old burned-out city cop like you may even be worth something."

Josh looked out the window and drifted off into the distance as he said, "No. My season is gone and past."

Lou leaned back and replied, "It didn't show by the way you kicked old Cliff's ass." Both men chuckled.

The waitress brought Josh his breakfast. Josh leaned back and said, "Wow. That's what I call a breakfast." The waitresses' big blue eyes brightened as she smiled and walked off.
Josh took a bite of toast, slyly looked around, and said to Lou. "I don't imagine that you have any ornerier varmints one could counsel around here for a free lunch?"

Lou smiled and said, "Just wait until dinner time when I get off. All the assholes are locked up now thanks to you. We gotta wait awhile for all the others to get ripe for pickin'!" "What brings you out here to Timber Creek?"

Josh stirred up the eggs, took a bite with folded toast, and replied, "Well, I heard that this was an exciting town and I decided to check it out."

Lou stirred his coffee, smiled, and said, "Yep. This is about the most excitement we've had around here in a long time. Ole Cliff here decided to bust the chops of his lady friend and run off last night. He hid out in the woods then after he sobered up, he came here to apologize. Then you came around and ended up ruining his day. Eight thousand people in this town and you just met the meanest and the sweetest at the same place at the same damn time. The waitress there, Kim, can melt the winter ice off the windshield of your car with just her smile."

Josh glanced out the window toward the calm and peaceful meadow shared by the carefree cows. He wondered how anything violent could come to this setting. He then saw a dark shadow out of the corner of his eye.

Josh started to speak but was interrupted by Lou's radio. Three beeps followed by, "Officer down! Officer down at 1200 Pine Dr. Responding units be advised that a county officer has been shot by an unknown suspect who fled Southbound on foot."

Lou squirmed out of the booth mumbling, "Shit! That's right around the corner and Carl is clear back at the station."

Josh said, "I'll go."

Lou ran out the door with Josh in pursuit and replied, "No. Well, shit! All right. I'm asking you for assistance. Get in!"

Chapter 2
"Officer Down"

Both men rushed into the patrol car that threw gravel into the calm quiet morning sky. Lou shouted, "Under the seat between your legs I keep a backup revolver."

Josh retrieved the .357 magnum, put on his seat belt, and said, "Now remember. I'm retired. Don't get me killed yet." Lou looked back for traffic and slightly grinned as he glanced over at Josh and slid the car sideways onto the blacktop road.

They only drove approximately ten seconds when Lou pulled over and stopped. Lou radioed dispatch Josh's description and advised that Josh would be assisting him.

Both men rolled out of the patrol car and ran up to the driver's side of the deputy sheriff's car that still had its emergency lights flashing. There were three bullet holes through the windshield and the deputy lied motionless with a hole above his right eye. His head was tilted back and formed against the head rest. Blood and brain matter oozed around his neck and drained a red stream down the front of his uniform. Both men momentarily lowered their eyebrows and tightened their jaw muscles. In front of the deputy's car was a white caprice with the engine running and no one in sight. Lou got on the radio and notified dispatch of his findings.
Lou glanced over and saw Josh staring down at the ground and asked, "What do you see?"

Josh replied, "A real problem. The shooter has a rifle. You better tell everyone." Josh reached down and picked up some rifle

casings with the first knuckles of his left index and middle finger.
"Looks like a .223."

Josh held the warm rifle casing as he turned and looked out between the houses while Lou spoke on his portable radio. His attention tightly focused as his right hand slowly came up to brush the handle of the .357 now tucked in his waist band. People began to look out their windows. A few screen doors opened.
Lou asked Dispatch, "501. Who's the reporting party?"

Dispatch answered, "The resident at 1603 Pine, Emily Soothers, whom we lost contact with."

Lou and Josh ran across the street and were met by a shaking woman at the door. "They ran that way. Is that officer alright?"

Lou anxiously asked, "What did they look like?" The woman gave a description which Lou relayed to Dispatch.
Lou asked for a return on the registration which Dispatch explained showed to be stolen as of yesterday out of Oklahoma City.
Lou looked at the white Caprice and said, "I bet those are the same bastards who robbed the liquor store up North and shot the clerk in the face with a .45."

Josh replied, "Well, they've stepped up to a rifle now and they're killing cops. You're going to be busy for the next several hours." A blue unmarked car sped toward the scene and skidded to a stop.

Lou replied, "Yep. The chief is here and you can bet there is going to be spit flying when they start arguing about jurisdiction over this one."

As the chief stepped out of the patrol car Dispatch announced, "501 and responding officers be advised that a neighbor reported that he just saw the suspects enter the back door of the residence at 1817 Pine St." All three men looked at each other. The chief radioed, "100. Officers maintain their positions." He then looked at Lou and Josh and said, "Grab your shotgun. We don't want any stray rounds in this neighborhood."

The chief gritted his teeth and said, "You boys hoof it over through the backyards. I'll drive up Pine and maintain a visual." Lou and Josh sprinted across the street and hurtled fences as they headed toward the address. Josh removed the pistol from his waist band and lengthened his strides as he ran along side of Lou.

Josh asked, "Are you robo-cop or do you simply run all the time?"

Lou replied, "I used to play football until my knee blew out." As they jumped a ditch both men hit the ground, rolled to their feet, and continued running.

Lou said, "Damn. If you hadn't said you were from Kansas, I'd swear your daddy was part Oklahoma greyhound."

Lou began to slow and said, "Ok. It's got to be one of those houses right ahead of us."

Both Lou and Josh kneeled down behind a bush and watched. Lou tossed Josh the shotgun.

Josh checked that there was a shell in the chamber of the shotgun, released the safety, held his trigger finger along the trigger guard and replied, "How many rounds do I have?"

Lou answered, "Eight buckshot with four slugs in the stock."

Lou and Josh moved forward just behind a metal shed. The rear door to the house was closed but the windows were open. The chief was giving instructions to Dispatch as he maintained surveillance three doors west of the residence. Lou got down on his knees, held his .45 pistol in one hand, and wiped the sweat from his forehead with the other as he peaked around the corner of the shed. Lou looked back at Josh, sighed, and said, "Man. I'm sorry I got you into this."

Josh smiled, "You didn't. I got me into this. But you will really piss me off if you get me killed my first day in town with that steaming beauty alone back at the diner."

Lou glared at the house, leaned back, and answered, "Well, seeing is all you're going to do with that sweet waitresses. Every stud in town has tried to get some of that. No one's scored yet."

Josh sat back and frowned, "How can you be so sure?"

Lou sat down and replied, "The cook there, Carl, he knows everything that goes on in town. He's a regular Cara Edwards."

Josh said, "You're too young to know about Cara Edwards."

Lou smiled, "This is a small town and we all watch Andy Mayberry." Both men chuckled.

Josh looked down the roll of peaceful houses and felt the calmness in the air. It didn't seem like evil could arrive in such an innocent setting. But the last twenty years of his life had taught him differently. He was accustomed to resting in calm waters and quickly feeling a tidal wave appear. Out of the corner of his eye he saw what appeared to be a shadow standing in the back doorway through the window. Josh blinked his eyes and it was gone.

The warm Oklahoma air quickly heated up as a terrified scream came from the house. Lou announced over the radio, "501. There's a woman screaming inside. We're making entry from the rear!" Both men rushed to their feet and ran for the back door. Lou quietly opened the door and paused inside the kitchen to listen. Josh stood on his left with the shotgun against his shoulder pointing at the ground and toward the living room doorway.

In the next room they could hear an angry deep voice say, "Bitch! I told you to shut up!" A soft timid voice was crying in the distance.

Lou and Josh rushed through the doorway.

In the living room stood a man holding a rifle with wide eyes that showed unfriendly intentions as he looked out the front window. Both Lou and Josh shouted, "Stop! Police!"

The man with the rifle began to turn toward Lou and Josh. As his shoulders turned square the gun battle began. Lou fired two shots with his .45 and struck the man in the chest. At the same time a shotgun blast struck the man also in the chest and threw his body backward. A second shotgun blast impacted the mortally wounded man and lifted his off his feet and sent him crashing against the wall. As Josh pumped another round into the shotgun the empty casing flew through the air as if in slow motion. Off to the right side of the room was a second suspect. Josh instantly pointed the smoking barrel toward the second suspect who stood behind the crying woman. The man held the woman tightly around the neck and fronted her as a shield. The woman gasped for air as blood ran from her mouth and split lip. A handgun was pressed to the right side of the woman's head.

The man's eyes were wide open and glaring like headlights on a semi as he profusely sweated and shouted "Put the guns down or she dies right now!" Josh slowly lowered the shotgun and moved to his left. The man had his full attention on Lou who was closer and moving slowly to the right. The perpetrator began to feel a second of relief which was about to abruptly end.

As the shotgun lowered toward the ground it quickly came up and exploded. Buckshot struck the man's left leg below the knee and sprayed bone and flesh across the room. Blood sprayed like a garden hose as the man's face turned to horror. Before his balance could give way a shot from Lou's .45 grazed his head. Josh pumped another shell into the chamber as the man fell to the left away from the woman. As the man's body neared the ground another shotgun blast struck him in the chest, spun him around in midair, and landed him on his chest. Josh quickly chambered another round and gently lowered the weapon that lay silent with a mild stream of smoke seeping from the barrel.

The woman fell to her knees shaking. Lou maintained his arms stretched outward with his .45 scanning the living room. He came upon a tiny crying girl in the corner whom he bent down to comfort.

Josh held the barrel of the shotgun upward and bent down to hold the traumatized woman. "It's alright. Is there anyone else here in the house?" The shaking woman shook her head.

Two bloody dead men lay motionless on the ground. Blood ran like a river out of their bodies and onto the carpet. Lou picked up the little girl and Josh helped the woman to her feet as they went outside to meet a parade of running police officers and rescue personnel.

The chief ran up to Lou and excitedly asked, "Are you alright?" Lou nodded his head and got a pat on his back by a passing officer.

Both the woman and the child were handed off to medical personnel. Officers entered the residence, checked the deceased suspects, and then searched the house to confirm that no one else was present.

The chief pulled both men together and said, "We're going to get you the hell out of here in a minute. I want you to both briefly tell me only about the shoot. I'm talking about a one-minute synopsis for the initial investigation and the media who should be slithering here any minute now. In 48 hours, we'll ask you to provide a formal statement and we'll have an attorney present for you. Remember; don't discuss this matter with anyone other than your spouses." The chief gently guided his arms around the shoulders of both men as he slowly spoke.

The chief then looked at Josh. "You must be new. Are you one of Bill's boys?" The chief was a tough well-seasoned looking man. He looked to be in his 60's with grey hair combed back. He reminded Josh of a shorter version of Clint Eastwood.

As Josh opened his mouth to speak Lou interrupted. "Josh is a recently retired Kansas officer who happened to be in the diner when the call came out. I knew help was several minutes away so I asked him to assist. He's also the reason Cliff's in jail right now with his clock cleaned."

The chief reached out his hand to Josh and said, "Name's Nate Baker. Thanks for your help." The chief motioned for another officer to come over and said, "Billy. Get this man's information and take him back to where he's staying. Make sure you brief him in complete detail."

Billy rushed over and replied, "Yes chief." Josh and Billy walked away and climbed into a parked patrol car.

The chief answered his telephone with his arm around Lou and stood motionless. He listened intensely as he began to slowly escort Lou to his patrol car and motioned for Lou to get in. Lou sat silent as his ears began to clear. He had never fired his weapon without hearing protection and the close quarters of the house had magnified the blast. His ears were ringing and he appeared to melt into the seat as the adrenalin dissipated from his shaky body. The chief listened intensely and finally asked, "Does the sheriff know all this? Print all of that and have Sara teletype for copies of those reports. Thank you, Lilly."

The chief folded his phone, placed it back on his belt, and looked at Lou. "Young man, it sounds like you and your friend are going to have your pictures on cereal boxes and such. Those two varmints back there are meth-heads and have been on a crime spree across the nation. They've left a trail of bodies and broken lives all the way to Timber Creek. In addition, that woman and little girl

back there are kin to the mayor. You've saved their lives and put
two evil bastards in hell where they belong. Damn good job."
The chief closed his window, turned up the air conditioner, and
calmly spoke in a comforting tone like a pastor in Sunday School.
"Lou. You're going to have a lot of unfamiliar feelings and
emotions going on inside your head for a while. This experience is
something we sign up for when we take the oath. You have accepted
the responsibility of trying to clean up all the crap that jeopardizes
the health of our community. The people here appreciate you
although they may not always show it and may not always realize
it."

The chief continued to preach and clinch his fist as he
emphasized, "Lou. Men like us take on this job because we can do it
and it needs to be done!" He then relaxed his hand, smiled, patted
Lou on the shoulder and said, "Lou. It's like a war out there. We're
warriors and we fight wars. We've just won this battle. Yes sir.
The good guys won this one. We took some lives in order to save
some lives. If those two men had gotten away there would have
been some little girl crying without her mommy."

Lou was a well-seasoned officer but the reassurance from the
chief added both confidence and relief. The chief was a true leader
who knew his men and looked after them. He was demanding but
fair. The entire community felt safe with Chief Baker looking after
them.

The chief continued, "In the next day or so a psychologist
will be calling you for an interview. Go see her and be open. Take

the next couple days to relax and be thankful that things happened as they did. You did well son. I am proud of you."

The chief then took out his pistol and handed it to Lou. "Now take this and hand over yours." Lou unholstered his .45 and traded weapons. "Once the investigation is over, you'll be reissued your weapon. You're on administrative leave per policy until further notice. Any questions?"

Lou adjusted himself in the seat and replied, "What's going to happen with Josh?"

The chief put the car into drive and replied, "Josh will be taken care of. He'll be treated like one of our own."

The chief drove Lou to the police station, shook his hand, and drove back to the shooting scene.

Josh exited Billy's patrol car at the diner where his car was parked. Billy had a chubby round face as Josh expected from a small-town cop. His belly rolled over his gun belt and bulged at the buttons.

Billy discretely whispered, "Don't worry. This is a good shoot and we have good support around here." Josh smiled and nodded as the patrol car drove off into the distance.

Josh walked toward the diner but stopped. He found that he was not in the mood for conversation. He had been in town for less than two hours and had already stomped one man and shotguned another. As he looked up, he saw the concerned face of Kim looking at him through the window. Kim half smiled and waved. Josh waved back, started the engine, and drifted across the rocky parking lot.

Chapter 3
"Paradise Motel"

The Paradise Hotel was just across the parking lot within sight distance of Sandy's Diner. Josh parked out front and walked in to meet the clerk. A rosy cheeked receptionist warmly announced, "Welcome. Would you like a room?"

Josh replied, "Yes. I guess I'll need maybe three days." Josh handed the lady his driver's license and a credit card.

The receptionists looked up with wide eyes and said, "Mr. Stark. I have orders that this reservation is to be billed to the sheriff's department. Just sign here please."

Josh smiled a puzzled sigh, signed his name, and asked, "Is there a gym around here with a weight room?"

The receptionists answered, "The community center is just North on Main Street and it's open until 10:00 or until Otis locks the door."

Josh grabbed the key and walked to his room where he entered and fell upon the crisp bed. White painted bricks upon the wall reminded him of his younger years in the military. The clean smell of the bedding was both soothing and inviting. After a brief pause, he got up, went to the community center for a weight work out, stopped by the liquor store for beer, and later stood in the warm shower with his left hand upon the wall and a Michelob Ultra in the other. As the warm water fell upon his face, he rewound the series of events that had transpired. After setting the thoughts into memory he turned off the water and stood naked in front of the steamy bathroom mirror.

Josh had a large muscular chest that gave shape to a V taper. As he lifted the beer to his mouth his bicep curled into a soft ball like shape. He was relieved to find that after all these years his stomach still tapered inward with distinct rolls of muscle. He leaned forward and looked closely into the mirror examining his eyes looking for any spots. He said to himself with concern, "If I keep seeing shadows, I'm getting these eyes checked."

He groomed himself, threw the empty beer bottle into the trash, and reached into the cooler for another but was interrupted by a knock at the door.

Josh threw on his jeans and opened the door.

There stood Lou in civilian clothes with a twelve pack of beer under his arm. "I know you were hoping for Kim but I thought perhaps some alcohol may cheer you up."

Josh smiled and said, "Well, no offense, but she's a lot prettier than you."

Lou laughed and said, "I'm glad you think so."

Lou walked in and handed Josh a beer. Josh smiled and said, "Bud light. In another ten years you'll be drinking that diet stuff, Michelob Ultra."

Lou replied, "Yep. I'll be sittin' back watching Andy Mayberry, scratching my Depends, and sucking on Michelob Ultras." Both men laughed as they sat down and opened the beers.

Josh sighed, "Things looking alright so far?"

Lou replied, "Yes. The chief is a good man and he'll make sure we're treated right. By the way, those two assholes had driven cross the Midwest on a killing and stealing rampage. God must have gotten fed up with them."

Josh looked out the window into the distance and took a drink of beer, "Yes. I recon we were in the right place at the right time."

Lou looked uneasy and said, "If I'm interrupting you, I can leave you be for now."

Josh quickly said, "No, no. I'm really glad you came by. Please down some beers and empty your mind."

Lou smiled a relief, took a drink, appeared solemn, and said, "Shooting someone was somewhat different than I had expected."

Josh turned from the window and replied, "It always is. It's situation specific and unique in every way. It brings with it costs and consequences. It contains its own little chapter in life's memories."

Josh took a drink, turned to look intensely at Lou and said, "But most of all it has its purpose, whatever that purpose may be at that particular moment. What we have to keep in perspective is what is good and what is bad. We are good and they are bad. That justifies it. It's that very simple. No need to look any further." Josh walked over to the bed across from Lou and sat down. "There's a cycle of events one must travel through during times like this. Go ahead and take that journey but keep it in perspective. They signed their death warrant not us. We did what we did because it was the right thing to do. That woman and little girl will have a tomorrow because of our actions. I think we did pretty damn good."

Lou tightened his lips and said, "Amen brother."

Both men tapped their beers together, tipped the beers back, and sat quietly. After a few seconds Lou smiled and said, "Old man. You're pretty damn good!"

Josh smiled and replied, "Well, I should be. I've been drinking this stuff for over thirty years back when you were in diapers."

Lou laughed and said, "And you can handle a shotgun like no bodies business."

Both Lou and Josh laughed and shared praises back and forth. They both felt rewarded that although they were from different walks of life and generations, they both found compatibility in each other's company. Lou was sixteen years Josh's junior and had a wife and two children to depend upon him. Josh possessed an inner quality that illuminated support to Lou and gave him comfort during this troubled time. There was a genuine bond that both men felt.

Stories passed, beers emptied, and the hours passed. Lou later telephoned an officer on duty who swung by and drove him home. Josh laid upon the bed and smiled up toward the heavens. He felt lonely but peaceful. He held confidence that God would lead him where He wanted him to go. His smile drifted him off to sleep. Outside darkness and quietness embraced Timber Creek. Stray dogs slept in the soft grass of the friendly fields. Cattle crowded under trees with timid tails that gently fanned the flies. An occasional

coyote would shout out to another who would answer with complimentary connotations. Even the stray cats laid in lazy motion upon porches and parked cars as the rowdy mice danced about.
A patrol car passed by the hotel with a sleepy police officer yawning while listening to country music playing from the FM radio.

 In the middle of town Kim lay in bed with her eyes looking up at the ceiling of her quiet bedroom. She thought about her life and the intriguing stranger who came to town. She had a special feeling about this person. He possessed a unique quality she admired and was attracted to. When she had looked into his eyes emotions were triggered that she never knew existed before.
As her heart began to beat faster, she quietly rolled out of bed and onto her knees. She prayed to God and asked for his help in calming this unfamiliar desire she had for this charismatic hero. She prayed that God would bring them together if it was His will. She then climbed back into bed to clear her mind for sleep.

 Kim was a descent, kindhearted, and respected lady in the community. She diligently pursued her responsibilities and asked for very little. Her personal ambitions and desires had been cast aside to care for her loved ones which consisted of her mother and those needy people within their community.

 As the years had come and passed Kim eventually found herself no longer a young woman. Although her dream to share her dormant love with a partner never appeared, she never gave up hope that her knight in shining armor would someday come along. As she continued to reflect and recall upon the day, she prayed that someone would rescue her from the sorrow of her lonely tears that fell in the night. She then thought about the handsome stranger who came to town.

Kim faded her thoughts and wishes to sleep. God had listened to the many nights when her tears had poured upon her pillow. He had a plan and would soon set events into motion which would soothe some lonely hearts and improve the world in which we live.

Chapter 4
"Kim Cooper"

At 0400 a.m. Josh woke up by routine and rolled out of bed to begin a series of pushups and crunches. He then performed some kata consisting of a series of blocks, kicks, and punches.

He stepped out into the warm Oklahoma morning and began to jog down the sleepy blacktop. As he ran, he did a series of sprints and jogged to listen to the dogs howling a song off in the distance. Timber Creek lay quiet as his shoes gently taped upon the blacktop. Cattle approached the barb wire and chewed inquisitively as Josh raced along the road.

After an estimated three miles Josh returned, stretched out, and drank a cup of hot green tea he had created from the portable coffee pot. He then enjoyed the warm shower as he wondered about what today may bring.

When Josh drew open the drapes, he saw the sun was just waking up over the horizon. He stepped outside and walked into the office. Sitting behind the counter with his head cocked back and his mouth wide open snoozed old Sam Clemmons.

Josh pulled the door shut and old Sam came to life. "Hot damn! I must have dozed off. Sam sat up, rubbed his eyes, and said, "mornin'." Josh answered the sleepy greeting and inquired about a newspaper.

Sam scratched his old grey beard and said, "Newspaper man's not been here yet. He usually hits Sandy's Diner first depending upon how drunk he got last night. Hank's one crazy son-of-a buck. They started lockin' him up for drunkin' driving awhile back and that kind of calmed him down a bit. You can still occasionally hear him and the misses hollerin' and a throwin' things late at night. Betty opened up his forehead many a times with a frying pan! Last year it took fourteen stitches to sew him shut! That Betty is a wild one. She dresses out to about three hundred pounds but she's as solid as a tree stump. I've seen her tote two fifty-pound bags of dog feed and drop kick ole Frankie their hound over the fence for pissin' on her porch! Ha, Ha!"

Josh chuckled as he helped himself to a cup of coffee from the pot on a nearby table.

Sam started to speak again and then paused, "Wait a minute. Might you be the feller staying in room 114?"

Josh nodded and answered, "Yes, sir."

Sam struggled to his wobbly feet and outreached his hand, "Good job son. Those sons of bitches got what they had comin'! May the Good Lord burn them in hell!"

Josh shook the man's arthritic leathery hand and answered, "I guess they came to the wrong town."

Sam excitedly replied, "Damn right! You know that Powell boy used to be one heck of a football player. He was only 225 pounds but he'd press double his weight and could run like a jack rabbit on white lightening! He graduated top of his class in college and ended up coming back here of all places just to tend to his momma. She's about 95 years of age but still gets around. That Lou's a good boy."

Josh said, "Lou seems like a first-class kind of guy."

Sam held his head up and said, "I hear tell that you can shoot a shotgun like Roy Clark can play the banjo."

Josh replied, "Well, I've fired one a time or two."

Sam whispered, "You know they've called in the State Police and the FBI on that deal. Rumor has it those murderous bastards have killed a lot of people."

Josh took a sip and said, "Well, they won't kill anymore."

Sam nodded, "Yep. Damn right!"

The old man talked about how mean the world has gotten over the years and Josh nodded in agreement. Josh had exhausted his attention but could not risk behaving rude and possibly hurting the old man's feelings. Josh leaned against the counter and glanced out the window to see Sandy's Diner illuminate inside. All of a sudden Josh got the craving for breakfast.

Josh stretched and said, "Well sir, I better let you get on with your day and get mine started."

The old man looked from side to side and said, "Yep. Oh! If you're out walkin' you best watch out for a blue pickup with the left headlight out. That's ole Hank. He's blind in one eye and can't hardly see out of the other. He's hit the fence post out there three times this month. He's liable to think you're a possum and just run you over - that crazy ole hoot!" Josh laughed and shook his head as he headed out the door.

Josh walked a couple hundred feet and as he got closer, he saw the attractive figure of a woman putting her long blonde hair back in a ponytail. He quickly recognized that it was Kim. He walked on and strategically darted around the ruts in the parking lot.

The cattle were back at the fence line chewing their cud and watching with their heads through the barb wired fence. Old gray jagged tree limbs were cut and patched as fence posts.

Josh looked over and said, "Yep it's me again. What? Is it my t-shirt or my tennis shoes with no coveralls that's confusing you?" The cattle up front stopped chewing and turned their ears forward. Josh opened the front door and stepped inside.

Kim smiled and said, "I saw you out there talkin' to the cows. Don't they have cows up there in Kansas?"

Josh smiled and said, "Yes we do. I thought that one up front resembled my Aunt Betsey." Kim laughed and poured Josh a cup of coffee.

Josh sat down and asked, "My lucky booth again?"

Kim replied, "Well, let's hope today is not as eventful for you as yesterday." Josh nodded in agreement.

Kim sat down across from Josh and said, "That woman and little girl whose life you saved yesterday are good friends of mine. They were on the telephone with me for two hours last night talking about it. I don't know what you're feeling right now but I can assure you that this whole town is grateful." Kim smiled and stood up to walk away, "Oh, and by the way. Thank you for what you did to Cliff yesterday. That bully has needed a whipping for a long time." Josh reached over and placed some equal in his coffee and slowly stirred it. He heard Kim say, "Carl, would you make the boys coffee for me today?"

A voice from around back answered, "Yes Ms. Kim."

As Josh took a sip, he was surprised to find Kim sit down in front of him with a cup of coffee. "The farmers will be in pretty soon for their morning coffee. God love 'em. All they've got to do these days is putter around their pastures and meet here every morning to talk about the old times."

Kim appeared confident yet down to earth as she spoke. Josh was caught by surprise and momentarily stared at Kim. Her bright inviting blue eyes glowed like unique sapphires that mesmerized him. Her light naturally tanned completion captivated his attention. Her smooth silky skin showed just enough essence to enhance the pinkish lip gloss that transferred to the side of the shiny coffee cup she cradled. Her blonde hair arched back above her ears, toward the top of her head into a pony tail, and flowed softly across her back. She reminded him of a model and not someone to be waiting tables at a café in some remote nowhere town. As she leaned closer toward him, he was possessed by the notion that she was not only beautiful but also eloquently charming.

Josh could no longer hold back the temptation and asked, "Kim. With all due respect, what are you doing here?"

Kim answered, "I often ask myself the same question? The bigger mystery is what are you doing here?"

Josh hesitated and answered, "I'm starting a new life but I'm not sure what or where it is. I just know it's somewhere other than where I have been."

Kim canted her face and asked, "What exactly are you looking for?"

Josh hesitated, took a sip of coffee, and answered, "Comfort, peace, meaning I guess."

Kim tilted her head and asked, "Meaning?"

Josh leaned closer and said, "I don't want to journey through a meaningless life and look back as a lonely old man to see nothing but emptiness."

Kim replied, "Are you finding meaning here in Timber Creek?"

Josh smiled and answered, "Do you want me to be honest?"

Kim smiled back, "Yes, I want you to be honest."

Josh looked around and then back into the bright blue eyes before him and answered, "I'm looking into the face of a charming and beautiful woman whom I do not want to offend by telling her so."

Kim looked back deeply into Josh's eyes and replied with a smile, "Well, with a respectful and complementing answer like that how could a woman be offended?"

Josh replied, "I'm not up to date on enticing women. I'm not young with a lot of time to beat around the bush. I'm not used to being caught off guard and being highly attracted to a woman. I do, however, have an intense desire to get to know you in a sincere and honorable sense."

Kim leaned back with folded arms, an excited aura, and said, "Well, here in Oklahoma a woman would be thrilled to hear those words coming from such a handsome and complementarily man. I guess she would love for him to ask her out."

Kim slid out from the booth with a smile.

Josh quickly spoke, "Kim. Will you have dinner with me tonight?"

Kim leaned over and whispered, "I'll meet you here at 5:00 prince charming."

Josh appeared stunned and thought to himself, "Gosh. That was easy."

The sun was coming up across the pastures and once again lifted the dew upward in a picturesque performance. The fog sifted along the low areas with magnificent mysterious connotations. Canyons and rustic old tree trunks peaked among the fog in an artistic greeting. To fully encompass the country impression a pack of three young dogs ran chasing and playing along the barb wired fence line.

An old faded pickup truck slowly pulled off the blacktop and onto the gravel parking lot. It swayed from side to side as it dipped in and out of the holes and ruts. Finally, it came to a halt and as slowly as it had arrived the door opened and out crawled an old farmer dressed in overalls.

The old man entered the diner and breathed heavily as he mumbled, "Good morning little princess." Kim stood holding a cup of steaming coffee as she patiently waited for him to slowly climb upon the counter stool.

She sat down the cup in front of him, placed her elbows on the counter and asked, "And how are those ornery hogs behavin'?"

The old man tilted his straw hat back and responded, "Houdini got out of the pen the other day and stomped through the miss's flower garden. She got after him with a shovel and chased him around the front yard. I laughed so hard I dang near soiled my britches!"

Kim's laugh was interrupted by, "Order up!" She turned around, retrieved a plate of food, and walked over toward Josh.

Kim placed the plate down in front of Josh and whispered, "You didn't finish your breakfast yesterday. Stan makes the best hash browns in the county. Some kind of special seasoning he puts on them."

Josh looked back to spot a timid wide eyed looking fellow with a white hair net intensely peeking over the order shelf at him. Josh took a bite of the hash browns and slowly chewed. He swallowed, stood up, and walked over to the counter where Stan was now shyly looking up with his head down.

Josh said, "Sir. These hash browns are the best in not only Oklahoma but the entire Midwest." Stan smiled from ear to ear as his cooking utensils chopped and turned the frying food on the grill with the skill of a samurai."

As Josh turned to return to his seat, he saw Kim was wearing an impressive smile. Josh then became detoured from his path as he saw a commotion in the parking lot.

Several pickup trucks had arrived to park. One of them had backed up and struck a car. Two young men were shouting at an old man who stood to the rear with his hands motioning in a downward manner in an unsuccessful attempt to calm the two down.

Josh quietly said, "You better call the police."
Josh approached the group and said, "It looks like we have a situation here that created an unfortunate event."

One of the younger men said, "Who the hell are you?"

Josh walked up close and said, "A messenger to remind you that you should understand that accidents happen and that you should respect your elders."

The other younger and much larger man stepped forward and said, "We don't need your ignorant advice." He then quickly extended his right arm as if to push Josh back. Josh answered the assault as he turned to the side, grabbed the large wrist, and twisted it aggressively to the outside. The large man impacted the gravel with such force that the thud could be heard inside the dinner. Josh then stomped the man's throat and turned him loose.

The talkative man stood in silence as he stared down at his friend. Josh stepped forward and said, "Do you get the message or do I need to explain it to you?" The trembling fellow shook his head. Josh said, "Now get out your driver's license and insurance card to exchange information. My breakfast is getting cold. I get really cranky when my breakfast gets cold."

As Josh turned to walk away, he stopped, turned around, and said, "If I have to come back out here you two are going to the hospital with missing parts."

The talkative one fumbled for his wallet and began talking with the old man who looked back at Josh in surprise.

Josh returned inside, sat back down, displayed a short smile at Kim, and continued to eat his breakfast. All the stools at the counter were full of old men who had turned around to audience the spectacle. One of them laughed, "Hah! A stranger comes to town and brings excitement with him. Good show young man!"

Kim gracefully walked over, placed her hand upon the booth, and said, "Well, you certainly have a way of communicating with people."

Josh chewed his food and replied out of the side of his mouth, "You've got to know how to speak their language is all." The large man eventually crawled to his feet and little by little leaned against the fender of the car. He rubbed his throat and coughed. A police officer arrived and spoke with all three men and completed a report. The vehicles cleared and the police officer drove off. Josh stood up and approached the register.

Kim looked over and said, "It's on the house."

Josh shook his head and said, "Thank you but I can't take advantage of your kind nature." He then walked over to the booth and placed a ten-dollar bill on the table. As he walked out, he paused and motioned with his mouth, "Five o'clock." Kim smiled. Josh opened the door and was met by a frantic elderly lady cradling an old leather dog leash. Kim rushed to the woman and leaned over to embrace her. The woman wore only a bathrobe and gravel-stained slippers. Her watery eyes were wide and darted frantically from side to side. Her mouth trembled upon her wrinkled and weathered face as she tried to desperately speak with shortness of breath.

Kim held her hands upon the terrified woman's shoulders and urgently asked, "Millie, what's the matter?"

Millie opened her quivering mouth and gasped to reply, "Sadie, I've lost my Sadie."

Kim tilted her head in remorse and said, "Oh Millie. Remember when Sadie became sick and we took her to Dr. Rouse?" Millie looked down in an attempt to recall. Kim continued, "And remember when Sadie hurt and would cry?" Millie looked up intensely at Kim. "And remember when Sadie stopped eating?"

Millie mumbled, "Oh."

Kim hugged Millie tightly, pulled back, and said with tearing words, "Millie, Sadie died."

Millie stood in silence and swallowed hard. Kim tried to appear strong and softly spoke, "Sadie is with God now. She doesn't hurt anymore."

Millie blinked her eyes and said, "Dear child. I am so sorry. Last night I dreamed about my Sadie. When I woke up, I found her missing from the foot of my bed. Now that I am fully awake, I can remember."

One of the farmers slid off the counter stool and said, "Come on Millie. I'm heading out and I'll drive you home."

One of the other old farmers replied, "We all forget things from time-to-time Millie. Ole Norman here forgets to get up out of bed when he goes to the bathroom at night." The group broke out in laughter.

As the farmer escorted Millie toward the door, she stopped, turned around and timidly smiled at Kim, "I still miss my Sadie." The couple drifted out the door and across the dusty parking lot.

Josh grabbed a paper napkin and handed it to Kim. Kim wiped her eyes half embarrassed and softly replied, "Thank you. Sadie was a Sheltie with a bad leg. She used to limp and Millie carried her everywhere she went. She died last month and ever since Millie has been lost." Kim then walked over to the coffee cups and began making more coffee.

Josh followed and asked, "Why doesn't she get another dog?"

Kim sniffed and said, "She said that she doesn't want another dog. But she's so lonely." Josh gently placed his hand upon Kim's shoulder. He then walked out the door, toward the motel, and was closely watched by Kim in the mirror.

Josh reached in his wallet, retrieved a business card from Lou Powell, turned it over and called the number written on the back. Lou answered and was excited to hear Josh's voice.

Lou asked, "Is today somewhat different than yesterday?"

Josh chuckled and replied, "I missed having you lead me across yards and over fences like a blood hound." Both men laughed. Josh asked, "I've got two questions for you. The first is will you and your family join me for dinner tomorrow after the deposition?"

Lou replied, "We'd be honored. Now what's the second?"

Josh discretely asked, "If you wanted to take a really special lady to dinner around here tonight where would you go?"

Lou laughed and said, "Oh my Gosh! You've got to me kidding me?!"

Josh replied, "That's what I said to myself also."

Lou paused and said, "Okay. Let's see. I'd take her straight East ten miles on highway 65 to Fantastic Fran's. I know it doesn't sound like it but they have everything especially healthy stuff like grilled chicken which Kim will probably prefer."

Josh replied, "Thanks. Fran's it is."

Lou said, "Oh before I forget. Did you have *words* with a couple of ole boys this morning?"

Josh said, "Yes by coincidence I did. They requested etiquette instruction on manners toward their elders."

Lou replied, "And I bet you graciously accommodated them."

Josh said, "I'm just here to lend a helping hand to those in need."

Lou replied, "Well, just watch that pretty 4-Runner while you're out. Those two turds are major thieves and troublemakers. They usually avoid our town because we have their number. But you hurt John's pride when you took him out so easily and he may be out to even the score."

Josh said, "Thanks for the heads up."

Lou replied, "Have fun tonight and don't be alarmed if you notice a patrol car following you around or watching your motel room. I had you put on extra patrol just in case."

Josh disconnected and returned to his quiet motel room. He laid down on the bed and closed his eyes to plan the day. This journey had been completely different than he had expected. He expected nothing other than laid back country folks and front porch hound dogs. Most of all he didn't expect to find a sweet and beautiful woman in this town of nowhere. As he fell deeply into a state of relaxation, he thought he'd just hang around this town for a while.

Timber Creek rested a little longer this morning. Saturday had arrived and most of the inhabitants who normally drove into the city sat at their kitchen tables or upon their front porches. Josh admired that this town displayed such a friendly neighborhood type atmosphere. People would wave at strangers and be seen conversing and laughing with one in other. Even the stray dogs that ran loose seemed to get along.

As 11:00 a.m. arrived Josh sat up and looked out the window. There those cows stood once again with their heads through the fence chewing their cud. He got up, walked outside, and approached the fence. "What are you still doing here now? It's the weekend. Oh, I guess you only rest on Sunday." The cattle once again turned their ears forward. One of them snorted.

Josh was excited for 5:00 to roll around. He felt like a kid back in high school.

A large truck hauling hogs pulled off the blacktop and into the rocky wavey parking lot. It slowly came to a halt and idled like a lion purring after a big meal. The mud flaps had mirrored images of a naked woman that rattled in rhythm with the singing diesel. The creaky driver's door opened, the engine shut down, and out slid what Josh had expected. An elderly bent-over truck driver dressed in overalls stumbled slowly. Josh folded his arms and walked over with half a smile. The driver placed his hands on the fender of the truck, stretched back, and groaned. His back snapped and popped like a hog eating eggshells and watermelon rinds.

"Whew! I'll need some Knob Creek tonight."

As the driver slowly twisted his body from side to side, he grunted his teeth and squinted his eyes while he looked up at the sky. He stopped, took a deep breath, and noticed Josh standing in puzzlement. The driver said, "Mornin' young man. Has Hank showed up with the newspaper yet?"

Josh replied, "No sir, I recon not."

The driver said, "Dang him. His wife probably whooped up on him again last night." You must be new around these parts, "Names Floyd Parker." His arm reached out and shook Josh's hand firmly.

Josh replied, "Josh Stark."

Floyd took a breath of fresh air through his nose and spit a stream of chewing tobacco the distance of about ten feet striking an empty beer can. "Watch them there hogs. They can squirt pee on you from ten feet away. They're going to market so I recon they don't feel like they have anything to lose. Ha, ha." The old man hobbled off toward the diner.

Josh climbed into his 4-Runner and drove Eastbound. He thought he'd check out the Fran's restaurant and become somewhat familiar with the area.

Josh opened his sunroof, cracked the back window, and felt the refreshing country air blow against his head. He reached under his seat and felt the handle of his stainless-steel Colt .45 still in place. He watched the wheat fields wave in the wind to welcome his presence. The hawks roosting upon the fence posts sat with attentive attention. A stray dog would occasionally perk up its ears and come running with its tongue flopping in the wind. A buzzard gracefully hovered overhead.

After about fifteen minutes of a relaxing journey, he saw the sign, "Meadville", up ahead. There off to the side was the restaurant just like Lou had described. He continued onward and into the small town.

He saw convenience stores with pickup trucks and older dusty domestic cars parked everywhere. Young children played about on bicycles and swing sets. Neighbors sat on the front porch drinking coffee, smoking cigarettes, and talking. People stared at him in an inquisitive like manner.

Josh noticed a drive-in theatre up ahead. He hadn't seen a drive-in for quite some time. He slowed and saw that the sign said, "Swap Meet Saturday." Josh said to himself, "Cool. I've got to check this out."

Josh parked his 4-Runner and smiled with amazement at the rolls and rolls of sellers. The parking lot was filling up minute by minute. Josh walked along the isles and saw all types of items for sales from antiques to simply junk. Josh loved antiques and the adventure of analyzing where they came from and what they were worth.

Josh found himself engulfed in the shelves of old tools and collectibles. He would converse and joke with the sellers and quickly felt comfortable and at ease. He found an old black man that sold knives and military bayonets. They spoke for several minutes. Josh ended up buying one of the bayonets.

As Josh looked at his watch, he found that his stomach agreed that it was time for lunch. He walked toward his vehicle and came across a little girl sitting by a box with a sign that read, "Puppies 4-Sale $20." Josh looked down and saw that they were Sheltie puppies. Josh said, "Wow. Those are some sweet darling puppies."

The little girl smiled and said, "We don't have papers for them but they are real Sheltie puppies."

Josh bent down and saw a smaller one in the corner. He asked, "Can I see that one there."

The little girl frowned, "I'm sorry but that one's defective." Josh laughed, "Defective?"

The little girl picked up the puppy and said, "You see her back leg has a birth defect and is shorter than the others. Momma said that I should bring her here anyway because she would be sad to not be with her brothers and sisters."

Josh kneeled down and said, "Well, I think I know just the right person who would love to have that puppy."

The little girl looked excited and said, "Really?!"

The little girl said, "You can have her for a discount if you want."

The puppy wagged her tail and curled up in the little girls' arms.

Josh smiled and said, "Here. I would feel guilty if I didn't give you $20 because she is so precious and well worth it." The little girl smiled from ear to ear.

Josh took out $25, handed it to the little girl, and said, "Here. For being such a helpful and professional sales lady, you deserve a tip."

The little girl's eyes widened and mouth opened. "Thank you, sir!!"

Josh was excited himself as he hurried to his vehicle. He grabbed a towel and threw it in the front passenger seat for the puppy to lie upon. The puppy lay still with its head down and eyes looking up. When he reached over to pet her, he was amused at the little tail that wagged excitedly from side to side. He then headed back to Timber Creek with a smile upon his face.

Josh pulled up in front of Sandy's Diner and jumped out with the puppy under his arm.

Kim rushed to the door to meet him with a smile, "What do you have there?" People in the diner all looked over.

Josh announced, "Folks. I need your help. Can you all sit tight here for ten minutes while this lovely lady and I run an errand?" Everyone nodded their heads. Some appeared puzzled. Several smiled.

Josh respectfully put his arm around Kim and said, "I need your help. Come on." Kim signed, "Oh. She's so cute. What are you…..? I don't believe it!"

Josh escorted Kim to his 4-Runner and said, "This better work because I'm too old to be raising young ins." Kim laughed. Josh and Kim drove up to Millie's and knocked on the screen door.

After a few minutes Millie opened the door and said, "Kim. Oh, you brought that handsome young man with you, how sweet. And…What do you have there?"

Josh held the puppy in his arms and tenderly said, "Millie. I got this puppy that desperately needs a home. She has a birth defect with one leg shorter than another. I can't keep her and the owner said that she's not good for anything. What do you think?"

Millie's eyes got big and her mouth opened, "Those silly people. She would be just fine for running off mice and warning when strangers come around. I limp around myself a bit but my grand babies like me learning them to build animals out of clay."

Josh handed Millie the puppy and said, "Would you like to hold her?" Before Millie could answer Josh placed the puppy in her arms. The puppy lay quietly, wagged her tail, and licked Millie's cheek. Millie smiled and gently petted the puppy with watery eyes. Josh asked, "I'm told that all God's creatures need love." Millie tenderly looked down and nodded her head.

Kim placed her hand gently upon Millie's shoulder and said, "How sweet. She sure does take to you."

Millie nodded and said, "I guess I could give her a home being that you are busy and can't care for her and all. Animals need people who have the time and patience you know. No offense."

Josh smiled and said, "None taken. Well, Kim here needs to get to work and I've got appointments to keep. If you change your mind, I won't be far."

Millie discretely sobbed and quickly said, "I won't be changing my mind. God bless you young man." The puppy looked back at Josh and wagged her tail.

Josh and Kim drove away in silence. When they walked from the 4-Runner and reached the diner door Josh noticed that he had been holding Kim's hand the entire time.

Kim looked down and with a smile and said, "That was really something back there."

Josh held his arms out and said, "The Lord works in many mysterious ways." He then opened the door for Kim to enter and placed his hand upon the old man seated at the register, "Sir. Did everyone behave themselves?"

The old codger replied, "Well, Ralph here passed wind but other than that all was calm." The entire diner burst into laughter as Josh walked out shaking his head.

Josh returned to his motel room and again rested upon the bed. He felt like he had accomplished something by matching the puppy with the needy old lady. He silently said a prayer of thanks to God. Throughout his journey in life, he had come to believe that God was always present. Although He did not always answer his prayers in the way that we asked he believed that God was always there listening. Josh often felt guilty for his lack of church attendance but made a commitment to bring the Lord into his new life.

After a few minutes Josh stood up and closed the blinds. He changed his clothes and put on a karate gee then practiced a series of punches, blocks, and kicks again. He worked hard and long until sweat filled the uniform. He felt his muscles pump and respond to the demand of the movements. He rehearsed scenarios over and over until his movements countered every imaginable assault. After an hour or so he was exhausted. He lay upon the floor in mediation until his heart rate slowed and clarity filled his senses.

His relaxation was interrupted by a vehicle that pulled up two doors down. Car doors opened and slammed in connection with young voices. Josh rose to his feet, took a shower, and realized in all the excitement he had forgotten lunch. He turned on the television and rummaged through a box for a protein bar and banana. After a few minutes he retrieved his laptop to check his e-mail and the news.

Josh often became irritated at watching the news on television because the liberal side always left out facts and projected a biased image. All the incidents he had been involved in showed fabrication and not reality. The most irritating ones were the police brutality videos where the news purposely left out the beginning where the suspect had cursed and punched the police first. It almost never disclosed that the suspect had been arrested on fourteen previous occasions for the same thing. Josh believed that he had never arrested a person that didn't need arrested and had never slammed someone that didn't need slammed.

Josh slipped a DVD into his laptop, watched some of the latest James Bond movie, and dozed off. After a couple of hours passed, he woke up, checked the time, and began thinking about what his next move would be. His planning was quickly interrupted by thoughts of Kim. He thought of her soft skin and gentle smile. He envisioned what she looked like with her hair down and out of the country ponytail. He thought about how it would feel to hold and kiss her. He then thought how he missed the scent of a woman and how he had better think about something else before his judgment became impaired.

Josh got up, straightened the room, and got himself ready. He then eagerly drove across the parking lot and parked in front of the diner. When he walked inside, he found a different group of old codgers gathered and drinking coffee.

One of the old men turned around and said, "Afternoon young man. We were hoping you would entertain us but you never showed." A voice from the end of the counter shouted, "We're much obliged for you straightening out those two varmints yesterday who got after Ed."

Josh smiled and replied, "Well, sometimes a kick in the butt can help lubricate the mind."

Another voice said, "If you're looking for Kim, she left about two hours ago. She was lookin' mighty perky."

A deep echoed voice from under the counter said, "She should be back momentarily. She said she's going out tonight." One of the men leaned over the counter toward the other who was bent down under the sink working and said, "Norm. The crack of your butt looks like the moon on a starry night." Laughter erupted from the counter.   Ned continued, "You better fix your britches before you start scaring off customers." Everyone laughed harder. Norm climbed to his feet, pulled up his pants and replied, "Now Ned don't get yourself all riled up or the police will be getting called about you chasing Beverly around the trailer again."

A laughing voice came from a booth, "Hey. Remember when we were playing cards and thought we heard thunder?"

A responding voice said, "Yea. It turned out ole Beverly was running through the trailer for the toilet!" Everyone laughed. Then Norm chuckled, "Yep. Then pretty directly I heard a crash and her screaming something awful. I ran in to find she had been on the pot and it had fallen thru the floor with her legs sticking straight up in the air!" People were slapping their hands on the counter in hysteria.

Norm leaned against the counter with his head back gasping for air, "The fire department came out and it took five of them to hoist her out!" The waitress slapped her legs and fell back into a booth as the entire diner busted up. Norm wiped his eyes, took a deep breath, and said, "Oh Lord! You'd look through the floor and there sat the toilet down in the gravel." People held their faces in laughter. "I told her, Baby, maybe you should lay off the ho-hos for a while. She wouldn't talk to me for two days!" Hands were pounding on the counter. "After she calmed down a bit she said, Norman; do you think I'm too fat? I told her, what do you mean by too?" Laughter roared. "That one cost me sleeping on the couch for a week." People reached for napkins and shook their heads.

As Josh regained his composure the diner door opened up. He turned around and stood stunned. All the faces turned and fell into a state of silence.

Kim rose up on her toes and said, "Well Prince Charming. Are you going to stand their joking with your friends or are you going to feed a hungry lady?"

Josh stuttered, "Uh…. Goodbye everybody."

Kim turned and said, "You boys leave Norm alone and let him finish his work. This weekend rate is costing me time and a half."

Norm shook his wrench at the crowd and replied, "That's darn right now. You be sure to tell your mamma that'll be one and a half apple pies this time!"

Josh followed behind Kim dressed in a blue flowered dress cut just above her knees. Her soft blonde hair flowed backward as she walked. Her hips moved in rhythm from side to side in perfect balance. The inviting lip gloss sparkled as she turned and smiled. As Josh followed to the passenger side door, he quickly reached for the door handle and pulled. Nothing happened.

He said, "Oh. I guess I better unlock it first." Kim smiled. Josh pushed the button on the remote and the door unlocked followed by a dim beep. Kim climbed inside and Josh slowly closed the door behind her as if he was staring at a sculpture of art.

Chapter 5

"Fantastic Fran's"

As Josh walked around the front of his vehicle he glanced thru the windshield. Kim was timidly staring back at him with admiration. She found his smooth and chiseled face appealing that was accented by his short and partial graying hair. His chest protruded forward beyond his belt line which she found both admirable and desiring. When he climbed into the vehicle, she spied from the corner of her eyes how his legs were tone with a trim behind. She felt like a young girl many years in the past. Her heart pounded and the blood circulated in ways she had not ever felt before.

Kim was not used to going out much. Many years had come to pass with her following the daily routine for managing the dinner and caring for her failing mother. She turned her back on those who chased her because she had been betrayed once before and vowed to never fall victim to it again. But today she felt differently. She felt an overwhelming need to open up and trust this person whom she was attracted to and beginning to secretly desire.

Josh started the 4-Runner, put on his seat belt, and bowed his head. "Kim."

She said, "Yes."

Josh replied, "I can't resist in telling you that I have never seen a more beautiful woman in my life." A euphoric feeling came over Kim accompanied by a sigh of relief for she felt the same admiration for him. Kim blushed and smiled. She felt authentic sincerity in his demeanor.

As Josh pulled onto the blacktop and accelerated Kim said, "This is a really nice car."

Josh nodded and said, "Thank you." The 4-Runner quickly reached the speed limit and purred down the highway. A mechanic friend back in Kansas had done some modifications to the engine to enhance its power.

Kim asked, "So, have you found your plans for your future?"

Josh said, "Well, I'm still trying to figure that out but things around here are looking might appealing."

Kim smiled and replied, "You've made quite an impact around here so far."

Josh turned to her and said, "Yes. I've got the number one catch in town sitting right beside me." Kim smiled.
Josh asked, "What are your plans for the future?"

Kim thought for a moment and said, "I've not given it much thought. I guess I perhaps someday need to."

Josh nodded, cleared his throat, and said, "Do you have any kids or ever been married?"

Kim looked out the window at the telephone poles passing by and replied, "I was married once. I thought that he was the perfect man until we discovered I couldn't have children and he lost interest. He ran off with someone else and here I am. What about you?"

Josh replied, "Well, I was married once many years ago. I allowed myself to fall into the trap of putting my career before anything else. I thought that was the way it was supposed to be. It was like a military career where you go off and fight wars. Well, police officers do their battles right where they live and often forget that they have other responsibilities." Josh cleared his throat and continued, "I met her after I had become a cop and being a cop was all that I knew at the time. She left with the baby and that's about the end of the story."

Kim asked, "Why haven't you seen your child?" Josh felt embarrassed to explain how she had moved several states away and made it pretty much impossible to see him. She then convinced the boy that his father was no good.

Josh continued, "She got remarried, has other kids, and contact just faded away. After the kid turned eighteen his child support ended and he disappeared. I had heard he joined the military."

Kim's eyes looked out the window as she said, "That's horrible."

Josh swallowed hard and said, "So, you focused your future in the diner?"

Kim replied, "No, the diner belongs to my mother. I just run it for her. My sister got killed in a car accident while I was away a college. So, I came home and here I've been ever since."

Josh felt the uneasy tone in Kim's voice. He paused for a moment of silence and said, "Well, you do a wonderful job there. Your devotion illuminates for miles and miles."

Kim smiled and said in an exaggerated southern draw, "I do declare. You Kansas boys sure have a way with words."

Josh appeared solemn and replied, "I'm telling you the truth and not trying to just impress you."

Kim moved closer, patted him on the cheek, and said, "I know. You don't have to stop either." Josh smiled. Their conversation continued and brought them closer together. The wrinkles on the edges of Kim's eyes showed as she laughed. Josh was relieved to find some age.

Finally, he said, "Kim, I'm 48 years old just in case you were wondering?"

Kim cleared her voice and said, "I'm 41 Josh."

Josh sighed and said, "Thank God. I thought you were only 30." Kim laughed and perked up in the seat with pride. The 4-Runner pulled into the parking lot and came to a stop. Both Josh and Kim climbed out and met at the front of the car.

Kim replied, "I hear the food is so fresh here you can hear them chase it around the kitchen."

Josh laughed and gently reached out for her hand and led her inside.

As they stepped inside, they were greeted by a friendly greeter and the sound of George Jones singing an old country tune. She smiled, "Welcome to Fantastic Fran's. Will that be a table for two?"

Josh paused as he scanned across the area. Off to the right was a small shop with t-shirts and ball caps displayed in cases and upon shelves. To the left was a room with "Arcade" illuminated over the entry way with kids scurrying about and laughing. Forward was a large entry way giving view to a high wooden ceiling with stuffed animals on the walls and black metal ceiling fans. Josh replied, "Yes. That would be fine. This would be a haven for a taxidermist."

As the waitress looked back, she said, "And I would assume nonsmoking."

Kim responded, "You assumed correctly."

Inside the main room tables were strategically positioned around the center of a dance floor. Off to the sides were several booths carved and recessed into their own secluded places. The waitress escorted the couple to a booth, handed them menus, and said, "Your waitress will be right with you."

Josh sat across from Kim and found himself looking at the menu but captivated by Kim.

Kim caught him and said with a smile, "What?"

Josh slightly nervously replied, "Oh, nothing."

She then reached forward, turned his menu right side up, and said, "Here. Maybe this will help." They both suppressed their laughter and finally erupted.

Kim smiled, "I guess I can take that as a compliment?"

Josh nodded, "Yes, very much so."

The waitress interrupted their giggle and chuckle session with a smile, "Good evenin'. Would you like to hear our specials for the night? Well, hey, Kim!" Both the women traded greetings back and forth. The waitress excitedly said, "You folks down there in Timber Creek have really had some excitement over the last few days! Ole Cliff finally got what he had comin'. You know he ended up with three broken ribs! Then there were those two ole boys from our town who got after the elderly fellow. I wonder if that hero was the same one who helped Lou Powel gun down those murderers."

Kim replied, "Well, I recon he just could be."

As the waitress stood with her hand on her hip in deep thought she looked at Josh, back at Kim, and said, "Who's this handsome fellow?"

Kim replied, "Oh, a friend from out of town."
The three conversed for a couple of minutes; the waitress took their order, and then quickly dashed away.
As Kim and Josh looked around the room, they pointed to the different memorabilia mounted on the wall. Shortly the waitress returned with their drinks.

Kim looked puzzled as Josh diluted his shot of Knob Creek Whisky with water, "Don't let these Oklahoma boys see you ruin their worshiped whisky or you'll be fighting some more."

Josh took a sip, smiled, and replied, "If I drank it like they did I'd be getting my butt kicked just like them." Kim looked down and laughed.

Kim took a sip of wine and asked, "Is that karate you used on those guys?"

Josh replied, "It's a combination of martial arts. I used to be a defensive tactics instructor for the police department and went to a number of schools. I also took karate and jujitsu until the years caught up with me. I suffered a shoulder injury that wouldn't heal. I later found that I had arthritis in my shoulders which limited my training. So, I still practice occasionally but not with so much enthusiasm."

Kim tilted her head and asked, "How do you know what to use when?"

Josh stirred his drink and replied, "It depends upon many variables and if there are any rules. Police officers have rules. There may even be rules of etiquette among minor rivalries in bar room brawls and such."

Josh took a drink and continued. "The more you learn the more tools you have in your toolbox. If a guy is a good boxer then I'll take him to the ground. If he's a good wrestler then I'll try to soften him up with kicks and punches. But a wise man once told me something that I have always lived by."

Kim intensely leaned forward, "What?"

Josh intently looked into her eyes and said, "You know, you have the most beautiful smile."

Kim blushed in surprise, "Thank you."

Josh leaned back, "Oh, yea. Everyone has a neck."

Kim smiled and said, "You mean like bull riding where you control the head you control the animal?"

Josh replied, "Well, yes, that's true also. But if you cut off circulation to the brain you turn the switch off. And the fight is over."

Kim took a sip of wine and said, "Have you ever lost a fight."

Josh laughed and said, "Sure. Everyone has if they're being honest. There are often costs involved at both ends. You may knock the guy out right there and walk away but your cracked rib will be there a lot longer. So, often it's difficult to say who really won the fight. Like wars, fights are a part of life. It is always better to avoid one. But occasionally some poor idiot needs his attitude adjusted. And those qualified dedicated carrying persons need to step up and honor that request."

Kim laughed, "You have an unusual approach to things."

Josh took a sip, "Well, I guess that's why I'm out here at this time in my life. I guess that I'm just an unusual kind of guy."

Kim replied, "Yes. And that's a good thing. I like it." The waitress appeared with their order and caught the couple looking intensely into each other's eyes. She sat the plates down, smiled, and said, "Would you like another drink?"

Kim said, "Maybe later, thank you."

Josh replied, "No. You can keep them coming for the lady but I'm driving."

Kim leaned forward and said, "Impressive. He's respectful and responsible."

Josh replied, "Oh, I'm versatile." The restaurant was starting to fill up. Men wearing cowboy hats approached the stage with guitar cases and large crates on dollies. A few applauses and whistles could be heard from the forming audience. The outer lights began to dim and the stage lights began to slowly glow. The animal heads upon the walls took on deep shadows with glowing eyes from the lighting effects. Ole Fantastic Fran's was coming to life.

Josh had many questions he wanted to ask Kim but he did not want to appear intrusive.

Finally, he asked, "Have you ever thought about leaving Timber Creek?"

Kim wiped her mouth and replied, "I've occasionally dreamed about it but everything would have to be just right."

Josh said, "Family roots grow, deep don't they?"

Kim smiled, "Yes they do. All the people in that town are very dear to me. Most of those gentle old farmers who sit at my counter now used to bounce me on their knees and sing me songs when I was a child. I feel I have a responsibility to care for them like I need to care for my mother who is desperately failing in health. We're all one big family."

Josh asked, "Tell me about your mother?"

Kim brightly said, "My mother is one of the most wonderful creatures God put on this earth. When I was little, she'd walk into the diner and glow with joy and enthusiasm with that fiery blonde hair up in a perfectly sculptured ponytail that flowed like a fountain. Every person who walked through the doors was very special and she'd make them feel that way. The parking lot would be packed every morning so tight that customers would have to come in shifts! My father had died when I was very young so mom had to raise us on her own. She did pretty darn well too."

Josh replied, "Yes I agree. She sure did well." Kim's smile was interrupted by the illumination of strobe lights and the pounding of a base drum followed by clapping and whistling. The lead singer was pouring out a Waylon Jennings tune that was rocking down the dust from the stuffed animals and sleepy windowsills. The adrenalin was flowing and capturing everyone's attention.

It didn't take long until boots were shuffling on the dance floor and smiles were glowing from the colored lights. Eventually the drum slowed down and began to mellow the audience. The old Marty Robbins tune *"Throw your arms around this honky tonk man"* came across the microphone. Josh thought he couldn't look too incompetent in his inability to dance this slow song.

He stood up, held out his hand, and said, "Shall we?" Kim smiled in surprise and quickly joined him.

The smooth voice and slow music quickly found the couple with their arms around each other on the crowded dance floor. As the song came to an end the lead singer winked at Josh and continued with another slow song. Kim laid her cheek against his chest as Josh gently rubbed her back. Josh lowered his chin to rest against Kim's soft blonde hair. Her fragrance was more than inviting. Her body felt to melt against Josh. As the song neared toward the end Josh slowed and brushed his cheek against hers. Kim raised her head up and turned her face toward Josh. Their lips met and Josh pulled her close.

As the song slowly ended Josh released his grip and felt Kim's warm and inviting body eased inward. Josh stared into Kim's eyes and felt them smile. She led him off the dance floor and back to the booth. She then stopped, turned around, and faded back into his arms. Josh quickly held her close as the music speeded up like a freight train blaring through a tunnel.

Kim smiled and slid back into the booth.

Josh folded his hands and said, "Well now. That's the nicest dance I've ever experienced."

Kim nodded in agreement then said, "Do you want to get some fresh air?"

Josh said, "Sure. The air here sure is getting smoky and thick."

Kim replied, "Yea. And the music is getting a little too loud."

Josh whispered, "And there are too darn many people around." Kim laughed.

Josh flagged down the waitress and paid the bill. As he started to get up, he quickly looked left and appeared startled.

Kim asked, "Is everything all right?" Josh replied, "Oh, yes. The shadow off that bear over there caught my attention." The couple then walked out the door into the parking lot and into a surprise.

As Josh approached his 4-Runner with Kim at his side laughing, he heard a voice shout, "Well now. It's Mr. Manners." Josh turned around and saw three large men approach at a trot. He handed over the key to Kim and said, "Here get in the car!" Kim got in the driver's seat and started the engine. Josh stood to face the three opponents.

This was a different scene for Josh. For now, the rules that had been imposed upon him for the past twenty years were no longer present. He was the minority and he was the one in defense. With three to one he felt he had an advantage. He had no limitations with nothing to hold back. The media would have no story about how a cop had used excessive force. A defense attorney would not be present to ridicule him on the stage. He felt relieved and free. His body felt energized with rocket fuel.

Josh moved to the right in order to gain an advantage of positioning. He then said, "Now fellows it's not polite to disturb a guy when he's out trying to impress a lady. You best be on your way and go back to tipping cows or whatever you do with yourselves."

A familiar voice stepped forward and said, "We're going to kick your cocky ass back to Kansas old man!" Josh continued to move right until he had two of the three lined up. He then stepped forward and delivered a palm strike to the nose of the noisy one. The palm strike enabled Josh to avoid damaging his fist which he had practice routinely to protect his hand in case he had to draw his gun. He then delivered a front kick to the groin and a low round house strike to the leg with his opponent's shin. The large man fell to the ground.

Directly behind the first was a second who momentarily paused in shock. Josh delivered a round house kick to the left side of his face which spun number two around and toward the ground. Josh quickly stomped the man's face lying on the ground. Blood sprayed like a fountain from his mouth and shattered teeth scattered about. Josh now concentrated on the third opponent who was positioned off to his left.

The third opponent swung at Josh with a powerful right hook which Josh pushed past him with his left palm. At the same time Josh had thrown his right hand under his left elbow which enabled him to grab the opponents left wrist.

Josh quickly glanced to check the scene for other opponents and aggressively pulled the man's arm downward. He then thrust his right knee upward and impacted the man's elbow with such force that it snapped. His right hand quickly shot inward and impacted the man's throat with a mighty crash. The man lost consciences and fell to the ground like a giant wet rag doll.

As Josh glanced over his right shoulder again to check the scene it was met by a smashing blow from a large hammer fist. Josh hit the pavement and bounced. A steel toed boot then kicked him in the ribs and lifted him upward. Josh's vision was blurry and his hearing began to fade. He felt weak and heavy. As a second blow from the large boot impacted his ribs as Josh instinctively grabbed the boot and held it tight to his body.

Josh began to feel intense anger which supercharged his survival techniques. He rolled toward his opponent and caused the adversary to fall to his back. He then climbed onto the man who attempted to claw and scurry to his feet.

Josh held tightly which gave him the opportunity to rest and regain his composure. He was now in the ground fighting mode in which he was very familiar. Judging by the frantic movements of his opponent he felt confident that his adversary was uncomfortable and thus entering a state of frenzy which was the neighbor to panic. Josh held his head down and mounted his opponent which forced all his weight upon the large man's chest. Labored breathing accompanied by grunts and groans from the large man assured Josh that he was becoming successful.

Josh looked over the scene to assure that another opponent was not closing in. He then directed an elbow strike to the man's face which was held steady by the unforgiving blacktop. The man's face split open and gave way to unconsciousness.

Josh then glanced again to confirm that no one had made their way to their feet. Josh rushed to his feet and found an opponent starting to get up. He fired a side kick to the man's knee. A snap sounded like a tree limb as the man fell to his back in agony. His knee was bent backwards with agony dripping upon his defeated face. He laid on the ground shaking in silence.

Josh stood motionless with heavy breathing. He was exhausted and engulfed with furry. He approached the only conscious opponent and dropped to his knees. The opponent looked up at him in fear as his foot lay folded forward. Josh grabbed him by the hair, lifted his face upward, and whispered, "If you or anyone else ever comes looking for me I will hunt you down and kill you all! Do you understand?" The man trembled and sweated profusely. Josh then fired an elbow strike to the side of the man's head and rendered him unconscious.

Josh's 4-Runner appeared in front of him with the headlights glowing. Kim appeared then grabbed him under the arm and said, "Let's go!" She then assisted him to the passenger seat and closed the door.

The 4-Runner then sped off across the parking lot spinning tires and sliding sideways onto the blacktop highway toward Timber Creek. The modified V-8 engine roared and quickly reached eighty miles per hour.

Josh put on his seat belt breathing heavily and said, "Thank you kindly, young maiden."

Kim looked at Josh with concern and worry. She sobbed, "Are you all right?"

Josh grabbed napkins from the glove box and held them to his bloody cheek and replied, "They're hurt. I'm only nicked a little." Kim eyebrows rose as she sighed in concern. She reached out and patted his shoulder.

Josh said, "These country boys sure do hold a grudge."

Kim shook her head and said, "Well, with what I saw you do back there I doubt you'll be hearing from them ever again."

Josh reached under the driver's seat between her legs then came up with a stainless steel .45. "Just in case of an emergency here is the safety. Just point with both hands and squeeze the trigger. They'll go away." He then slipped it back into position and leaned against the head rest.

Kim breathed heavily and swallowed, with sobbing eyes and said, "Two of those guys were the ones from the accident in our parking lot. Why can't people just leave well enough alone?"

Josh leaned forward, wiped his left hand upon his pants, and then gently stroked the side of her face. "Princess, Ms. Volts taught me in fifth grade science class that for every action there is an opposite and equal reaction. This is simply the cost of admission to life."

Kim replied, "Somehow I feel kind of responsible for what happened."

Josh smiled and said, "Well, yah. If it wasn't for your irresistible smile and charismatic personality, I'd be minding my own business right there alone in that exciting motel room watching UFC movies."

Kim wiped her tears, smiled, and said, "You don't have to act like a youthful warrior taking on all the evil solders on my account."

Josh replied, "Remember that warriors fight wars, I'm not all that young, and besides it was all worth it just to hold and kiss you." Kim sniffed and smiled.

The 4-Runner came to a stop in front of room 114. Josh staggered out and was met by Kim who rushed to help him out. Josh looked in the right-side mirror and examined the damage to his face. "That's not too bad. Is it?"

Kim reached up, turned his jaw, and said, "It looks pretty darn good to me." She then kissed him.

Josh said, "Maybe we should go inside where we can get a closer look." Josh unlocked the door and the couple walked inside. Josh took his shirt off and examined his ribs in the mirror. "These country boys sure have big feet. At least nothing is broken." As Kim closely looked over Josh, she felt a little uneasy. She was highly attracted to Josh but wanted to retain his respect also. Although she wasn't getting any younger, she still valued the importance of acting a lady. She ached for Josh to hold her tight like back on the dance floor. She further felt her heart shaking as her craving lips had touched his. As Kim lowered her head in confusion Josh caught her thought.

He reached out and pulled her to him. "Hey. Thank you for what you did back there looking out for me and all." He then kissed her on the forehead.

Kim smiled and said, "Thank you for the wonderful dinner and also the amazing entertainment. Now I don't know how they do things in Kansas but down here in Oklahoma if you take a lady home before ten o'clock it means you're not interested."

Josh jumped back and said, "Give me five minutes to clean up and change then we'll be up for round two!"

Kim waltzed to the door and said, "I'll just wait outside." The door closed and Josh shook his head in admiration.

The Oklahoma moon was glowing up above. Bugs were swarming around the parking lot light with horned toads eagerly staged below. Off in the distance the moon light was reflecting off the cattle pond. There were still a few cars across the way at the diner with a younger crowd sitting at the counter. The cattle across the road lay under the shade trees all gathered together. The sound of yelping coyotes could be heard off in the valley. Kim took a deep breath as the wind gently brushed her flowing soft hair behind her back.

Josh came outside smiling and said, "Well, what do you say we go out cow tipping or frog gigging?"

Kim laughed, "That's the kind of thing you can do with your buddy Lou. Why don't we just take a stroll through town and visit?"

Josh reached out his hand and said, "Lead the way dear princess."

The couple smiled and strolled off into the moonlight across the gravel and onto the blacktop street. Shallow ditches lined the streets followed by picket fences, barking dogs, and friendly faces. Occasionally a distant voice would shout, "Hush up", at a barking dog. Rocking chairs creaked on the wooden porches and youngsters played hide and seek. Some porch lights illuminated groups of people laughing and sharing conversation. An occasional voice of greeting would shout out in a welcomed fashion.

After several blocks the couple reached the city park where Josh was excited to find a large vintage steam locomotive resting on a section of track. Josh stopped and stared in delight. "That is beautiful! Look at the front of that. Can you imagine how many cows that front stoop must have scooped out of the way?"

Kim laughed. "There's a ladder on the other side."

Josh excitedly grabbed her hand and said, "Let's go!"

The couple climbed up and inside the engine room. Josh looked out the window and said, "You know. I've always wanted to ride in one of these."

Josh turned back around quickly and found Kim looking into his eyes. He gently pulled her close and felt her arms around his back. He kissed the side of her face and slowly progressed forward to her waiting lips. The couple kissed passionately for several minutes. Their breathing increased along with their caressing. Kim slowly broke away and pressed her cheek tightly against his chest as she held him tight.

Kim said, "Josh, I don't just go out with any ole man that happens by."

Josh replied, "I know."

She continued, "I'm not the kind of woman who kisses men and lets them hold me."

Josh softly whispered, "I know."

She quietly whispered, "And I don't normally become so darn attracted to someone I just met."

Josh smiled, "I know."

Kim replied, "You know, you seem to know a lot."

Josh smiled again, "Well, all I really know is that I've traveled a great deal in my life and finally found an amazing woman who has me stopped dead in my tracks. I've had feelings lay dormant for so many years and it's hard to restrain them."

Kim looked up at him and said, "Well, then don't." The couple then continued to kiss until their mouths got tired.

As they stood in silence holding each other Josh said, "Tomorrow after the deposition I've invited Lou and his family out to eat. I was hoping that you would join us."

Kim smiled, "I would be very much pleased to accompany you, my gentle warrior." Josh laughed. The couple climbed out of the locomotive and walked throughout the park trail sharing thoughts and stories. They acted as if they were in high school laughing and holding hands.

Kim looked down at her watch, "Oh my gosh! It's almost midnight!"

Josh gazed deeply into her eyes, "Well, we better get you back before you turn into a pumpkin."

As the couple walked quickly Kim said, "My car turns into a pumpkin not me." They both laughed.

Josh escorted Kim back to her car and said, "Just in case the spell is over tomorrow can I have one of your shoes?"

Kim laughed hard, "You've held my heart in your hand tonight gentle warrior. I shall not forget you."

Josh said, "Great. I'll call you tomorrow after the meeting." Kim started her car and slowly drove off as she blew him a kiss. Josh wondered back to his motel room in a daze. He plopped himself down in a chair, checked his messages, and decided he better telephone the Sheriff's department to report his run in with the three men at the restaurant. He was told that they had all been at the hospital claiming that a bull had thrown them. The deputy said that he would complete the report for informational purposes only. Josh took a shower and drifted off to sleep with Kim intensely on his mind.

The next morning Josh went to the community center and lifted weights. He then dropped by the Baptist Church in town to attend the early Sunday morning services. Since he was wearing his suit in preparation for the meeting, he felt he could use a little spiritual assistance. The preacher was intriguing but still held an aggressive stance regarding hell and damnation. Josh always believed that the message of the Lord should be approached out of love and appreciation, not threats about going to hell. When the congregation was dismissed, he found himself in the lobby confronted by several citizens. Warm smiles and pats on the back were a surprise and quite over whelming. He felt honored to be in the company of kind and caring people.

As he started to open the door for an elderly woman, he caught a glance of the soft flow of golden hair off in the distance. Her eager eyes were glowing toward him. He continued to hold the door open and stepped to the side as he waited for Kim's arrival. Kim excitedly approached Josh with her mother at her side.

She said, "Momma, this is Josh."

Josh slightly bowed his head and said, "It is a pleasure to meet you Mrs. Cooper."

The elderly woman smiled, reached for his hand, and replied, "Pleased to finally meet you Joshua Stark. Kim's been burning my ears about you." Kim blushed. Mrs. Cooper then said, "Don't be embarrassed child. I was just as excited about your daddy. Will you join us for tea?"

Josh was caught off guard and replied, "Well, yes. That would be wonderful. I have an hour before I need to be at a meeting."

Kim smiled with excitement as the three walked toward the parking lot absorbing the delicate Oklahoma breeze. He then followed them to the Cooper house where he parked his car and rushed to assist Mrs. Cooper out of Kim's car. The group climbed the four porch stairs and waited patiently for Mrs. Cooper to retrieve her old brass key to unlock the door.

Mrs. Cooper then said, "There seems to be so much meanness out there now days that people have to lock their doors. Isn't that a shame?" Both Kim and Josh nodded in agreement.

Mrs. Cooper opened the front door and there laid a large German Shepard with its head down. Kim rushed in and said, "Arrow! Are you alright?!" Josh walked in and Arrow sat up, walked toward him, and sat down.

Josh held out his hand petted the dog and said, "Hello girl." Both Kim and Mrs. Cooper looked astonished.

Mrs. Cooper said, "Arrow never does that with strangers. As a matter of fact, she does not like men."

As Josh petted Arrow, he looked around to see the morning light reveal antiques, bright throw rugs, and glamorous glass lamps. Josh felt that he had just walked into a museum.

Mrs. Cooper said, "Well, you sure have a way with animals, don't you Mr. Stark?"

Kim held her mother by the arm and escorted her to the living room and into her rocking chair. The elderly woman appeared frail as she paused to take deep breaths and rest her cane across her lap. A small wagging dog entered the room and quickly jumped into her lap.

Mrs. Cooper smiled at the dog, placed her cane on the floor, and said, "Won't you sit down Mr. Stark. Mitsi here is my little girl. Arrow belongs to Kim."

Josh sat down upon the couch that was covered with hand stitched throws. The warm sun glowed in through the windows with glass that was thin and wavy from many years gone past. The dark stained windows were equipped with the old style of rope and pulley. Hand stitched drapes accented the antique picturesque setting.

Mrs. Cooper said, "Kim. Would you go make us some tea while this young man and I get to know one in other better?" Kim nodded and left the room while glancing back at Josh.

Mrs. Cooper looked deeply in Josh's eyes and gently petted her sleepy dog as she spoke. "Mr. Stark my Kim has taken quite a liking to you. She doesn't take to people in such a way and I've been quite amazed at her excitement. I can tell by your eyes that you are an honest and sincere man. You project off an inviting and friendly aura. As you make your journey through life, I pray that you will forever retain your good intentions in a Christian like manner. Her father is not here which leaves this old woman to bring these words to your attention. She is all I have left and she will always be my baby."

Josh listened intensely cleared his throat and replied, "Thank you for your openness and words of wisdom. I give you my word that I will always honor your daughter with respect."

Mrs. Cooper smiled and said, "Well then. With all your excitement over the last few days do you have any direction for your life's journey?" Kim entered the room carrying a tray with a shiny antique tea pot and three elegant cups. Vanilla wavers were articulacy placed about. She poured the tea and then sat down beside Josh. Both Mrs. Cooper and Josh nodded in approval and thanked her.

Josh replied, "Well, I see that you have a university about 20 miles west of here. I thought that I'd gather my resume and pay them a visit."

Kim's eyes lit up as she said, "You mean teach?"

Josh replied, "I don't have a teaching degree as such but I have a master's in management which would perhaps qualify me for some instruction. According to their web site they teach some law enforcement courses there which I believe I could qualify to teach."

Kim grabbed his hand and excitedly said, "That's wonderful!"

Mrs. Cooper smiled and said, "Twenty miles is not such a long way to commute."

Josh quickly replied, "A twenty-minute drive is just right. Besides, everything else I need is right here."

Mrs. Cooper spoke up, "Yes. I heard that you two were dancing in the park last night. Did you fall down and bruise your cheek?"

Josh replied, "Well, something like that. You've got a community center here, the wonderful park, and this wonderful dance partner. What more could anyone ask for?"

Mrs. Cooper said, "Yes. That Fantastic Fran's can get mighty wild at night.   And I've heard that dance floor can get quite slippery."
Both Kim and Josh smiled.

Josh took a drink, looked at his watch, and said, "Goodness. I need to get going. Thank you for the wonderful tea." Mrs. Cooper nodded and smiled. Kim got up and escorted Josh to the door.

She stopped and held both his hands out in front of her and said, "I am so excited about the university!"

Josh replied, "Me too. I'll give you a call as soon as the meeting is over." He then gently pulled her close and kissed the side of her face.

Chapter 6
"The Deposition"

Josh pulled up in front of the police department and went inside where he was met by a police officer who escorted him to a conference room. Along the way Lou Powell approached wearing a suit and a tie. As they passed Lou smiled, held his hand up, and discretely slapped Josh five.

Josh entered the crowded room and shook hands with everyone present. Everyone was wearing smiles and appeared very friendly as if they were attending a football game and not investigating a shooting. Josh was struggling to appear friendly but also professional and reserved.

The chief of police and the sheriff were present along with members of the district attorney's office. Other people announced their names and titles which Josh did not remember. They offered Josh a glass of water and then began their rehearsed speech. A detective explained that they had spoken with both the woman and the small child along with Officer Powell. They just wanted a brief explanation of what had happened from his point of view as the detective handed a piece of paper for Josh to sign. Sitting beside Josh was a distinguished woman who said that she was present to represent him as his lawyer. She shook Josh's hand and said that she was Cynthia Brown and all fees were being paid for by the city.

The detective said that he could begin at any time with the date, time, and place already noted in front of Josh. A stenographer was seated beside him and punched away at her machine at a rapid pace.

Josh took a drink and said, "I was speaking with Officer Lou Powell who was investigating the assault which I was a victim of involving a suspect I know only as Cliff. As we conversed, I heard a triple beep come from his radio. The Dispatcher announced that there was an officer down. Based upon my training and experience I recognized that an officer had most likely been shot and that my assistance may be needed. This assumption was confirmed when Lou said that the call was just around the corner and his back up was a distance away. I told him that I would go. He told me all right. He then asked for my assistance."

Josh looked intensely at the audience and explained that Lou had given him his back up .357 revolver which he did not use due to later being given a police shotgun issued by Officer Powell. Josh said that he has qualified with several shotguns for patrol duty including the Smith & Wesson which had been given to him.

As Josh continued the series of events, he reached the part when he and Lou were outside the residence where they believed the suspects had entered.

Josh explained, "As we waited outside the residence for assistance, I heard a woman's scream for help. Both Officer Powell and I rushed to our feet as he notified Dispatch what we had heard and that we were entering the residence. The agonizing scream led me to believe that a woman was being attacked and that if we did not come to her aid that she would be killed or severely injured."

The detective asked, "Would be?"

Josh said, "Yes. They had already killed a deputy and had nothing to lose."

Josh continued, "Officer Powell entered the back door first with me following closely behind and to his left. I heard a different crying sounding voice, which I concluded was a second voice, which I believed was a small child. As we entered the living room doorway, I saw a white male holding a rifle. I had previously determined that the deputy had been shot by a rifle based upon the casings found in front of his patrol car. Both Officer Powell and I shouted, Stop Police. The male turned his body and lifted the rifle up toward our direction. I felt my life was in danger with the need to immediately stop the threat. Both Officer Powell and I shot the male. I fired the shotgun until I felt the threat was gone."

The detective asked, "How did you determine when the threat was gone?"

Josh answered, "When the male was no longer pointing the rife toward our direction."

Josh continued, "Officer Powell and I then stepped through the doorway where I believed a second male was present. I heard a woman sobbing and a male ordering her to shut up. As I stepped into the room, I saw a male holding a pistol to a woman's head. He ordered us to lay down our weapons or he would kill the woman. I lowered the shotgun and stepped to my left in order to set up a shot on the male without injury to the victim. I believed that the woman was in grave danger and the male would kill her. I then quickly shot him in the leg followed by at least one more round to the body."

The detective asked, "What did Officer Powell do?"

Josh replied, "I was concentrating on the male and heard a couple of shots which I believed came from Officer Powell's side arm. I don't remember how many times I fired but I continued to fire until the male had lowered his pistol from the woman's head."

The detective asked a few questions for clarification, looked at the chief, and said, "Does anyone have any further questions?" Everyone shook their heads in content followed by smiles.

The chief got up and shook Josh's hand. "Well done young man! The D.A.'s Office will file the necessary paperwork to help prevent any of the suspect's relatives from filing lawsuits."

The sheriff got up and also shook Josh's hand. He said, "We've looked over your qualifications and concluded that if you ever should decide to reenter law enforcement you won't have far to look." Josh thanked them but said that twenty years was enough. After another round of shaking hands Josh left the room with several business cards in his hand. The police chief gave him a card of a psychologist and urged him to call her.

Josh opened the door and was met by smiling Lou. "We're done buddy. Let's get some food."

Chapter 7
"Lou and Darla"

Josh walked out relieved and asked, "Where's your family?"

Lou said, "The kids are at grandmas and the wife is waiting for us to pick her up."

Josh replied, "Great, give me one minute to make a call." Josh called Kim who said that she was ready anytime. Josh and Lou climbed into Josh's 4-Runner and sped off. They picked up Kim and then swung by Lou's place to pick up his wife. No sooner had the car stopped then the house door opened and out ran a tall attractive woman smiling.

Lou jumped out the back door and held it open, "Hello baby. Climb in here and meet Josh Stark. Josh Stark this is my much better half Darla."

Darla reached out her hand to Josh and said, "A real pleasure to meet you Josh. Hello Kim." Kim smiled and said hello. The 4-Runner took off westbound.

Josh asked, "Do you folks imagine there is a non-violent place to eat up around the university?"

Kim replied with a smile, "Yes. I'm sure there are plenty of places." Darla and Lou nodded in smiles and agreement.

The Sunday afternoon was kind and pleasant to the travelers. Josh opened the sunroof and cracked the rear window where the soft gentle wind whistled a serenade and cordially caressed their heads. Kim leaned back and felt the refreshing wind against her face. Josh struggled to resist from touching her soothing hair.

Lou and Josh spoke about the deposition and the relief that it was over. Josh said that it had gone too smoothly and was extremely brief. Lou agreed but explained that it was mainstreamed for formality purposes.

Kim asked, "What exactly does all that mean?"

Josh turned and said, "They did their jobs, completed the routine check list, and will send it off. They were seeking justice and not someone's head."

Lou replied with a sigh of relief, "Amen brother."

Kim discretely looked at Josh and motioned with her lips only, "University job." Josh said, "Oh by the way. I've decided to apply for a job at the university."

Lou replied, "You Kansas boys are sure full of surprises. What kind of degree do you have?"

Josh replied, "My master's in management but with my law enforcement certifications I think I can perhaps find some work there." Kim looked back at Darla who winked and smiled.

Lou said, "Well old man. If you're going to stick around, I'll just start you a list. Plus, we've got some bad biker dudes who come through here about this time of year that we could use some help with."

Kim said, "No thanks Lou. I'd rather have him save his energy for me and not waste it on punching some criminals." Everyone laughed as Kim looked out the window and blushed. The couples ate at a local restaurant, shared conversation, walked around the square, and headed back toward Timber Creek.

Lou asked, "Are you going to look for a place to live out this way?"

Kim quickly answered, "No. He's staying in Timber Creek." Darla nodded and smiled. Josh drove Lou and Darla back to their place.

As Lou exited the car he said, "In a couple of days I was figuring on having the guys over for a couple of beers if you interested."

Josh was about to speak when Darla interrupted, "The ladies will also be meeting out on the back deck for some wine if you're available Kim."

Kim appeared caught a little off guard and said, "Well, what a nice thought. How about if we give you a call and get back with you?"

Lou smiled and said, "Sounds good." He then shook Josh's hand and climbed out of the car.

Josh asked Kim, "Do you have a few minutes to stop someplace with me?"

Kim smiled, "Sure." He then drove to a modern vacant house with a two-car garage.

He stopped out front and said, "Let's go." Kim appeared puzzled and followed. "What do you think about this place?"

Kim said, "It's wonderful. It's the Miller place. Her daddy built it for her but she ran off and got married to a rich guy in Colorado."

Josh nodded, "Mr. Miller has agreed for me to rent it from him."

Kim was ecstatic and cried, "That's wonderful! But isn't it mighty expensive?"

Josh said, "No. Not too bad. I agreed to assassinate his neighbor who continues to allow his dog to poop in his yard." Kim laughed. Josh pulled out a key and said, "Let's take a look."

Kim and Josh walked around the inside with Kim in slow pace with her mouth open. "Oh, my goodness! It has a fireplace and even one in the master bedroom!" Josh toured Kim around the main floor, the second floor where the bedrooms resided, and then the finished walkout basement. Josh handed Kim the key and said, "Actually it was pretty cheap. It turns out that the three thugs we encountered at Fantastic Fran's had robbed Mr. Miller a while back. The police could never prove anything although they knew who did it. When Mr. Miller got a call from a police detective explaining what had happened to the thugs, he was excited and appreciative. He extended his appreciation my way."

Kim said, "Oh, my gosh!"

Josh said, "Yea. That bull ride they took that night really cost them." Kim hugged Josh and busted up laughing. Josh said, "Oh, by the way, that key is yours in case I'm ever locked out or you feel the desire to come visit."

Chapter 8

"Kim's Assault"

The days went by and Josh settled into his new place. Kim paid daily visits and could be found waving at passing neighbors from the front porch with Josh.

One evening Josh was looking over some course work when the doorbell rang followed by the entrance from Kim. "Hey. You're getting this place furnished really well!"

Josh reached for Kim, picked her up, twirled her around, and said, "Lord you look good!" Kim smiled and slid down to where their lips met. They passionately kissed then Josh carried her away and said, "We've got to stop being apart so long."

Kim locked lips with him again, pulled away, and replied, "Yea. I bet it's been six hours!" They both giggled. Kim asked, "What's new?"

Josh smiled and held up a letter, "This is the formal acknowledgement where I'll be starting next week as an adjunct professor!" Kim jumped down and clapped. Josh said, "Starting out the money will pay the bills with only a little left over, but I've got full medical benefits, a retirement, and full education benefits!"

Kim hugged him and said, "I'm so proud of you."

Josh said, "Hold on. That's not all. You can take night classes to complete your degree at the same time I am working slowly on a teaching degree."

Kim got quiet and said, "I've always dreamed of finishing my degree and maybe teaching at a university somewhere. I'd like to help people make a difference in their lives."

Josh said, "Well, it's right around the corner."

Kim said, "But how can I afford to pay for it?"

Josh replied, "That's no problem. Things will work out. Trust me." Kim hugged him and got watery eyes.

The couple talked for a while and Kim said, "I've got to get home and check on momma. I'll see you in the morning at the Diner?"

Josh said, "Ok. Here, let me drive you."

Kim said, "Now Josh, I'm a big girl and I think I can handle walking four blocks by myself through the neighborhood I've grown up in."

Josh said, "Well, it's pretty dark out there. I'd feel better if I drove or walked you."

Kim persisted, "No. You go ahead and finish that paperwork. I'll see you in the morning, my gentle warrior. I'll call you to let you know I've safely arrived home." She then kissed him and walked out the door.

Josh felt uneasy but then again, he was used to being over sensitive toward safety first. After all he did not want to appear to smother Kim. He desperately wanted to tell her that he loved her but was afraid that it was way too soon. As he watched out the window she faded off into the darkness. Then he turned around, and felt the overwhelming need to follow to assure that she made it home. When he turned toward the door, he saw a shadow outside. It was the same familiar shadow he had seen prior to the fights and shooting. Josh bolted out the door and ran down the street.

As he reached the corner, he was horrified to see that Kim was nowhere in sight. He stopped in a state of panic and closed his eyes while his heart pounded in anticipation. He concentrated intensely then heard a commotion thirty feet forward in the bushes. Josh leaped over the bushes like a mad man and found a large figure on top of Kim.

Kim had been approached from the rear and was thrown to the ground. The impact had knocked the wind out of her. The assailant pressed all his weight upon her which compressed her chest and prevented her from breathing. The assailant had then lifted her dress and torn off her panties.

Josh climbed upon the assailant and applied a modified choke hold. The assailant gagged and gasped for air. Josh pulled him off Kim, who laid in a convulsing state of panic. Josh quickly wound up and applied a powerful elbow strike to the side of the man's head. The man fell hard with a loud thud.
Josh pulled Kim up off the ground, turned her around, and held her gasping body.

The assailant climbed to his knees but was quickly caught by Josh fueled by an animal like rage. Josh impacted the assailant chest to chest and knocked him flying to the ground. He then rolled the large man on top of him and wrapped his legs around the man's waist. Josh had his left arm around the back of the assailant's neck with his hands clinched palm to palm. Josh squeezed with his forearm bone tightly pressing past the flesh and into the nerves of the assailant's neck.

The adrenalin ignited Josh's mussels with every controlled breath. Like an anaconda snake he was squeezing tighter and tighter. Josh was locked in and focused in the attack mode with all his strength and power as he twisted and abruptly arched his back. A large pop echoed throughout the neighborhood.

Kim was sitting up gasping for air. Neighbors were turning on lights and running to her rescue. Josh rolled the lifeless assailant off him and reached out for Kim. Kim melted into Josh's arms and sobbed long deep cries followed by gasps for air.

Two police cars arrived followed by an ambulance. The police officers checked the neck of the assailant for a pulse and holstered their weapons. They looked at each other and then back at the couple closely embraced.

Ambulance personnel rushed to Kim and asked her questions. Kim tightly grasped Josh to the extent that her nails had broken the flesh on his arm. She stared straight ahead and sobbed followed by two large gasps for air over and over. Josh picked her up and carried her toward the ambulance.

The paramedics quickly gathered their gear and approached. Josh opened the rear door and carried her inside where he placed her upon the gurney. Josh shouted with authority, "She needs oxygen! Hurry up!" A paramedic grabbed an oxygen mask, placed it over her head, and turned it on. The other checked her vital signs. Kim tightly held Josh's left hand in a panic like state.

The paramedic sympathetically asked, "Did you lose consciousness honey?" Kim gasped and nodded.

A police officer opened the side door and said, "We've got a 10-40 out here. One of you better take a look.

Josh sternly replied, "The hell with him! This victim needs to get to the hospital!" He then turned to a paramedic and said, "Let's get the hell out of here."

The paramedic looked at the officer and said, "We're 10-6 and enroute to the hospital. I'll call you a backup." The police officer looked at Josh with slight embarrassment and closed the door.

The ambulance transported both Kim and Josh to the local hospital. Josh was impressed with the professional care given to Kim. It turned out that she had not been injured or penetrated by the assailant. She was however quite traumatized and shaken up. A detective quickly arrived at the hospital and spoke with Josh. Because the assailant had been on top of Josh and had suffered a broken neck it was much easier for the detective. He just contacted the coroner who ordered the body held for an autopsy.

The detective pulled Josh aside and said, "Hey, I know you're a friend of Lou's so I will tell you that the guy lying on the slab at the coroner's matches the description of a suspect involved in three rapes out west. DNA will tell the truth." Josh thanked the detective and asked to speak with the police officers at the scene. The detective pulled out his radio and requested the officers to telephone him on his cell phone. He then handed his cell phone to Josh.

Josh spoke to the officer who had come into the ambulance. He apologized for his outburst. The officer thanked him for the apology and explained that he made the request based upon procedure and not desire.

Kim refused to stay in the hospital and declined medication to make her relax. A police officer later drove them back to Josh's house.

Josh told Kim, "I'll drive you home."

Kim spoke out, "No. I don't want to be alone. Please take me inside and sit with me."

Josh picked up Kim and carried her inside. She melted into his arms with wide opened glaring eyes like a frightened fawn. He sat speechless on the couch with her in his lap. As he gently caressed her hair Kim asked, "How did you know to come for me?"

Josh replied, "Well, I felt troubled with you walking home alone and something strange happened."

Kim tilted her head and asked, "What?"

Josh said, "You're going to think I'm crazy but ever since I came to this town, I have seen a shadow figure just before something bad is going to happen." While I was contemplating following you home, I saw a shadow figure outside from the living room. I just knew it was a warning and immediately ran full speed after you.

Kim hugged him tight and said, "I think maybe these are apparitions but can be a long list of possibilities. I think you should visit the old Indian who lives outside of town tomorrow. Part of this town used to be an Indian burial ground. Maybe one of the spirits is looking after you."

Josh sighed in relief, "So you don't think I'm crazy?"

Kim gently kissed his lips, "No baby, never."

Josh let out a deep breath and said, "Thank God."

Kim stood up and said, "Maybe it's an angel. Can I take a shower?"

Josh excitedly replied, "Sure. I've got an extra toothbrush, a robe, disposable razors, and whatever you need." Kim held her hand over her mouth and laughed.

She then approached Josh and said, "Even if you didn't save my life, I would love you anyway." Josh pulled her tight and realized that she had almost been taken away from him.

Deep from his heart he replied, "I love you too." Kim slowly walked to the bathroom escorted by Josh who explained where the towels were.

Kim smiled and said, "I'm sure I can manage."

Josh shouted through the closed door, "I'm afraid that I could use a beer."

A sweet tender voice answered, "I'll join you in a few minutes."

Josh took a drink of beer, sat down, stood up, walked around the room, and sat back down. He then approached the bathroom door where he heard Kim inside sobbing. He stood outside the door pacing and shaking his head in puzzlement. He wanted desperately to help her but he did not know what the proper thing to do was. As he stood in confusion the door opened.

Kim stood completely wet with a towel held by one hand covering the front of her. Her head was lowered and she sobbed.

She reached out her other hand and Josh took it. He walked forward and hugged her tight. She stepped back, dropped her towel, and gently pulled off Josh's t-shirt.

Kim softly said, "Please hold me."

Josh stripped down and accompanied Kim into the warm shower. Kim melted into his arms and closed her eyes as her cheek lay against his chest. Josh reached for the bar of soap and gently washed her back in a slow circular motion. She slowly turned around and pressed her back against him as his soapy hands caressed her entire front. Her head leaned backward as her mouth opened for increased breathing. She turned quickly around and met his lips with hers. As the water rinsed her body Josh dropped to his knees and slowly kissed her athletic body. Kim arched her back with rapid breathing and the pulling of Josh closer until he held her collapsed and quivering body in his strong and yet gentle arms.

The couple quickly dried off and in full embrace climbed onto Josh's bed where they remained romantically connected.

At 4:00 a.m. Kim was still held tightly in Josh's arms. She kissed him with a smile and saw his sleepy right eye open. Kim whispered, "You need to get me home before mamma and the neighbors wake up."

Josh blinked and said, "Yep. You're right." Kim ran into the bathroom, took a quick shower, and threw herself together. She then opened the door to find Josh fully clothed and all groomed.

She asked, "What did you climb into a telephone booth or something?"

Josh laughed, "Nope. I wish. The secret is having a second bathroom in the next room."

Josh drove Kim home and departed with a long kiss. He asked, "Are you feeling better?"

She answered, "Yes. Your therapy cured me."   She timidly whispered, "Well, I guess I didn't scare you too bad this morning."

Josh replied, "Nope. I could get used to that."

Kim kissed his cheek and replied, "Me too." Josh sat in his 4-Runner and watched Kim's elegant voyage to the front door as she gently swayed her trim and graceful figure. She waved and blew him a kiss as she entered the doorway. Josh smiled as a thought entered his mind. He quickly drove to the all-night convenience store and bought a bouquet of roses.

He then reappeared at her front door and waited patiently for her to exit for work. She came outside and was surprised to see Josh standing with his hands behind his back. She smiled a puzzled smile and started to say, "Hey honey. What are you….?" She then gently tilted her head to the side with watery eyes and said, "Ooo. They're so beautiful."

Josh gave her a kiss on the cheek and said, "I thought you could use some cheering up."

She blushed, "You've already done a wonderful job at that, but these are nice too."

Josh returned home and stood looking at his empty bed with just the thought that Kim had been lying there less than an hour ago. He walked over and smelled her fragrance on the pillow. He became concerned about how he had become attached to her in such a short period of time. They seemed to connect so well together. He strongly believed that this would be the start of a new life. He felt a level of comfort that he had never felt before among this quiet and comfortable community.

As he poured a glass of water, he couldn't help but feel there was a storm coming. He looked up at the sky and softly said, "God. Do you send me into trouble or am I just a shit magnet?" He then looked down at the glass of water and back up at the sky, "I know. It's all part of your plan. Well thanks for all the beauty you have shown me. Thanks especially for Kim."

Josh rushed to the community center for a workout and then to the diner where he found Kim lining the counter with coffee cups and glowing with beauty.

She quickly approached him, snuck him a kiss, and with a big smile said, "Good morning! How are you today?"

Josh returned the smile and replied, "With the experience I had last night this has to be the best morning ever."

Kim smiled, "Well, mine started off pretty rough but went the other direction and was the best! You cured me of my trauma." Pickup trucks arrived and old wobbly bodies came through the door with cheerful smiles and hellos.

A couple of them quickly approached Kim and wrapped their arms around her. One of them said, "Are you all right princess?"

Kim looked down and said, "Yes. Thank you."

The door opened wide and in came a loud boisterous voice, "Little princess! Come give me a hug!" Kim smiled and ran to him.

She patted him on the back and said, "I'm all right Norm, thanks to Josh."

Norm turned to Josh, shook his hand and said, "Well done young man. Well done. Wish you'd put more of those rotten bastards in hell where they belong!" He then climbed upon a counter stool and quietly took a sip of coffee, "Goodness. Not only are you the prettiest girl in town you make the best darn coffee too. Just don't let the misses know that because she'll be after me with the shovel."

A few chuckles came from the counter. A voice sounded, "Yep. Both you and your hound will have matching knots on your heads." The others joined in and once again it was like an orchestra of laughter and one liners.

Josh saw a patrol car quickly pull up in front. In walked Lou Powell who gave a friendly greeting to everyone and sat down. He then spoke to Kim, "Nothing for me today Kim. I've got to run."

Lou said to Josh, "I see you were busy again last night cleaning the scum from our city. Today the detective should complete the photo lineup and, in a few days, we'll know about the DNA match. I think I'm going to suggest that we just have a detective, and maybe a coroner, follow you around to make our investigations more efficient. How are you doing?"

Josh smiled and said, "I see Cliff and his lady friend have patched things up." Lou looked out the window and saw the couple walking toward the diner.

Lou replied, "Yep. Ole Cliff is back in AA again and claims to be turning over a new leaf."

The door opened and in walked Cliff followed by his girlfriend. Lou smiled and nodded. Cliff stopped and said, "Mornin' Officer Powell."

He then turned to Josh, extended his hand and said, "No hard feelings mister?"

Josh shook his hand, smiled, and replied, "Name's Josh and there's no hard feelings." The big man smiled and followed his lady friend to a booth and sat down.

Lou said, "Hey. I just wanted you to know a bad ass biker gang is coming through the area. The highway patrol has been following them and stopping them for anything. They arrested about a dozen of them or so for suspended driver's licenses and warrants. If you get into it with them, they'll swarm you like a pack of wolves."

Lou stood up, placed his hand of Josh's shoulder, and whispered, "You better start packing some heat." Lou walked out the door and said, "You folks have a nice day!"

Kim walked over and leaned up against Josh. He appeared troubled.

Kim asked, "Does Lou's conversation mean that you'll be seeing that shadow again soon?"

Josh patted her hand and said, "Perhaps."

Carl shouted, "Order up!" Kim walked away as Josh turned to watch her graceful hips gently roll back and forth. She glanced over her shoulder and winked at him.

Josh got up and waved a goodbye gesture at Kim. He stepped outside and paused to digest the sweet smell of country. The wind was gently passing across the pasture and bringing with it the fragrance of wheat and fresh vegetation. A large hawk elegantly floated aside the bright blue sky patiently waiting for breakfast. Two stray dogs wrestled along the grassy ditch and took turns acting vicious.

Josh eagerly wanted to get moving and accomplish something but he was concerned about the bikers and leaving Kim alone. He knew Lou would keep a watch out when time permitted but what if he was on a call? He took two steps forward in contemplation and caught glimpse of a shadow figure again. He quickly turned his head and ran to the side of the building where he had seen the vision. He nervously looked around but found nothing. He then turned to see several people inside the diner looking at him in surprise.

He then walked back inside the diner and sat down. One of the old timers asked, "Did you see something out there Josh?"

Nate replied, "Yea. He saw that wind you blew earlier form a dust bunny and met aphorize into a being." The crowd laughed.

Josh replied, "I just thought I saw something but it turned out to be nothing." Kim glanced over at Josh from the end of the counter and appeared concerned.

Chapter 9
"Outlaw Bikers"

The early morning innocence was quickly interrupted by the thunder of loud motorcycle engines. The parking lot was quickly filled with a cloud of dark dust. The rumbling slowly decreased and left troubled silence. The dust slowly cleared and gave way to unfriendly figures slowly walking through the gaze toward the door. The door opened and in walked a crowd of leather jacketed dust infested problem people with chips on their shoulders.

Josh slowly stirred his coffee and discretely examined the hierarchy of the gang. He rehearsed a plan and came to the conclusion that he would probably need to kill someone today. Several large men strolled inside and disgustingly blew kisses at Kim. Josh felt energy enter his body and his muscles throb. He controlled his breathing and began to focus on a battle. One of the men walked back toward Cliff's table and sat down beside Cliff's girlfriend.

The dirt covered biker put his arm around her and quickly caught a huge impact from Cliff's right fist. The large man hit the floor and several bikers turned with tight jaws to glare at Cliff. Josh quickly sprang from the booth, grabbed a kitchen knife resting on a napkin, and impaled s biker's hand into a bar stool.

The large man groaned and shivered in pain. Josh turned to the crowd, drew his .45 from his waist band, and pointed it to the head of a biker standing near his booth. "Tell them to slowly walk outside now."

The man was the leader of the gang with a chiseled bearded face and large tattooed arms. He smiled and replied, "I don't think you'll use that."

Josh quickly smashed the butt of the pistol into the face of an enforcer who stood across from the leader. He then grabbed the woman who snickered beside the leader by the hair and dragged her backward. Josh pointed the .45 to the woman's head and said, "Before I blow your frickin' brains out, you'll get the pleasure of watching what little brains she has splatter the window. Look into my eyes. Don't test me boy."

The leader hesitated then roughly spoke up with clinched teeth, "Everyone outside, now."

It sounded like the shuffling of cattle as bodies glared at Josh then followed out the door.

Josh threw the woman to the floor with a stern focus in the eyes of the leader. She slid across the floor and slowly crawled to her feet and staggered out. Josh retained a deadly focus upon the leader ordered him to sit down then sat down across from him.

The leader folded his arms upon the table and stared back at Josh. Josh stuffed the .45 back in his waist band and placed his elbows upon the table then sternly said, "You've got a problem. Perhaps I can help solve it for you." Kim leaned back against the counter shaking along with the cook, Carl.

The leader roughly spoke, "I'm looking at a dead man."

Josh smiled, "We all die sooner or later. Besides, something tells me you'll be first in line."

The leader smiled, "What's your plan cop?"

Josh replied, "I'm no cop. Think of me as something of a messenger."

The leader continued, "Maybe you're not a cop now, but you used to be. Your presence tells me you're a man of action but you are way out of your league on this one."

Josh stood up, walked to the counter where he retrieved two cups and a pot of coffee. He then sat back down, poured two cups, slid one over to the leader, and replied, "I'm many things but unprepared is not one of them." He poured a packet of sweetener into his coffee and calmly took a sip. "The simple things in life can bring such joy can't they young man?"

The leader appeared somewhat caught off guard and said, "You disrespect me and then pretend to entertain me?"

Josh leaned forward, "I just saved the life of your big turd that only has a hole in his hand. Then there is you. If you think the local cops would throw a fuss if I had blown your brains out then you're as stupid as the bitch who had stood beside you. I've been on this planet longer than you have so you should listen."
Josh had the leader's attention, "people like you don't like people like me because we're called conformists. The reality is that we live by rules because we believe that people must live by order and follow rules in order to retain their rights and protect the rights of others. A person like you likes to do what they want regardless of what others think is right or wrong. There brings conflict."

The leader took a sip of coffee and replied, "Nice speech. Now explain why it is of my best interest to not hunt you down."

Josh emphasized, "You have the responsibility to lead your gang. Killing them is not protecting them. If you make me fight, I will kill a multitude with the first being you. Then the police will respond along with some deputies followed by state troopers. More of your people will die because of your poor judgment. You're getting a heck of a deal here by being able to simply ride out of this county. A shake of your hand will honor your word. We're still men whatever walk of life we come from."

The leader leaned back, paused in deep thought, and slowly extended his hand. As the two men shook hands the leader said, "I'd love to take you on just you and me."

Josh replied, "Yea, me too." They internally smiled and gradually broke their grip.

As the leader walked toward the door he stopped and respectfully said, "You take care of yourself, old man."

Josh replied, "Continue making good decisions and perhaps you'll live this long also."

The leader walked out the front door and stood in front of his gang. One Native American sat on his motorcycle, tilted his head back, closed his eyes, and said, "Lighthorsemen."

Another biker asked, "What you say?"

The leader replied, "Lighthorsemen."

The Native American said, "This is Choctaw land. We are trespassing. Lightorsemen are big, big medicine. A tribe's greatness is measured on how great its enemies be. There is no shame to ride away from this fight." He then lowered his head and stared at the leader. The leader looked over his shoulder at Josh who took a sip of coffee, slightly nodded, and tipped his cup.

The leader said, "Leave the Lighthornsemen be. Let's ride." The riders got onto their motorcycles, but this time there was no thunder. Just a deep rumble of engines that slowly drove out the parking lot and onto the black top then faded off into the distance.

Josh dialed his cell phone and shortly said, "Lou. It's Josh. As a favor I'd like your boys to let those bikers head out of town."

A voice on the other end replied, "I'm sittin' here with a shotgun in my lap ready to swoop down on that diner. You got it. I'll spread the word. You've got to tell me all about this one buddy."

Josh replied, "Drop by anytime tonight and bring your drinking hat." Lou laughed.

Kim ran to Josh and jumped into his arms. Josh lifted her off the ground with one hand and gently held her close. She then buried her cheek in his chest and said, "How did you do that!"

Josh kissed her and said, "You've got to speak their language and add a lot of luck," Josh then turned around and walked toward Cliff who stood like a guard beside his girlfriend.
He extended his hand and shook Cliff's hand, "Good show young man."

Cliff smiled with pride, "You did one hell of a performance yourself sir."

Josh turned then paused to say, "Maybe so, but your courage was mighty impressive and set it all in motion. Thank you." Cliff sat down and began to swell with pride.

The old timers at the counter shook their heads and began to applause. Kim sat down beside Josh and held him tight.

She then said, "I thought you were going to shoot that guy."

Josh kissed her cheek and replied, "Yea, me too."

After regaining his composure Josh exited the dinner and felt relieved. He thought to himself if anyone had doubt about a God then they should have been there at that diner. Josh gently tucked the .45 back into its holster under his seat and slightly trembled as he drove off. He thanked God for the outcome as the soft Oklahoma wind massaged his head and pointed his car toward the university.

As the 4-Runner purred down the highway Josh sat his cruise control, leaned back, and turned up Randy Travis on his C.D. player. When he got out of town, he felt an intense feeling that someone was calling him. He looked around and saw a dirt road up ahead. His cruise control shut off and Josh braked to turn right. He came to a stop, picked up his cell phone, and called Kim.

He asked about the old Indian she had spoken of. He came to find out that he lived just outside of town in the deep of wilderness. He followed Kim's directions and before they disconnect Kim pleaded, "be careful! No one goes up there because they say there are ghosts. The last hunters who went in there did not come out!"

Kim's mother, Sandy Anderson, had given birth to Kim three years after the birth of her older eldest daughter Cami. Kim's father, Jake, was kicked by a horse and killed when the girls were very young. Sandy struggled to make ends meet and worked long hard hours six days a week. It wasn't unusual for her to shuffle back and forth from the diner to her house to care for the girls. Helpful caring neighbors were always at her home providing helping hands.

Sandy never remarried, although she very easily could have. She was known as having the best-looking legs in the county. She was tall and trim with long blonde hair that came together at the top of her head to form a flowing spectacle like a waterfall. Her blue eyes sparkled and her face always displayed a smile – even when she broke a dish over a customer's head for patting her behind one day. A couple of regulars made sure that no one ever violated Sandy again. The pest was punched in the face and thrown out the door into the parking lot.

Kim and Cami were extremely close and grew up quickly together because of their time together keeping house and doing chores. Both girls were excellent cooks by the age of twelve. They pretty much raised themselves throughout those years. Sandy continued to work grueling hours and when she got home each night she would run in the house, grab the girls, and smother them with kisses. Then every night she would kneel beside her bed in prayer and ask God for help. In addition to her asking she also give thanks for everything He had given them. God was listening, heard the sobs, and felt her tear-soaked pillow every night.

One day a man named Carl came looking for a job. Sandy hired him on the spot out of desperation. As time passed Carl became her right-hand man. He was an artist at preparing food out of simple basic ingredients. A chicken or any piece of meat for that matter was transformed into a delicious extravagant dish. When Cami and Kim turned fourteen, they began waitressing at the diner and everything gradually changed. Other high school girls were hired to fill in the gaps. The bills were getting paid on time with some left over. Sandy was able to slow down a little to rest her tired and weary legs, but sadly it was all too late. Her legs simply wore out. All those years twisting and turning, rushing here and there, combined with long hours shut her down. Then one day a man dressed in a suit carrying some papers came into the diner and asked for Sandy. Sandy came in from the back and apprehensively accompanied the man into a booth. The man smiled and said, "Ms. Anderson don't be worried, I come with good news." Sandy relaxed and listed to the man explain and stretch out papers upon the table. He was there to issue her an inheritance check from a neighbor who had recently passed.

Sandy had been kind to the neighbor and was always lending her a helping hand in between trips back and forth. The neighbor had no next of kin and had named Sandy her beneficiary. Sandy instantly thanked God, laid her head upon the table, and cried.

Sandy took the money and paid off debt. She even gave some to Cami and Kim. When Kim turned eighteen and graduated high school, she received a full college scholarship to run track. Kim could run like lightening. She set many school records and placed in the state championships every year. Cami, on the other hand, was too wild to settle down and read books. When not working she was always racing around in her modified '54 Chevrolet Pickup. Neighbors would always be shouting, "Cami! Slow down!"

In Kim's third year of college during one cold and rainy night she was woken up by the college dorm supervisor. Two state troopers were there to talk to her. Kim sat in her chair as one trooper got down on one knee in front of her. He softy spoke and explained that Cami had been killed in a motor vehicle accident.

Kim telephoned her mother and the two cried together until they could weep no more. That next morning Kim packed her belongings and when she opened her dorm door, she found all the girls in her dorm were lined up to hug her and cry with her. They helped her carry her belongings to her car and found the entire track team lined up with their heads bowed.

Kim drove home and collapsed into her mother's grieving arms.

The state troopers determined that the rain had caused water to flood across the darkened roadway. Cami had run into the water, lost control, and slid off the road into a tree.

Kim now would spend the next eighteen years working the diner and bringing comfort to her heart broken mother. Sandy still helped out from time to time but could not tolerate standing on her feet very long. Still, most every afternoon Sandy would be seen sitting in the back booth reading her Bible and cross-referencing scriptures with a concordance. Her mornings and evenings were typically dedicated to Bible studies and visiting the needy. Sandy was known throughout the town as the charming charitable princess.

Although Sandy's hair is now gray and eloquently wrapped up upon her head, she is still a beautiful woman at 65 years of age. The empty hole from the loss of her beloved Cami was more than filled with the love and loyalty poured out from Kim.

Josh and Sandy had instantly hit it off. Josh reminded Sandy of her late husband Jake. Jake was known to be a "scraper" who held no pause to come to her rescue or for anyone else in need. The reputation Josh held was admired by Sandy because she knew Josh would protect and respect her Kim. Josh was always greeted by Sandy with a hug.

Chapter 11
"The Choctaw Indian"

Josh followed the twisting and turning dirt road. The soft red sand pulled the car toward the earth and sucked it downward. Josh engaged four-wheel drive to maintain the speed. The narrow road had many treacherous washouts which caused him to stop and traverse on and off the red clay roadway. Judging by the bumpy surface it had been a long time since any vehicles had been up this way. He wondered that if he found someone if they would still be alive.

There were no old wooden fence posts or decapitated barns to provide any suggestion of civilization. Josh drove on. Black birds sat silent in the trees and an occasional squirrel could be seen scurrying about.

As he came to the top of a hill Josh stopped the 4-Runner and got out. His eyes carefully canvassed the area but found nothing except a worn walking trail leading up into the woods. He continued onward on foot.

After about a mile he came across a clearing where he got a glimpse of an old log cabin.   As he proceeded onward the leaves gently swayed in the trees and groaned a sinister song.

The quiet was so intense that he could hear his feet walking upon the soft cushioned sand.

Josh followed the old ancient path and came to the old wooden shack beside a slow-moving stream. An elderly Indian man was sitting on the porch in a rocking chair. What appeared to be a large wolf sat beside the old man and closely watched Josh.

The leather faced old man wore long grey hair, a tan weathered leather hat, a plaid long sleeved shirt, and faded blue jeans. His chin protruded slightly forward as if he carried no teeth.

As Josh stood admiring the ancient spectacle before him the weathered face spoke, "I have been expecting you, gentle warrior." Josh stepped forward in surprise and stood before the steps. The ancient voice said, "Come, sit with me."

Josh approached the distinguished old man and slowly sat in the chair beside him. The Indian projected a friendly yet royal like aura.

Josh asked, "Are you a chief?"

The voice answered, "No. White people always think old Indians are chiefs." The Indian slowly said, "I am Sitting Wolf, great grandson of Choctaw Lighthorsemen Running Bear. You are the gentle warrior whom the spirits have summoned."

Josh leaned forward and asked, "Why have I been summoned?"

Sitting Wolf continued to stare straight and without expression replied, "It is your time."

Josh appeared puzzled, "Time for what and why?"

Sitting Wolf extended his left hand and the wolf sat up to receive the stroke of the Indian's old leathery hand. "The blood of the ancient warriors runs through your veins. The visions you see are the spirits guiding you. It is a great gift that one would be honored to be given."

Josh leaned forward, turned his head, and paused with his mouth slightly open. "As a child I heard that my great-great grandmother was an Indian. I have heard relatives mention the word Lighthorsemen also. What does it mean?"

Sitting Wolf spoke with great authority, "Lighthorsemen were brave Choctaw law enforcement officers who courageously maintained the peace between the many Indian tribes who were forced to come together by the white man in this land. They were highly dedicated and educated warriors."

Sitting Wolf slowly turned his head toward Josh, "You, gentle warrior, possess the spirit of the Lighthorsemen. You are gentle in spirt, but a warrior at heart. The white of you is gentle yet you hold fists of iron. You are skilled with rife and many weapons. The Lighthorsemen inside of you seeks to destroy evil and bad doers. It is powerful medicine. But with powerful medicine comes much responsibility."

Josh slowly asked, "What kind of responsibility?"

The warm wise eyes of the Indian replied, "Service. You will come to the aid of others when evil spirits come to call."

Josh asked with an overwhelmed tone, "How? Who will show me the way?"

The Indian stood to his feet and spoke as he slowly walked toward the door, "The spirits guide you Lighthorseman."
The Indian stopped and continued, "The spirits know and tell many things. The evil spirits are restless. They have entered the hearts of willing men and have come to battle with you Lighthorseman. The evil spirits seek war. You have a shadow spirit looking after you to

show you the way. Your journey is one of great honor. Walk by sight in the light. The spirits will watch for you in the night. That is enough for now, gentle warrior." He then opened the log cabin door and disappeared inside.

Josh stood frozen for several seconds. He then stepped off the porch and turned to find the large wolf sitting up closely watching. It had blue ghost like eyes that intensely glowed. Its large frame was both muscular and magnificent.

The Oklahoma wind blew silently through the trees. Josh looked down to observe goose bumps on his arms. He then slowly travelled back to his 4-Runner and slowly sat inside. As he started to start the engine he wondered if he should leave a gift out of respect. He opened his glove box, felt around, and came out with a large collectible Gerber folding knife dressed with a serenaded blade.

He returned to the log cabin and placed it on the small table next to the rocking chair. The ghost like eyes of the wolf followed him without expression.

Josh jogged back to his 4-Runner to drive off and glanced at his front passenger seat. There in his amazement lay a beautiful hand-made hunting knife with a bone carved handle and leather pouch. The leather pouch was dressed in feathers and beads. Josh thought to himself, "How in the…?" He reached for the knife and examined the delicately sharpened blade that sparkled in the sun light. He placed the knife in his door pocket. He then looked toward the dancing clouds in the sky and slowly drove off along the sandy and treacherous blanketed road.

Chapter 12

"The Gentle Warrior"

Josh was torn between the need for seclusion and yet the craving to be with Kim. He drove home and collapsed in the hand me down recliner. The last thing he wanted was to be on some mission from God or anybody. Still, he could not deny his vision of the shadow person and Sitting Wolf's convincing words about the spirits. And how was it that he had come to a seemingly quiet town and had gotten into more confrontations in just a few days than big city cops experience in weeks?

A voice message left from the detective had confirmed that the DNA from the deceased rapists matched that of the three victims out west. Surely all of these incidents could not possibly be of mere coincidence. He picked up the phone and called Kim to ask her when she got off work.

Kim replied, "If you need me to, I can take off any time."

Josh hesitated but said, "I saw the Indian, and I could really stand to see you."

Kim joyfully replied, "I'll be right there."

It only took a few minutes for the door to open and in rushed Kim. Her appealing and feminine figure coupled with her warm smile made Josh forget about his troubles and erased his notion of seclusion. She climbed upon his lap and greeted him with a passionate kiss.

He leisurely said with a smile, "I just felt a breath of heaven."

Kim gave him another long kiss and said, "Now tell me about our Indian friend."

Josh rambled on and on with Kim intensely listening with only the occasional response of, "Oh, my gosh!"

After over thirty minutes of rapid talking Josh stood up with Kim in his arms, "I need a drink and I'm sure you do too." Kim laughed. He sat her on the counter as she giggled, poured two large glasses of wine, and he carried her back into the living room as she laughed and balanced their glasses.

They sat on the couch, held their glasses up, and together said, "To Sitting Wolf." Josh asked, "What do you think?"

Kim cleared her throat and replied, "Well, first of all as outrageous as it sounds, Sitting Wolf makes sense. Historically the Lighthorsemen did exist and Indians do believe in the purpose of shadow people. Then you have me who would not be here today if you would not have come to my rescue, my gentle warrior."

Josh excitedly leaned forward, "That's another thing! He called me gentle warrior!"

Kim covered her forehead with her hands, "Oh, wow this is all too weird! I had never heard that term until it popped out of my mouth that night!"

Josh got on his knees in front of Kim and held her hands, "Kim. I don't want this assignment or whatever it is. I left where I was and all that responsibility back there with the job."

Kim smiled, "Josh. Maybe it's a calling from Him. You know, part of His plan."

Josh said, "I don't believe that God pushes buttons and steers us around like figures in a video game. I do believe that he does intervene though. Do you think it's a possibility that God has sent 'me' here?"

Kim took a sip of wine and responded, "I don't know, but I'm sure glad He did!" She then said, "Maybe this is a do over. You know your second chance at life. You even said yourself that you were looking for something that you were not sure what it was."

Josh nodded in deep thought, "Perhaps."

Kim then continued, "Maybe it's like the guy on the airplane that crashes and everyone dies but him. Maybe God had a plan for him as he does now for you."

Josh's eyes widened and he stood up fast. Kim asked, "What's the matter?" He sat down his glass of wine, placed his hand on the back of his head, and began to pace.

Kim stood up to confront him, "What?"

Josh held Kim by the shoulders, "When I was driving out of Wichita a truck swerved to avoid a ladder or something on the highway. The load must had shifted in his trailer because he started to swing and lost control. I swerved for the outside shoulder but his trailer whipped around in front of me and occupied that inside shoulder."

Kim's eyes widened, "And then what?"

Josh appeared out of breath and replied, "Kim. There was a concrete barrier in that median so how did I get past him? When I looked in my rear-view mirror, he had come to rest occupying that outside shoulder and all three other lanes."

Kim pulled Josh's head down to her shoulder and with a shaky voice said, "Oh, my God what does this all mean?"

Josh trembled and said, "Well for one thing it means I need some Knob Creek."

Kim busted out laughing and said, "I love you Josh Stark."

Josh led her by the hand toward the kitchen and said, "Just hold that thought. Whatever I am I promise to be anything but boring."

As Josh mixed a glass of whisky Kim leaned against the counter and said, "I knew the way you held me and touched me you couldn't be human."

Josh smiled, "Oh. I'm human alright. I'm just not sure about being normal."

The telephone ran and Josh answered, "Hello Lou! Oh gosh, I'm sorry I forgot. What? Hold on a second." Josh cradled the phone against his chest and asked Kim, "Do you mind if I invite Lou and his wife over?"

Kim kissed his cheek, "Not at all. I want to see his eyes bug out when you start talking about the shadow people."

Josh suppressed his laughter and said, "Hey. Why don't you grab Darla and the kids and come on over? We've got a swing set out back for the kids. Plus, I've got a story that will raise the hair on the back of your neck. Oh, and by the way. Hurry up. I've gotten into the Knob Creek." Josh held the phone away from his ear and extended his arm where Lou's laughter echoed throughout the room.

He sat the phone down and found Kim consumed with laughter. Josh cradled Kim in his arms and said, "Anymore wine for you and you'll be spending the night."

She presented a provocative smile and replied, "If that's an invitation you're on." Josh picked her up high and nibbled at her stomach. Kim kicked her feet and laughed.

After a few minutes the doorbell rang and in walked the Powell family. Josh and Kim gave everyone a tour and the two children ran for the swing set. Kim helped Josh fix some drinks and asked Darla, "Would your kiddies like some juice?"

Darla smiled and said, "Oh I'm sure they would." The two women poured a couple of glasses and walked out back.

Lou stared at the women as they walked out the door, "Those are two fine lookin' ladies there."

Josh took a drink in stare and replied, "Yep."

Lou continued, "Kim seems to fit in really well around here."

Josh smiled, "Yep."

Lou asked, "Are you going to have her move in with you?"

Josh quickly said, "If I did, I'd have Mrs. Cooper after me with a shovel like Betty, or whomever she was, that worked over her hound dog."

Lou laughed. Josh continued, "I've already had conversation with Mrs. Cooper and would not bring disrespect toward her. Besides, Kim's not a live-in kind of girl."

Lou nodded, "You got that right buddy."

The two men walked into the living room and Lou asked, "So, what is it you have to say that will cause the hair to rise up on my neck? Wait a minute. Does it have to do with ghosts and goblins?"

Josh said, "Well, kind of."

Lou put his hand up, "Then wait just a minute. If I'm going to be shaking and all I'll need Darla holding my hand!" Josh laughed.

The two ladies walked in and entered the living room. Darla said, "Josh, I really love your house, especially the master bedroom."

Josh smiled, "Thank you. That's my favorite room also." The couples smiled.

Josh said, "Well, everyone top off their drinks and sit back and relax while I enlighten you to my bazaar dilemma."

Josh started at the beginning with the truck in Wichita, seeing the shadow figures, and the visit with Sitting Wolf. Lou and Darla sat speechless for the thirty-minute dissertation with their mouths half open. When Josh finished, he sat down with Kim's arm around him and asked, "What do you think?"

Lou stood up, walked toward the kitchen, and said, "You got any 7-Up or Sprite to go with that Knob Creek?" Josh, Kim, and Darla laughed and got up to join him. As they all refilled their drinks Darla looked outside to check on the kids and followed the group back into the living room.

Lou took a drink, started to talk, took another drink, and said, "Wait a minute." The others then laughed again. Lou finally spoke rapidly, "There is too much here to suggest anything other than something or someone is watching over you. Your conversation with Sitting Wolf suggests that there are spirits involved. My momma has told me many stories about the Indian spirits. Whether we believe it or not does not discount the fact there is some connection with you. Are you a descendent of the Choctaw?"

Josh said, "I don't know. I did hear the term Lighthorseman as a child though."

Darla said, "Maybe you coming here woke up the spirits or something."

They all turned to her as she continued, "What I mean is that Timber Creek was built over an old Indian burial ground many years ago. Even the old timers can't tell for sure where it was. As a child they used to tell old stories about seeing totem pole figures and giant birds dressed in beads late at night."

Josh stood up, "Well, whatever it is I'm not happy about it. I didn't drive all this way to be part of some spiritual mission."

Lou put his hand on Josh's shoulder and said, "But you're so good at it!" The group laughed as Kim put her arms around Josh and squeezed.

Lou continued, "You know you can't dismiss the fact that you were instrumental at saving a lot of lives and clearing some important cases. I wonder what would have happened if you hadn't come to town." The group got silent.

Kim smiled, "I know that I'd be awfully lonely."

Josh tenderly hugged Kim and replied, "Yea, me too."

Lou said, "Do you believe this guy's 48 years old? You know I think this guy is the spirit that came to town and woke all the others up!" As the group laughed Lou's cell phone rang.

Lou answered, "Yes. Ok. At what time? I'll be there." He then hung up and shook his head.

Darla asked, "What's up baby?"

Lou placed his phone back on his belt and said, "Special surveillance tomorrow at 7:00. For the whole darn shift. I'll be sitting out there watching the tumble bugs."

Darla said, "Take Josh with you. His ghost stories will keep you both entertained and awake."

Josh said, "Yea. I find tumble bugs enjoyable to watch."

Lou replied, "Yea. That way he can tell me some more spooky stories where I won't be able to sleep at night."

Darla stood up, put her hands-on Lou's shoulders, winked and said, "We'll just have to come up with some way to take your mind off all that scary stuff at night." The group laughed. Lou rounded up the kids and staggered out as he handed Darla his car keys.

Ten p.m. rolled around and the house lye silent with only Kim's gentle breathing against Josh's shoulder upon the couch. Josh gently caressed her face and saw a smile slowly appear. Her eyes opened to be met by a tender kiss.

Kim slowly pulled away and said, "I think I'm going to take a shower."

Josh smiled, "Just yell if you need any help."

Kim stood up, reached out her hand, and said, "Come on. I have some hard-to-reach places." Josh kissed her, picked her up, and carried her upstairs to the bathroom.

Kim's soft trim body felt more than inviting as the warm water soaked their heads and ran down their bodies. The steam gently raised and brought mystic romance to their rapidly beating hearts. Josh tenderly caressed her body and felt her trembling lips move around his face and cheeks. He then slowly cradled her with his left arm around her back and his right arm below her bottom. Kim wrapped her legs around him as he gently kissed her neck and felt her chest melt upon his.

After the soothing water had rinsed the soap away Josh opened the shower door and carried Kim to the bed with one arm after grabbing the two hanging towels. As he gently laid her upon the bed, he gently padded her silky body. Two hours passed and found the couple lying intensely embraced with only the Oklahoma moon smiling in through the window.

Kim sat up on her elbow, kissed Josh's forehead, and asked, "Josh. Will you love me forever?"

Josh looked deeply into her eyes and sincerely responded, "Yes my beautiful princess."

The alarm came to life faster than what it seemed it should. Kim's eyes opened to find Josh standing at the bed with a silver tray. She sat up with delight glowing in her eyes.

Josh bent down and gently whispered, "Good morning beautiful. How about some nourishment to start your day?"

Kim smiled, "I would be delighted if you slipped in here and joined me." Josh sat down beside her and shared the breakfast. The couple then got ready to start the day.

As Kim went out the door she ran back inside and passionately kissed Josh. "Have a nice day. I'll see you tonight."

Josh rushed to the community center and got in a quick workout. He then showered, returned home, and made some green tea. He placed a concealed holster on his right hip and filled it with a stainless steel .45. He then placed a magazine holder containing two spare magazines on his left side. He downed a loose-fitting shirt to cover everything.

Josh walked out the front door holding a small cooler and breathing the fresh morning air. He sat down in the cushioned chair and slowly sipped from his cup of tea. A squirrel in the tree above nibbled on an acorn. His fluffy tail occasionally flickered as he sat with his front paws carefully manipulating his breakfast.
As Josh sat upon the porch chair admiring the beautiful view before him, he thought how close to heaven he felt. Never in his life had things felt so right and good. His relationship with Kim was like a dream come true.

As he sat daydreaming a boy on a bicycle drove by and said "Good morning Mr. Stark", and threw a newspaper.

Josh reached out and caught it with a smile. "Excellent throw young man. You'll be playing for the Scooners in a few years with that arm."

The smell of wheat and country filled his mouth along with the drink of sweet warm tea. People began to stir and walk out to their porches with cups of coffee and friendly greetings. Josh heard the smooth purr of an engine and looked to see an unmarked patrol car stop in front of his house. He walked out to the road, put his head in the window, and said, "Good morning. Are you ready for ghost stories?"

Lou smiled and replied, "Hop in. You'll never believe what we've got going down."

Josh climbed in, shook Lou's hand, and said, "Let's rock and roll country boy."
The patrol car drove off and headed out of town.

Lou appeared anxious and upset. Josh said, "Are you all right?"

Lou wiped his lips and said, "Man. We've got a real problem. Someone is running meth out of the county in a real big way. The chief is all riled up and wants everyone out covering assigned posts. We are to operate completely silent with no radio transmissions and cell phones only for emergencies. There was a guy dressed in a suit wearing a serious expression sitting in the chief's office. He had to be some spook from a special operations department. Probably a fed."

Josh squinted his eyes and said, "What the hell would the feds be doing in a spare of the moment investigation out here?"
Lou shook his head and drove out of town down country roads.

Chapter 13

"Friendly Fire"

As Lou backed the patrol car up upon the shoulder Josh asked, "Lou. Were you told exactly where to park?"

Lou looked concerned and replied, "Yea. Why?"

Josh cleared his throat and with a troubled tone said, "Let's park across the way where we can see this area."

Lou replied, "Let me guess. You just saw your shadow friend again?"

Josh half smiled and nodded his head, "Yep. I'm afraid so."

As Lou repositioned his patrol car under some trees in a nearby field Josh got on his cell phone, "Hi honey, it's me. Listen don't leave the diner today until you hear back from me. Ok? I'll explain later." He then handed his phone to Lou, "Here, call Darla and unlock that rifle of yours." Lou glanced around the area and made the call.

As the two sat patiently in the car Josh sipped on his cup of tea. Lou asked, "What is it you put in that stuff?"

Without taking his eyes off the view of the windshield he handed his cup to Lou. Lou took a sip and said, "Hey brew master. That's pretty darn good! If we live through this you've got to make me a cup."

Josh took the cup back, took another sip, and replied, "You got it pal."

Lou turned off the engine to prevent the grass from under the vehicle from catching fire. The cool Oklahoma breeze was kind today. An eagle flew overhead and rested upon the utility pole. Lou asked, "You don't recon that's old Sitting Wolf do you?"

Josh said, "Nope. But it's probably one of his friends." The grass gently danced as the wind echoed a sweet tune across the prairie. Cattle off in the distance drank from a pond and would give no notice to the soon to come changes of events.

Lou asked, "Is it silly to ask if you need the .357?"

Josh replied, "It won't be necessary today."

Lou smiled, "Good thinking."

As the two men sat quietly, they exchanged thoughts back and forth. They quickly came to the conclusion that they could only trust and depend upon each other right now. Lou asked, "Have you ever been shot?"

Josh replied, "No. That's one area I'd rather give than receive. I hope to keep it that way."

Lou looked out the window and softly said, "Amen brother."

Josh sat up straight and said, "Why don't you hand me that shotgun." Lou removed it from the center and handed it over. Josh slid the slide back about a half an inch from full stoke and began removing the buckshot from the magazine. He then removed the slugs from the stock and began to load them. "Do you have any more of these slugs stashed?"

Lou opened the glove box and handed him three boxes, "Here. Why the slugs?"

Josh smiled, "You only have to hit them once with these babies. The impression is ever lasting and they'll burn right through car doors."

Lou shook his head, "I'm glad you're on my side."

An old blue pickup slowly topped the hill. Josh asked, "What's this?"

Lou looked through the binoculars and counted, "One, two, and three. Oh, that's only Amos, Earl, and his other brother Earl."

Josh asked, "Two Earls?"

Lou sat down the binoculars, took a sip of energy drink, and said, "Yep. There's a story behind it."

Josh laughed, "I can't wait."

Lou explained, "Well, many years ago, as the story goes, Amos Hicks was born and named after his daddy's daddy. Three years later Earl came along named after his momma's daddy. The two boys took after their grandpas and were not quite right. They'd sit in the pasture eating dirt then run-in circles chasing butterflies with sticks. One day Amos, who was about six, took little Earl to play in a tree house. Now Earl was too little to make the eight-foot climb so Amos got the bright idea to tie a rope around both his and little brother's waste to pull him up. Amos made it to the top and got little Earl about two feet off the ground when Amos lost his balance and fell off backwards. Little Earl shot up and was knocked unconscious by a tree branch as Amos fell crashing to the ground. Amos panicked, shouted for Earl to hold on, and untied the rope from his waist. Now little Earl came loose crashing toward the ground as Amos desperately circled to catch him."

Josh asked, "He didn't catch him, did he?"

Lou replied, "Correct. Little Earl landed on his head and stuck in the dirt like one of those metal yard darts. Amos scooped him up and ran him home. Mr. Hicks carted him off to the hospital where Earl laid in a coma. The doctors said that Earl was brain dead, would never recover, and would soon pass on to a better place."

Josh thought and said, "So, the Hicks have another child and name him Earl to make up for the dead Earl who is not actually dead and later recovers."

Lou answers, "Correct again. About two years later dead Earl wakes up and is as good as new. Only, as fate would have it, better. You see the knock on dead Earl's noggin did something to his brain function and actually made him slightly smarter than his two brothers. He drooled less, lost his appetite for dirt, and actually started reading books."

Josh asked, "So, is he like the Einstein of the three?"

Lou finished his drink, shook his head, and replied, "No not exactly. More like the Moe of the Three Stooges."

With the car engine off and the windows open the sound of gentle blowing grass massaged their minds and provided a relaxing atmosphere. An occasional car could be heard approaching from far off down the road. Josh said, "You know they may very well know we're out here and if so, will be heavily armed."

Lou nodded his head, "Yep. You recon there will be some deputies involved in this?"

Josh stretched, took a deep breath, and replied, "They've got to be. There's no way that much methamphetamine can be moved out of here without their involvement. I just hope it doesn't go all the way to the top."

Lou shook his head, "I honestly don't believe that the sheriff is. He's too connected to the community to lower his morals and be involved."

Josh quickly turned his head, brought up the binoculars, and said, "We've got a blue van coming our way. They're slowing down to make the turn."

Lou said, "Why are they stopping out there?"

Josh replied, "Perhaps they're expecting somebody." Two men with assault rifles exited the rear of the van and disappeared into the wooded area. Josh slowly crawled from the patrol car with the shotgun in his hand, "You better make that call now."

Lou quickly flipped open the cell phone and spoke to Dispatch. He then closed it, snapped it on his belt, and rolled out with the rifle.

Josh whispered, "Start the car and roll up the windows."

Lou complied with Josh's request and moved to the back of the patrol car and said, "Let's move on back behind those trees and wait." Josh nodded.

Josh and Lou crawled on their elbows through the high wheat field and back behind a patch of trees about a hundred yards back. Josh watched the blue van through the binoculars.

Lou whispered, "Are those two still out in the woods?"

Josh ducked down and said, "Here they come." Lou hugged tightly against the ground and listened intensely.

After about five minutes they saw four figures surround their patrol car. Josh depressed the safety button on the shotgun and crouched up into a kneeling position with the barrel pointed toward the group. Two men approached the side of the patrol car while the other waited at the rear. Lou then noticed a fifth man seated inside the van watching with binoculars wearing a headset. Lou mentioned the man in the van to Josh.

The silence of the field was broken by gun fire as the two figures near the patrol car started spraying it with bullets. Then all four approached closer.

Josh said, "Can you hit the guy in the van from here?"

Lou hesitated and said, "Yea. Once you hear the shot go off start pumping lead into our four friends there."

Josh answered, "Amen."

Lou steadied the rifle against the tree and squeezed off a shot. The gentle silence of the cool Oklahoma prairie had been broken once again.

The bullet penetrated the windshield of the van and knocked the man out of view. Before the barrel of the rifle came down the blaring of shotgun blasts filled the scene. Once a slug fired out of the barrel the casing was ejected out the side and another eager shell was quickly chambered and rushed another slug down range in a firing frenzy. The first man at the driver's door got shot in the chest and flew backwards into the wheat field. The second one was at the passenger side and caught one in the stomach which launched him forward and into the ground. The two at the trunk turned to return fire.

One of the men at the trunk fired a rifle round which struck the tree beside Josh and caused him to flinch. He sent a burning slug into the man's neck. Lou fired three rounds into the chest of the last man and watched him fall backward upon the trunk. The prairie once again laid in silence.

Josh maintained a visual down range and loaded more slugs into the shotgun magazine. He then said, "Come on. Let's check them out." The two men ran to the patrol car and checked the four bodies for any sign of life. Josh asked, "Do any of them look familiar?"

Lou said, "No. Thank God. Let's check the van." Josh dragged the body off the trunk and got in the patrol car as Lou drove across the prairie and pulled in behind the van. Broken glass filled the seats of the patrol car and blood dripped from the fenders. They both exited the patrol car and found only one lifeless body in the van. Lou got on his cell phone and notified Dispatch.
As the two leaned up against the hood of the patrol car Josh turned to Lou, "Do you think it's safe out here?"

Lou started to speak and was interrupted by a marked sheriff's car that skidded to a halt. Two uniformed deputies pointed handguns at Josh and Lou.

Lou said, "You can holster those weapons boys. The enemy is out there - dead. We're with the Timber Creek Police Department." The faces of the deputies showed no expression among with the mirrored sunglasses and straw hats.

Chapter 14
"Betrayed"

A second marked sheriff's car arrived occupied by two more deputies. They also exited their car with their pistols drawn. One of them handcuffed Josh, removed his .45 from his holster, and slammed him upon the hood of the police car.

Lou shouted, "Hey take it easy! He's on our side!" An unfriendly pistol struck Lou in the jaw and spun him around. Two deputies grabbed Lou, handcuffed him, and took his pistol. They then smashed him against the patrol car door as they thoroughly searched him.

Lou was placed in one patrol car and Josh in the other. They were then blind folded and given an injection. They later found that they had been taken out in the country to some remote barn modified as a fortress.

Josh woke up and found himself still handcuffed but now seated in a chair in some small room. His head throbbed and he felt hung over. He gagged and nearly vomited. As his vision began to focus, he looked for an escape. There were no windows. Only two metal shelves containing some cardboard boxes.

The door opened and in walked a man in a suite accompanied by a larger man who looked like he worked as a lumber jack. Josh said, "I don't know what you gave me but can I have a pillow?" The man in the suite smiled and leaned over. "You're going to make a telephone call to your sweetheart and ask her to meet you east of town."

Josh whispered, "No I won't asshole." The man in the suite stood up and stepped back as he nodded to the large one. The large man grabbed Josh by the throat and slammed two crushing blows to his stomach. Josh bent over and gasped for air.

The man in the suite leaned over again with his hands folded behind his back, "Have you changed your mind or should Honk persuade you some more?"

Josh struggled to speak, "Screw you and your Honk." A large fist struck Josh in the side of his face and sent him sailing with the chair against the wall.

As he lay unconscious the man in the suit said, "Not so hard next time Honk, if you bust him up too bad, he'll be no good to us. Let's have conversation with the other one."

The two men left the room and Josh slowly regained consciousness. He felt lucky he had been able to duck slightly before being struck. If the massive fist had hit his jaw it would have broken it. Josh stood up and slowly walked over to the shelves where he turned around to feel inside the boxes. He smiled as he found what felt like a paper clip among some papers. He straightened it out and fed it along the latch where it slipped the handcuff open. He then brought his hands around in front of him and smiled to himself, "Damn. It does work." He had learned the method in an officer safety seminar. He then easily removed the cuff from his other wrist.

Josh then returned to the door to listen. He then positioned the chair slightly facing the door and began to search through the cardboard boxes for any kind of weapons.

He eventually tipped one of the metal shelves on the side and quietly stepped on a leg to bend it down. He then bent it back and forth until it broke loose. He then had a slightly jagged edge about ten inches long which he felt he would give Honk as a present when he returned. He then returned the shelf to the up-right position and leaned it against the wall to appear in tact.

Josh then sat in the chair with his hands behind his back holding the piece of metal. After a few minutes the door opened again and in walked the man in the suite followed by Honk. Josh pretended to had been asleep and opened his eyes to say, "Did you bring me my pillow?"

The man in the suite replied, "No, you won't need a pillow when Honk gets through with you."

Josh replied, "Well, I've been thinking about that phone call. Will you promise not to harm Kim?"

The man in the suite smiled, "Sure. We just want to find out what you've told her."

Josh leaned forward and said, "Great." The man in the suite removed his cell phone as Honk stood with his hands folded. Josh quickly jumped up and drove a lightening front kick to Honks groin. Honk moaned and leaned forward. Josh then drove the jagged metal shelf leg into his throat with all his strength. Honks eyes bugged out and he fell to the ground with a mighty thud. The man in the suite stood momentarily in shock until Josh delivered five rapid strikes to his stomach. Josh then followed him to the ground where he sat upon his chest.

Josh pressed his forearm bone against the man's trachea until he gagged and gasped for air. Josh then asked him, "Who do you work for?"

The man said, "They'll kill you."

Josh grabbed the man's right hand and quickly snapped his index finger. The man's attempt to scream was silenced by Josh's forearm against his trachea. Josh punched the man in the solar plexus and grabbed his middle finger to snap in the other direction. The man groaned in agony. Josh whispered in the man's ear, "The way I figure it, you have eight more chances before I start working on your arms. Now what's it gonna be?" The man nodded in agony.

Josh released the pressure on the man's throat and received satisfaction to his questions. The last question was where Lou was being held. When the man answered Josh patted him on the cheek and said, "Thank you. Goodnight." He then slammed his elbow into the man's head and rendered him unconscious. Josh handcuffed the man to the chair and searched him. He took the man's cellphone and his 9 mm pistol. Josh then dug through the pockets of both men until he found a handcuff key in Honks pants. He slowly opened the door to check the hallway. He then crept down the hallway and to a room where the man in the suite had described.

Josh opened the door and found Lou handcuffed sitting in a chair. Lou looked up with a bloody face to find Josh say, "What are you doing?"

Lou smiled, "Waiting for you. I'm bored with playing with these boys."

Josh replied, "I think it's time for the elimination round."

The two men found themselves slowly creeping down the hallway looking for a window to give them some sort of orientation. The walls were all made of concrete blocks with a poured concrete floor. The stairwells were all made of metal and reminded Josh of a military instillation.

Lou asked, "Where is everybody? They wouldn't have left just two guarding us."

Josh said, "I want to get my hands on those deputies. Are you sure you didn't recognize any of them?"

Lou replied, "Yes but they sure looked legitimate."
As the two searched about they came to an office door. Josh drew the pistol,

Lou asked surprisingly, "Where did you get that?"

Josh replied, "I talked that nice fellow wearing the suite out of it."

Lou said, "What about the big guy?"

Josh whispered, "He won't be playing anymore." Lou silently chuckled as he slowly opened the door.
Once inside they found what appeared to be a waiting room. As they slowly entered, they could hear voices coming from another doorway inside.

Josh said, "You open the door and I'll rush inside first. Anyone who looks to be a bad guy I'll shoot them and you get their gun."

Lou asked, "Just like that?"
Josh replied, "Well, I'll shoot them quick."

Lou flung open the door and Josh rushed inside with the pistol displayed and shouted, "Stop." Four surprised faces in deputy uniforms stared at them like deer on a country road staring at the headlights of a semi. One of them started to draw his weapon and Josh quickly shot him in the face twice.

Josh said, "These 9 mm always seem to have a sensitive trigger for some reason. Does anyone else feel anxious to die?" No one moved. Lou took the pistol from the dead man and handcuffed the other two after placing them on the ground.

Lou started to ask questions and Josh interrupted, "Lou, take those two fellows outside and wait for me." Lou looked at him with his head cocked. Josh said, "Wait. Give me his knife. This last fellow and I are going to have conversation." The door closed and all that remained was Josh and the worried man whom Josh handcuffed and pulled to the floor.

Josh quickly wrapped the man's right leg in a leg lock and removed his shoe and sock. He then stood up and said, "Just a minute. Don't crawl off." Josh opened some nearby doors and found a bathroom. He tore the mirror off the wall and returned. He placed the mirror in front of the man sitting up where the man could see behind him as he lay on his stomach. He then tore a seat cushion from a chair and placed it under the man's chin.

Josh then wrapped the man up in a leg lock again and said, "I want to make sure you can see everything that's happening. I'll slice slowly so you don't miss a thing."

The man's eyes got big. Josh asked, "First of all, what's your name?"

The man stuttered, "John Clark."

Josh said, "Well John, here's how the game works. I ask the questions, you give answers, and as a prize you get to keep all your toes. We'll start with the little one that went to market and work our way up. Just keep in mind that your big toe will significantly impact your ability to dance." Sweat poured down the man's face as he trembled.

Josh asked many questions and got all the answers plus more. He came to the conclusion that John either liked his toes connected or really cared about his dancing career.

After several minutes Lou opened the door and asked, "How's it going?"

Josh patted John on the head and replied, "John and I are doing fine. How's your friends doing?"

Lou replied, "I think they're uncomfortable with our company." Josh stepped out into the hallway and conversed with Lou. They both concluded that the interrogated John was probably being truthful and they did not want to spend any more time there than necessary. They returned to the other two men and tied their feet together to prevent them from escaping.

Lou telephoned Darla but Josh was unable to reach Kim. Lou then telephoned Dispatch to provide their location. As they toured the building, they came to a large room that contained a multitude of containers of meth.

Lou shook his head, "Somebody is going to be in a lot of trouble. Can you imagine the millions of dollars in street value sitting here?"

Josh replied, "Yea. Let's get upstairs where we can see outside. This ground hog setting gives me the creeps."

Lou smiled, "Wow. Finally, there's actually something that makes you uncomfortable?"

Josh looked around and said, "Here's another for your list, these tiny 9 mm pee shooters."

Lou said, "You know hanging around with you is no picnic."

Josh replied, "Hey. This is your call. I just came along."

Lou said, "Yea. But you're the one with the guiding ghosts, and the one who keeps turning live men into dead men. But in a good kind of way."

They climbed a stairway and opened the door to find the cool Oklahoma wind blow gently in their faces. Josh smiled, "Freedom at last. Now, be sure that these responding patrol cars are friendly this time."

Lou replied, "Unless they are marked Timber Creek Police Department we're going back inside!"

Patrol cars arrived along with a state police helicopter. Men in suits arrived in unmarked cars. Lou said, "The feds."

Josh said, "You're going to be typing for the next two weeks."

Lou put his hands on his hips, "Hey buddy. You volunteered to play in this game so you've got to start typing too."

Josh replied, "Yea. I recon so, but since we shot those guys, we've got a couple of days rest first."

Lou smiled, "Yea. Good thinking."

The chief ran from his car and put his arms around both Lou and Josh. "Hot damn boys, we got the biggest drug bust in Oklahoma history! And we've got I bet a half dozen deputies involved in this scandal. Are you two all right?" They both nodded. The chief paused and turned his attention to Josh, "Young man. Your Kim is missing but we've got roadblocks in place and we'll find her I promise. Witnesses said a dark car pulled up in front of the dinner and two men rushed inside and grabbed her. The cook tried to fight them and almost got himself killed."

Josh stood in silence then turned to Lou, "I need you to take me back home, now."

The chief walked to the rear of his patrol car, opened the trunk, and took out a stainless steel .45. He asked Josh "Does this look familiar?"

Josh replied, "Yes sir."

The chief said, "I thought it looked too fancy to belong to one of my boys." He then handed his car keys to Lou and said, "Here. Hurry up and don't get it full of bullet holes." He then walked away.

Chapter 15

"The Rescue of Kim"

Lou turned to Josh, "Where do we start?" Josh said to follow him. The two men turned around and returned inside the building and quickly walked downstairs where the two handcuffed deputies were being escorted down the hall.

Josh walked between the escorting officer and grabbed John by the arm and said, "This one will be with you in just a minute. We have something to discuss." The officers stood back as Josh kicked open a door and threw the man inside.

Lou closely followed, turned to put his hand out in the direction of the officers, and closed the door. Josh threw the man into a chair and smashed a table with his elbow. He picked up a chair and threw it against the wall. The chair shattered and knocked a picture off the wall.

Josh leaned over John with maddening eyes and with a growling voice and said, "Where did they take Kim!!"

John shook and stuttered, "Thompson's place. He's got her in the guest house or in an upstairs bedroom."

Josh's rage cooled as he said, "Thank you."

As Josh headed for the door John said in a shaky voice, "Be careful. They have cameras everywhere and will know you're there before you do. Behind the barn is a blind spot but it will only get you near the house." Josh nodded in approval.

The two men ran from the building and jumped into the chief's patrol car. Lou drove back toward town with Josh sitting in

silence. Josh had never served in a war during his four years in the
Marine Corps but he felt he had trained and prepared for it his entire
life. This was the moment of truth. He only wished that he was
younger and faster. The thought of losing Kim was beyond
comprehension. He knew he had to get her out fast before they
found out their empire was crumbling and they had nothing to lose.
Josh said, "Tell me about this Thompson house."

Lou replied, "Old man Thompson kicked off a
few years ago and left everything to his two boys.
One of them disappeared overseas somewhere and
never returned. Rumor has it that the older boy
created an empire in overseas trade in the prescription
medication industry."

Josh replied, "It sounds like medication is not the only thing
he's importing."

Lou said, "Yea. Well today it's all going to come crumbling
down."

Josh saw that the clock showed late afternoon. There was
plenty of sunlight left which would make things tricky. He leaded
his head back against the head rest and turned to watch the clouds
gently wave across the sky. The crooked trees turned and twisted in
fine character that decorated the rugged countryside.

A large turkey buzzard flew up ahead. Lou said, "Come on
this way you greasy devil. We'll feed you." Josh smiled.

Finally, Josh spoke, "Let's stop by my house for a minute."
Lou entered town and soon pulled into the driveway and stopped.
Josh jumped out and said, "Come on inside." Lou followed.

Josh pulled out two bottles of energy drink and threw one to Lou. He then grabbed a bottle of Tylenol and two power bars. "Sit down and relax for just a minute." Josh ran upstairs and returned with two AR15 rifles, two ammo belts, and a .45 pistol for Lou. The rifles were hand me downs of the Vietnam War era equipped with semi-automatic fire only.

The light weight and pistol grip provided easy maneuverability. The only limitation was the delicate stock which prevented butt strokes, but that's what elbows and knees were for. Still the benefits outweighed the limitation. He tossed one to Lou and said, "Partner tonight will be one you'll remember. And so, will many others. Let's go." Josh then put on a backpack and headed out the door.

Lou asked, "what's in the backpack?' Josh replied, "All kinds of surprises."

The two jumped back into the car and headed out toward the end of town where the Thompson residence quietly waited for the arrival of war. The unmarked car drove across a pasture entry and came to rest behind some trees. Josh finished his power bar and gulped his power drink, "Let's rumble!" The two followed the tree line, crossed the fence behind the barn, and watched quietly behind the barn. The Thompson residence had been built before the civil war. It was magnificent with large white pillars in front. A large circular driveway curved around the front with over hangs. It was white in color with black shutters beside all the windows that lined the main and top floor. Colorful flowers in decorated boxes were beneath the many windows. The front landscaping was nothing less than a spectacular flower garden.

Josh said, "This place is beautiful. Too bad we have to destroy it. Have you ever been inside?"

Lou shook his head, "No. But there are rooms and guards everywhere."

Josh said, "I've got an idea. Let's get us a guard." Josh laid his rifle on the ground and said, "Wait here. I'll be right back."

Lou peeked around the corner and thought to himself, "I gotta see this."

Josh crawled along the side of the barn where the shadow from the sun provided some concealment. He then hid behind a bush and waited until the front door opened and a guard made his rounds. As the guard approached the barn Josh leaped out and punched him in the face. The guard fell backward stunned. Josh grabbed his feet and pulled him behind the bush. As the guard shook his head and regained his composure Josh crawled upon his back and tightened a choke hold.

The guard started to pass out but Josh loosened his grip and allowed him to come back. Josh whispered in the guard's ear, "Where's the girl?" The guard mumbled. Josh applied the choke and felt the guard go limp. He loosened the grip and the guard came back around. Josh whispered again, "I don't have time to play games with you. You have one more chance before I break your neck. Now I'm getting pretty pissed off about now. Where's the girl?"

The guard mumbled and gasped, "Upstairs the first bedroom on the right."

Josh said, "Thank you." He then administered an elbow strike to the side of the guard's head and rendered him unconscious. Josh then pulled some rope from his backpack, tied the guard's arms and legs, then placed a gag over his mouth. He then crawled back to Lou.

Josh said, "Well, the guard said she's in the first upstairs bedroom on the right."

Lou asked, "Do you think we should wait until dark?" Josh said, "I really don't want her in there that long."

Lou replied, "Yea. I wouldn't want Darla in there either. Now what?"

Josh said, "Let's see what's inside the barn?" The two crawled along the other side away from the house where they found a window.

Josh glanced inside and said, "Perfect all I need you to do is drive that tractor there with the hay wagon up to that second story window. You hop off and provide cover fire first at the door and then through every window on the first floor."

Lou said, "And what are you going to do?"

Josh replied, "I'll waltz right in the front door, kill everyone in sight, run up the stairs, kill a few more, enter that bedroom, rescue Kim, and jump out the window into the hay wagon with Kim in my arms. Now you'll need to hop back up on that tractor and drive us through the fence and back to the car."

Lou said, "What?!"

Josh replied, "Don't worry. I can provide cover fire from the back of the wagon."

Lou shook his head and said, "Josh I know you're a hot shot and all but this is crazy."

Josh replied, "I know. That's why it's going to work." Josh then put his hand on Lou's shoulder, "Buddy If Darla was in there, I would be saying the same thing."

Lou nodded his head, "I know. Let's go kick some ass."

The two climbed in through the barn window, that Josh had managed to pry open, and approached the tractor.

Lou climbed upon on the tractor, flipped the fuel switch, and said, "Josh. Do you believe your shadow figure will help us out here?"

Josh replied, "I don't know but I do believe in God. And I think we'll need His helping hand on this one."

Lou started the tractor and whispered to himself, "Heavenly Father, please be with us."

Josh opened the sliding door to the barn and climbed upon the fender of the wagon. He then began firing rifle rounds at the door and windows. Lou also pointed his rifle and fired with one hand. When the wagon lined up with the bedroom window Josh jumped off and ran for the door.

He kicked the door open, dove on the floor, and sprayed the area with rifle rounds. He quickly reloaded a fresh magazine and continued firing. Beautiful plush sitting chairs and lamps exploded with the impact from the rifle rounds. Priceless paintings tore and came crashing down.

Two men returned fire from the main level hallway. Josh fired into the plaster wall and silenced them. He then ran up the curved staircase and went down to a knee as pistol rounds impacted the wall around him. He fired upward at the top and struck a guard in the groin and the chest. Pieces of the beautiful oak hand railing was splintering and filling the air.

The sound of gun fire filled the house and echoed throughout. Bullets were ricocheting everywhere. Josh felt his legs sting but detected no malfunction. He quickly reloaded a fresh magazine and continued firing first ahead of him and then behind him. Glass was shattering and plaster dust was flying everywhere.

Josh climbed up the staircase and continued firing. When he reached the top of the stairs, he desperately ran for the first bedroom door. He kicked the door open and immediately jumped to the side. Bullets sprayed from inside at a rapid rate. Josh felt bullets come through the wall at him. He ducked down and rolled in front of the opening and fired at two men standing with automatic weapons. The men took rounds to both the chest and the head before falling.

Josh rushed inside and found Kim tied to a chair. He closed the door, quickly retrieved his knife, and cut her free. Kim removed the handkerchief from around her mouth and jumped into Josh's arms.

Josh turned around, fired a few rounds through the door, and said, "Let's get out of here!"

He then grabbed a chair, shattered the window, and picked up Kim. He climbed up on the windowsill and jumped with Kim tightly clinching around his neck. When they landed in the hay wagon Josh rolled in front of her and continued firing at anything he saw.

Lou climbed upon the seat and drove toward the fence with Josh continuing to spray bullets. Lou shouted in joy and crashed through the bright white picket fence toward the patrol car. Josh changed magazines and continued firing toward the house. Guards came running from around the house but were quickly either cut down by Josh's rifle rounds or dropped rolling to the ground. The tractor crossed the road, entered the field, and came to rest beside the waiting patrol car. Josh grabbed Kim and rolled out the back of the wagon. Lou got behind the wheel and started the engine while Josh pushed Kim inside. Lou accelerated rapidly and threw dirt and grass as he headed across the field.

Lou shouted to Kim, "Get down!" Josh leaned out the window with his rife. As the patrol car spun onto the black top Josh continued to point the rifle toward the direction of the house until they got safely out of rifle range.

Josh pulled Kim up out of the seat and passionately kissed her. She held him tight and sobbed. Josh asked, "Did they hurt you?"

Kim sobbed, "No."

Lou shouted, "Yes! Hell yes!! Man, what a fight!" He reached his hand back to Josh who broke loose one hand to grasp Lou's. Lou got on the radio and announced, "501. We've got many 10-40s and injured suspects at the Thompson residence. You better send in the National Guard and show me enroute to the hospital."

Dispatch hesitated and replied, "10-4 501!"

Kim continued to hug and kiss Josh as he tried to speak to her. Her tears were flowing but she refused to slow down her joyful embrace.

Lou pulled up to the hospital and found the barrel of the rifle still warm and smoking. Josh limped out the back and pulled Kim to his side.

Kim appeared frightened and said, "Oh my God! Are you hurt?"

Josh replied, "Naw. It's just a scratch." Lou jumped out and ran around the side to put Josh's arm around his neck as he and Kim helped Josh limp through the emergency entrance. Nurses ran to his aid with a wheelchair and took him back into triage. Kim stayed with him closely followed by Lou.

The nurses asked, "What happened here?"

Lou replied, "He had a run in with a whole lot of bullets and some may have struck him."

A nurse asked, "Is this person your prisoner?"

Lou laughed, "Nope. He's just someone who came to save our town."

The nurses checked out both Josh and Kim. One bullet had penetrated his leg. Several others had nicked him. He was released shortly thereafter and driven home by Lou.

As the days passed the investigation revealed that the heirs of the Thompson estate consisted of two sons. One had become hooked on methamphetamine and organized their property as a main hub for distribution. They had employed a half dozen deputies and over two dozen private security guards. When all was said and done over twenty-four people were convicted and later sent to prison. Eighteen bodies were carried out of the house that day. Although the sheriff's department was under investigation it appeared that only a handful of deputies had been involved in the illegal activities.

The days passed and Kim religiously came to Josh's house on a daily basis. He maintained his position at the university which quickly grew into a full-time position. In the evening time when Josh was not stretching and performing light workouts, he would sit on the front porch with his leg elevated while he read and drank tea. The neighbors were all friendly and pleased to have Josh as a neighbor.

The neighbors quickly found that Josh had a pleasant way about him and was easy to talk to. He could be found helping a neighbor work on an old car or playing catch with a youngster. One early evening Kim was delayed in coming by and Josh sat on the porch as a neighbor kid walked by with his head down. Josh shouted, "Conrad. How come you're not riding your bicycle today?"

Conrad stopped with his head down and answered, "Hello Mr. Stark. I thought that I'd just walk today."

Josh replied, "Well then, how was school? Did you put any snakes in the teacher's desk?"

Conrad slightly smiled and replied, "No, sir. I couldn't find any snakes today."

Josh laughed, "Well, one day I bet you'll lose interest in snakes and put more attention on the girls." Conrad slowly walked over with his hands in his pockets, climbed up the steps, and sat down. When he sat down, he quickly leaned forward with a wrinkled face. Josh asked, "What's wrong little buddy? Are you hurt?"

Conrad shyly replied, "I'm ok. I got a whipping' last night from my step-dad."

Josh noticed Conrad's watery eyes, "It must have been a big whipping'."

Conrad nodded. "I may not be able to play catch with you for a while because mom says we may be staying with grandma for a few weeks."

Josh replied, "Ok. I'll keep the glove warm for when you're ready again. There's some juice in the refrigerator." Conrad slowly got up, went inside, and returned with a juice. He slowly sat down with watery eyes again and said, "Thank you Mr. Stark."

Josh said with growing concern, "Conrad. Tomorrow I'd like you to visit the school nurse and talk with her about any worries you might have. Maybe she can give you some suggestions to make you feel better. Will you do that for me?"

Conrad nodded, "If you really want me to."

Josh said, "Well, we're buddies and buddies look out for each other. Don't they?"

Conrad took a sip, nodded, and asked, "Can she give mom some medicine too?"

Josh answered, "Maybe you should ask her." Conrad sat in the chair with his legs rocking back and forth. An occasional car would drive by accompanied by a friendly wave. A few birds conversed in the elderly oak tree and a couple of squirrels danced

about in the limbs above. Quite as the evening sat it was quickly
interrupted.

Conrad's step-father, Sam, came storming down the street
toward Conrad. Conrad looked nervous and said, "Oh, oh. Step-
dad's coming and he's been drinking a lot of beer."

Josh replied, "I'll have a talk with him."

Sam stormed up to the porch and said, "Get your butt home
boy!" Conrad looked up at Josh who nodded with fear. As Conrad
jumped to his feet and walked past Sam, he was slapped Conrad hard
on the bottom. Conrad let out a whimper and began to cry as he ran
home. Josh stood up and limped down the steps. Sam took a step
back with his right foot and appeared to square off.

Josh said, "Maybe you'd like to abuse someone your own
size?"

Sam slurred, "You think you're a real bad ass don't you Mr.
big shot?"

Josh sternly looked into Sam's eyes and said, "If you ever
abuse the boy again, I'm going to look you up and tear you a new
asshole. Understand?" Sam's eyes saw red but before he could
react Josh grabbed him by the throat and drove his right thumb deep
into his larynx. Sam gagged for air and Josh grabbed his right arm
by the elbow and slammed him against the side of the house.
As Sam struggled to gasp for air Josh released and punched him
several times in the stomach until Sam fell to his knees in surprise
and agony. Josh then grabbed him by his hair, pulled his close, and
whispered into Sam's ear, "Today I will allow you to keep all your
teeth. If we ever have to have this conversation again, you'll be

pissing blood. Do you understand?" Sam nodded. He then released his grip.

As Sam leaned over with his hands on his knees he gasped heavily for oxygen.

Josh said, "Sam. Tomorrow I want you to come over here and visit when you're sober. We're neighbors and I think our conversation will have a positive impact upon your health and your future. Is that agreed?" Sam nodded. Josh said, "Good. Now go home and be kind to your family."

Sam staggered home with his large frame bent and broken like he had just been spanked. Josh was glad that only the neighbor across the street had seen the spectacle. The neighbor, Mrs. Golf, rocked in her chair and slowly nodded in approval. Mrs. Golf appeared to be a kind and wise old widow woman in her eighties who helped maintain the friendly atmosphere of a small town. She routinely walked and brought cheer to the neighborhood and was well respected. She often had kind and wise comments that she would share with others.

Josh sat back down in his chair and recalled the many people like Sam he had encountered in his profession. He knew that the likelihood of Sam changing was very slim but sometimes people wise up and see the light. Perhaps there was a chance.

The next morning Josh went to the community center for a light workout and then drove to the diner and nervously asked Kim to come outside with him.

Chapter 16
"The Proposal"

As the couple stepped outside a dirty pickup truck with only one headlight came bouncing across the parking lot and toward Josh's car. The couple retreated to the door as the dusty vehicle skidded to a stop. Kim shouted, "Hank! You slow down!"

A skinny old man with a soiled ball cap slid out and said, "Oops, sorry about that. This here shiny car sort of blended in with the gravel. Well, hello Miss. Kim!" Hank carried a stack of newspapers inside the diner as Josh released the suppressed laughter. Kim held her hand over her mouth and turned her head.

Kim accompanied Josh to his 4-Runner and sat inside. She appeared concerned and asked, "Is everything, all right?"

Josh gently brushed her soft beautiful hair and cleared his throat, "Well, Kim I've been thinking a lot here lately about us."

Kim replied, "Ok. Well, I constantly think about us too Josh. Is something the matter?"

Josh said, "Well, kind of. You see with all we've been through I've come to the conclusion that we're quite the match."

Kim kindly interrupted, "Yes. I'd sure say we are."

Josh reached into his pocket, opened a small black velvet case, and said, "Will you marry me Kim?"

Kim bowed her head as tears poured from her eyes. She pressed her lips together in surprise and smiled, "Yes my gentle warrior. I would be honored to be your wife." She then passionately kissed him. The door to the dinner flew open and everyone stepped outside clapping and whistling. Kim smiled as Josh took out the diamond ring and placed it upon her finger.

The clouds above appeared to part as the Oklahoma sun brightened the sky. A large hawk soared over head. Hank smiled and displayed what was remaining of his tobacco-stained teeth and clapped along.

Kim said, "Why wait? Let's go to the courthouse now."

Josh replied, "Well shouldn't we tell your mother?"

Kim said, "Sure. Let's stop by and take her with. You can call Lou and have him meet us there also!"

Josh said, "Why not." As they drove toward Mrs. Cooper's house Josh telephoned Lou. "Hey Lou, are you busy? Why don't you and Darla meet us at the courthouse while Kim and I get married?" The phone got silent and Josh said, "Lou, are you still there? Ok. See you in about fifteen minutes." Josh disconnected and laughed.

Kim asked, "What did he say?"

Josh replied, "He dropped the phone!" They both laughed.

As they pulled up in front of Kim's mother's house Josh said, "Why don't you go inside yourself and tell her? I've already been here and shown her the ring."

Kim smiled, "You have?"

Josh replied, "Well, yes. Since she's going to be my mother-in-law I wanted to get off on the right foot and get her blessing." Kim kissed him and ran into the house all excited.

The group convoyed to city hall. Josh was impressed by the grandeur of the city building. Large concrete pillars stood proudly at the top of the steps. The spectacle reminded him more of an ancient Greek cathedral. The front doors were tall with large brass handles and made of thick glass. When they stepped inside their heels echoed upon the polished floor. Dark oak trimmed the windows and the doors. Above the doors were antique tilted windows partially opened which allowed the breeze and friendly gestures to permeate.

Josh escorted Kim to the door where a sign hung indicating, "Justice of the Peace." A friendly bearded man was leaning against the counter laughing with two elderly grey-haired secretaries. He looked up and said, "Well hello Kim. And I see you've brought your mother with you. How are you Mrs. Anderson?" Everyone smiled and he politely continued, "Well, there's Officer Powell and his misses." He shook the men's hands and identified himself as Henry Marshall. "What brings you in today?"

Kim smiled as she clinched Josh's hand, "We'd like to get married."

Henry's mouth flew opened, he smiled, and said, "Oh yes! You're the man I've heard so much about. Splendid! Come on in!" Everyone crowded inside Henry's tiny office filled with bookshelves and antique furniture. The session went fast and within ten minutes Josh had himself a wife and Kim herself a husband. As the couple walked out the building they were applauded and confronted by handshakes and pats on the back.

Kim asked, "Where did all these people come from?"

Darla replied, "I guess news travels fast."

Lou grabbed Josh's shoulder and whispered, "You haven't been visited lately by your shadow friend, have you?"

Josh replied, "Nope, not lately."

Lou said, "Great. We both need to rest for a while."

A voice shouted, "Where's the honeymoon?"

Kim looked at Josh, "Gosh, we never thought about that."

Josh asked Kim, "When can you get away and for how long?"

Mrs. Anderson spoke up, "You two love birds can leave tomorrow. I've got some part timers who can watch things."

Josh said, "Well, I guess we can leave tomorrow."

Darla spoke up, "Wait just a minute. You be at our house tonight at 6:00 for the party!"

Kim smiled, looked at Josh who nodded in agreement, and replied, "We'll be there."

Several old men wearing ball caps with pressed coveralls were clapping. One of them shouted, "Will you have some of that spiked prune juice for Ned here?"

Laughter erupted and Darla replied, "Yes. And your wives are welcomed."

One of the old codgers softly said, "Why would be bring our wives? We wanna have fun!"

Another replied, "To keep you from dancing on the table in your boxers you old coot!" The crowd harmonized in laughter.

As Kim and Josh climbed into his 4-Runner to drive away, they looked back to see over a hundred people clapping and waving. Josh said, "It must have been your mother's doing. I never told anyone else." Kim just smiled and rested her head upon his shoulder.

Josh drove straight to his house and carried Kim inside, closed the door, and ravenously kissed her. Josh asked, "So, what's the first thing you intend to do to OUR house?"

Kim smiled, "Since I'm the one who decorated it in the first place, nothing. I'll just bring the rest of my clothes over and Arrow."

Josh carried her upstairs and said, "Speaking of clothes."

Kim asked, "Where are you taking me Mr. Stark?"

Josh smiled, "Where you don't need any clothes, Mrs. Stark."

Hours went by and eventually found the couple dozing in each other's arms. Kim gently whispered, "Josh, I have a confession to make."
Josh kissed her forehead and replied, "Ok, go ahead."

Kim said, "Would it be un-lady like to say that the first day I saw you I wondered what it would feel like to wake up next to you?"

Josh replied, "Well, honestly I craved holding you from the moment I saw you."

Kim smiled, "Me too."

When 5:45 rolled around the couple walked to the door hand in hand. Josh pulled her close to him and kissed her cheek and then her ear. Kim tilted her head back and said, "If you don't stop that we're going right back upstairs and will be late."

Josh lifted her off the ground and said, "Yea, it would be rude to keep them waiting." As Josh and Kim walked down the steps a little boy rode by on his bicycle and smiled. Josh shouted, "Conrad. Keep an eye on the place for me buddy. I'll be back next week and will have a surprise for you." Conrad smiled and gave him thumbs up.

As the couple drove off Kim tightly held Josh's arm and said, "Josh. I have a question to ask you that has been bothering me." Josh said, "On this beautiful Oklahoma afternoon what's on your mind?"

Kim asked, "Does it bother you that I cannot have children?"

Josh stopped at the stop sign, looked deeply into her eyes, and replied, "Honey. I and forty-eight years ago and I'm relieved that you don't expect children from me. Besides, there are enough children running around this neighborhood as it is without us adding anymore of 'em." Kim glowed in relief.

The Powell's lived in a new neighborhood about a mile away. Most of the houses were three-bedroom ranch styles with poured concrete floors and two car garages. The couple arrived at the Powell's house to find cars parked everywhere, people waving and clapping, and a large banner that read, "Congratulations Kim and Josh." They walked inside to find everything decorated and presents on the table.

Josh whispered in Kim's ear, "How did they manage to get this all together so fast?"

Kim whispered back, "Us country hicks are just full of surprises."

Josh smiled, "You got that right."

Lou rushed over and was quickly embraced by Josh. Josh said, "My goodness. Thank you so much! You outdid yourself!"

Lou handed Josh a bottle of Michelob Ultra. Lou got a serious look on his face and said, "I've been thinking about that day out on the stakeout. If I would have been alone, I would have been parked where I was told to be and I wouldn't be here today."

Josh smiled and said, "The Lord works in many mysterious ways." Lou smiled. Josh continued, "Oh. Thank you for the help at the Thompson place. If it wasn't for you, *I* wouldn't be here today." Lou smiled again and patted Josh on the back.
Josh held Kim's hand and asked her what she would like to drink. As he turned around Darla handed her a glass of wine.

Josh reached out and hugged Darla and whispered in her ear, "Thank you."

Music played and people danced. Several old folks got up and line danced. Josh was fascinated with the skill and the talent of the seniors. They all seemed to move and play off each other like a finely tuned dance team. The smiles and sincerity electrified Josh and brought forth a festive feeling of joy. He felt blessed to be in such pleasant good-natured company.
Hours passed and people began to drift in and out of the party. A huge mountain of presents piled up.

As people laughed and moved about Josh saw a small figure enter through the front door. Darla kneeled down and spoke with the little figure. As Darla stood up, she looked around the room and pointed toward Josh with her arm around a little boy. Josh approached and was met by a smiling little boy. "Hello Conrad! How's my little buddy?"

Conrad stood shyly in a pressed shirt with tie and dress pants. He smiled and stretched out a brightly wrapped present. "This is for your Mrs. Kim."

Josh tenderly kneeled down and reached out to receive the gift. "Thank you, pal. How have you been?"

Conrad smiled, "Step-dad's a lot nicer since you had a talk with him."

Josh patted him on the head, "Sometimes dads need to be reminded of things just like anyone else."

Conrad smiled, rushed into Josh's arms and said, 'Hurry home. I'm getting that fast ball down pretty darn well."

Josh smiled, "Keep practicing and I'll see you in about a week." The little boy turned and walked to the door where his mother patiently waited outside with a precious smile.

Josh turned and found himself face to face with Darla and said, "Wow. These Timber Creek folks sure are generous."

Darla replied, "Yes. Kim is very special to us all. She is as genuine as they come and you're pretty much admired also."

Josh looked down at his drink and said, "Yes she is quite an angel." Josh then cleared his throat and said, "Darla, thank you for all you've done here tonight. I apologize for putting your husband in harm's way."

Darla took Josh by the hand and said, "I've given it much thought and have come to the conclusion that you first and foremost saved his life and afterward you asked for his help in saving Kim's. You did well and conducted yourself just like Kim calls you, gentle warrior."

Josh nodded, "Well you see I had an amazing partner."

Darla placed her hands on her hips as she smiled, "Listen here gentle warrior, the fight is over, they're all gone. Now relax, have fun, and most of all enjoy your wife!" Josh nodded and looked to see Kim seriously looking at something in her hand in the presence of an old lady.

Josh approached and saw that the old lady was holding a little dog. Josh put his arm around Kim and said, "Hello Millie. How's your little Sadie doing?" Before Millie could answer Kim unfolded a beautifully embroidered piece of artistic material with their names and date. The artistic design was unique and glowed with richness. Kim's eyes watered as she smiled at Josh. Josh cleared his throat, touched the soft fabric, and said, "Goodness Millie, it's beautiful."

Millie smiled and replied, "I wish you a happy life with our Kim. I pray that you will fare well." She then slowly shuffled away with her Sadie tightly held in her arms.

Josh turned to Kim, "Wow. You sure are popular around here."

Kim said, "And who is it that stormed a fortress to save my life after taking down the largest drug cartel in the state of Oklahoma?"

Josh replied, "That was easy. When a man finds the greatest treasure in his life, he will find a way to protect her." Kim smiled and hugged him.

Josh was quickly attacked by pats on his back. Laughing voices said, "Good catch young man." "Congratulations!" "Good job on those drug bastards!" Old men dressed in pressed coveralls and faded ball caps circled and applauded.

Josh smiled and laughed as he conversed with the group. As the night lingered on his attention focused on Kim. She turned and met her eyes with his. Her lips continued to move in conversation but her attention was focused on Josh across the room. Her face gave an intimate expression away from her immediate domain and increased as Josh approached.

Josh's voice slowed as he arrived and pulled her away from the conversation. Her beautiful eyes sparkled and fired intense emotion toward him. He gently placed his cheek against hers and felt her energy transfer into him. She struggled to control the emotion but her strength was not powerful enough. She closed her eyes and melted into his warm embrace. His arms gently cradled her as her breaths increased to accommodate his attractive response.

Josh whispered, "You know this is great, but I really want to be alone with my wife now."

Kim intensely responded, "And I want is to be with my husband."

Josh looked around and found Lou watching from across the room. Josh's half smile was acknowledged by Lou's nod. The couple slipped outside and away from the crowd.

As Josh's 4-Runner departed from the friendly vices he placed his arm around Kim. She tilted her head against his shoulder and quickly produced a smile upon her lips.

Within a few minutes Josh pulled into their driveway and parked in their garage. He pressed the button beside his sunroof which closed the door. He then slid off the seat with his arms tightly wrapped around Kim. He cradled her in his left arm as he shut the car door. He then carried her inside as she warmly molded into his arms.

Josh squeezed out of his tennis shoes and slowly climbed the stairs across the upstairs hallway and into the master bedroom. He gently laid her upon the bed, removed her shoes, and kissed her ready lips. He unbuttoned her blouse, dropped it on the floor, and slowly slipped her dress below her trim and smooth legs. Her left leg slowly rose with her breathing and gently brushed his neck. His head turned and gently kissed her ankle and traveled upward where she trembled and arched her back.

As the minutes turned into hours the couple was later found relaxed in silence with the moonlight glowing through the window. Soft breathing harmonized throughout the bedroom and created an atmosphere of sincere attachment and love. Their hearts beat together a devoted sound of love and romance.

When 4:00 displayed on the clock Josh's eyes opened. He turned his head to check the time and smiled as he found Kim lying beside him. He then tenderly kissed her face and quickly faded back to sleep.

As the morning woke by the timid sun Josh carried Kim into the shower with giggles and smiles. The warm water relaxed their ambitions and brought them passionately together in each other's arms. Kim whispered, "Did I dream or was what happened last night for real?"

Josh kissed her ear and replied, "If you did, we both had the same glorious dream." Kim held her diamond ring up to her face and cried a happy tear. Josh gently brought her hand up to his mouth and kissed it. He then dropped to his knees and kissed her warm and soft stomach. She gently caressed his head, slowly backed her shoulders against the shower tile, and arched her trembling back. Josh cherished every touch he shared with Kim. He was extremely attracted to her sincere character and gentle approach to life. He respected how she truly cared about others and was exceedingly tuned to people's feelings. During their romantic embrace he found that her body was as an artistic miracle. He found her athletic design was a man's dream. In his eyes she carried her forty-one years as the master of beauty.

Their shower once again escalated to uncontrollable proportions. When the shower was over Kim blinked her excited eyes and collapsed into Josh's arms. She trembled and smiled in fulfillment.

The Oklahoma sun peeked in through the window and whispered that the couple must move onward. They quickly got themselves dressed, packed their bags, and loaded up the 4-Runner. As they drove down the street neighbors resting within their porch swings waved and clapped. Josh said, "Before we head out, we need to make a quick stop by the bank."

Kim said, "Ok. I guess we better have some cash." The 4-Runner pulled up in front of the bank and stopped.

Josh said, "We need to go inside where we can get your signature on my account."

Kim replied, "Oh! With all the excitement I forgot about the financial stuff. We need to get your name on my account also." The couple walked into the bank and quickly met with a friendly officer who brought out the records and presented them. Kim's eyes lit up. "Is there a mistake? Is this amount correct?" The bank officer and Josh smile. Kim signed her name in a daze and displayed a puzzled smile.

The bank officer said, "Congratulations Mr. and Mrs. Stark. Here's my card if you should ever need anything at all." The couple thanked her and headed toward the door. Josh pushed open the large glass door and escorted Kim to the 4-Runner where he opened the door for her.

When Josh returned to his side and climbed inside Kim asked, "Josh. We never discussed financial matters much. How did you end up with that much money? Did you cash in your retirement?"

Chapter 17
"The Honeymoon"

Josh smiled, "Honey. When I left Kansas, I sold my house and everything I owned. The hundred and eighty thousand dollars was the equity I had in the house plus all my savings. I get over two thousand dollars a month in retirement."

Kim took a drink of water with wide eyes and said, "Oh my gosh! The Miller house you're living in would cost less than a hundred."

Josh stroked her hair and replied, "Little princess, Mr. Miller wanted eighty and I told him that I felt the price was too low. Besides, I wanted to assure that I could capture your heart."

Kim smiled, "First of all you captured my heart when you brought Millie that puppy. Second of all, with all due respect, Mr. Miller has more money than he can possibly spend. I would not feel like I was taking advantage of him by taking him up on his generous offer. He only said it to help you out and share his wealth."

Josh started the engine and said, "You see. I knew I was marrying not only a beautiful woman but a smart one at that. When we get back, I'll pay Mr. Miller a visit. If you're sure you really want the house."

Kim leaned back and said, "Honey, that house takes my breath away every time I walk into it. But not as much as you do."

Josh said, "Okay. The house is yours."

Josh thought to himself how fortunate he was to have found Kim. He felt that any man would do anything to have her and that she was a much better catch than he deserved. He prayed that God would continue to bless him and Kim. He turned to Kim and said, "Kim. Thank you for being my wife."

Kim tenderly smiled and replied, "You're welcome, my gentle warrior." She then kissed him on the cheek.

The 4-Runner headed off toward Branson. Josh turned on the radio and smiled as Kim tapped her foot to the country music. She opened the sunroof and smiled as the sunlight sparkled in her hair. Josh reached out and gently stroked the side of her face as she closed her eyes and leaned her head back. She softy said, "You don't have to spend a lot of money on me Josh Stark. I would be content with just laying in your warm and tender arms beneath the stars."

Josh started to speak but felt his throat squeeze. He swallowed, smiled, and gently pulled her face toward him. He looked into her eyes and kissed her warm passionate lips.
The warm Missouri breeze feathered Kim's hair in harmony with the wholesome country music. Bright billboards covered the highway and brightened the imagination of the travelers who eagerly followed the road toward entertainment. The highway cut through rock and history like a rainbow leading to a treasure. Although commercialization reached out, easy country living lurked beyond the trees and canyons. Josh imagined how it used to be many years ago. He visualized the rafts drifting down the river with laughing children as farmers tilled the land and women scrubbed the clothes on metal washboards.

The highway climbed hills and quickly descended into the valley below. Canyon rock wallpapered the shoulders and brought grandeur to the picturesque rugged setting. Kim leaned back in comfort as she held Josh's warm and contented hand. She felt secure like she had never felt before. She was still overcome with the security and dedication Josh had offered her so warmly. With her eyes closed she prayed and gave thanks to God.

Highway 76 was just up ahead. Josh slowed the powerful engine and welcomed the ramp. Kim opened her eyes and said, "We're here already?"

Josh said, "Well yea. You've been asleep my sleeping beauty for the past two hours."

Kim smiled and stretched, "I've been saving my energy for later."

Josh replied, "Good. With the way you look right now you're going to need it." Kim laughed.

The 4-runner cruised into the downtown area and came to rest in front of the hotel along the river front. Josh climbed out with Kim by his side. Roman like pillars proudly stood out front and protected the entrance through the large tinted doors. Exotic flower plants brought warmth and beauty to the atmosphere. The hotel was magnificent with plush carpet and cheerful bell hops rushing about. The couple approached the front desk to conduct their business.

The desk clerk smiled as he quickly typed on the keyboard. "Good afternoon Mr. and Mrs. Stark your room is 515. Would you like me to note your credit card number for room service and additional services?"

Josh replied, "Yes that would be fine. Mrs. Stark may decide she needs some refreshments." Kim smiled as the clerk handed room cards.

The clerk smiled politely and said, "The pool is on your left along with the exercise room. The restaurant is available twenty-four hours a day. If I may be of any further service please press zero on your room phone. Is everything in order?"

Josh looked at Kim who smiled and nodded her head in approval and replied, "Yes everything looks wonderful."

The clerk smiled and said, "Have a nice stay."

Josh nodded and escorted Kim to the elevator and up toward the room. As they walked along the clean plush carpet, they found comforting chairs and miniature sitting rooms near the elevators. When they entered the room Kim's eyes lit up. "This is beautiful!" There was a large king size bed with a large oak entertainment center against the wall. A refrigerator was beneath the counter with a sitting room off to the side. A balcony overlooked the river and the shops below.

Kim slowly entered the room and stood with her mouth open. Josh took her by the hand and directed her into the bathroom. On the right was a large Jacuzzi with a shower beside it. The marble countertop contained bottles of soap and bath beads. A panel of switches was upon the left door. Josh pressed one of the switches and a series of lights around the mirror lit up. Another switch illuminated the Jacuzzi.

Josh asked, "What do you think?"

Kim replied, "I think that we can manage for a month or so right here." Josh laughed. The couple walked out onto the balcony and leaned against the rod iron railing which overlooked the shops below and the nearby slow-moving river. Josh moved behind Kim and wrapped his arms around her. She sank backwards into his arms, smiled, and tilted her head back. Josh lightly kissed her neck. Her smile grew and from her soft plush lips came, "If you keep that up, we won't make it downstairs for lunch."

Josh whispered, "Well we can't have that. We've got that bottle of champagne that needs to get in the ice. Tonight, we're going to try out that Jacuzzi for at least a couple of hours."

Kim kissed him and replied, "I hope that bathroom is soundproof."

Josh smiled and said, "I'll get some ice and be right back."

Kim replied, "Wait. I'll go with you." The couple entered the hallway and received friendly nods and hellos from passing tenants and housekeeping personnel. They filled their ice bucket and headed back to the room.

Kim said, "Everyone here is so friendly. It's like a big small town. I've never stayed in a fancy hotel like this before, have you?"

Josh shook his head. "No. I never had a reason to up until now." Kim hugged his arm and smiled. The couple returned to the room and back onto the balcony. Josh put his arm around Kim and asked, "Where do you want to eat?"

Kim looked both left and right and pointed, "How about right there."

Josh picked her up and carried her back inside as she giggled and kicked her feet. Kim asked, "When I get to be seventy years old are you still going to carry me around like this?"

Josh stopped, contemplated a moment, and replied, "Even if I have to cart you around upon my lap in a wheelchair!"

Kim laughed, "Well then, we better make sure we visit that exercise room during our stay otherwise you'll be seeing a chiropractor."

Josh laid her upon the bed and began passionately kissing her. Kim's stomach growled and Josh asked, "What was that?"

Kim frowned and said, "I'm hungry."

Josh stood up with Kim's legs wrapped around his waist and said, "Let's get you fed so you'll have energy for tonight."

Kim replied, "I think you're going to be in trouble tonight buddy after I get some of that champagne in me."

Josh kissed her chest and said, "I can't wait."

The couple walked out the hotel into a spectacle of shops with mesmerized tourists. There was a large fountain which sprayed water over fifty feet in the air with multi -colored lights. Side jets shot streams into the center with large arches. Families sat around the edge and reached out to touch the clear refreshing water. Every thirty feet or so an old-style metal streetlight was seen positioned along the sidewalk. Large flowerpots contained speakers that played warm country music. The lights upon the speaker boxes would change colors occasionally. An open trolley drove up and down the center of the street driven by a friendly man dressed in with black hat as an old-time railroad engineer. Smiling and excited children waved and cheered as the trolley slowly drove by and rang its bell.

Kim excitedly squeezed Josh's hand and said, "This place is so beautiful and homey." Just then they came across a commotion up ahead. As they approached an Irish Pub several people were crowded around the outside patio. Many wore troubled faces. Kim said, "It looks like someone is fighting."

Josh turned and caught glimpse of a familiar shadow by the building up ahead.

Josh replied, "That's unusual entertainment for around here. Let's check it out." As they approached the crowd an apprehensive man wearing glasses stood with his arms around a teenage boy. The teenager had blood running from his mouth which was being gently padded by a woman who appeared to be his mother. The mother sobbed and shook as she gently comforted the teenager.

As the couple approached a large build man sat at a table and argued with the apparent father. "The little punk needs to watch were he's going."

The mother replied, "It wasn't necessary for you to slap him you animal."

The man stood up as if to approach the family. Josh gently moved Kim behind him and stepped forward. "For some reason I think you owe these people an apology."

The man glared at Josh and angrily replied, "Keep yourself out of this if you don't want hurt."

Josh smiled, "I'm not so sure you can stand up to anyone larger than a timid teenager. Can you boy?"

The man was accompanied by several rowdy looking men who looked at him in anticipation for an appropriate response. The man approached Josh with an angry stare as he wrinkled his nose. Josh quickly accessed the scene and concluded that this group of bullies was just a bunch of unfriendly people who desperately needed guidance. He felt he was equipped and perhaps obligated to provide such guidance. Especially since an innocent family was involved.

The large man aggressively approached Josh with his fists clinched. The crowd stepped back in anticipation. When the man got within range Josh thundered a side kick to the man's solar plexus which sounded like a sledge hammer striking an oak tree. The man bent over with a groan as Josh followed up with a crippling round house kick to his leg. A chop to the side of the man's neck dropped him to the ground.

Josh turned to see two companions of the injured man stand to their feet. Josh quickly stepped forward in a fighting stance and aggressively said, "Don't you make a stupid decision like your friend here. I won't be as gentle!"

One of the men stepped forward and appeared younger and more athletic. Josh quickly decided to dial up the power and held nothing back in order to set the right tone and discourage the others from participating.

The athletic one took a boxing stance and made his approach. Josh delivered three quick jabs before he made contact with the man's nose. The impact threw the man's head back just long enough to distract him. Josh threw a lightning-fast front kick to his abdomen followed by two quick punches. The man leaned over and covered his bloody face.

Josh moved to his left where he could see the group of aggressors watching in surprise. He then delivered a round house kick to the side of the man's head which echoed a loud pop. The man paused and struggled to recover but Josh was fired up and delivered additional kicks and punches. The sounds of the impacts began to imitate the rapid fire of a machine gun. As the man got weaker his arms dropped which gave way to more powerful and direct punishment. Josh knew that eventually his deliverance of strikes would destroy the man's ability and desire to resist. The fight had now turned to almost a workout session on a bag in the dojo. The man fell to the ground, brought up a knee, and started to stand. Josh shouted, "Stay down!" The man stood to his feet where he quickly encountered a front kick to the jaw. Teeth and blood sprayed through the air as the man fell to the pavement with a mighty thud.

The crowd stood silent as Josh rushed to the group of aggressors. He kicked a chair and sent it slamming against the table. Like a wild tiger he grabbed one of the men at the table by the collar and pulled him to his face. As the veins in Josh's neck and arms electrified, he spoke, "You and your buddies collect what's left of those two animals and get your asses out of here! If we ever have to cross paths again, they will not be able to put you back together again!" Josh released his grip and carefully watched the group collect their friends and stagger off.

As Josh took some deep controlled breaths to calm himself, he heard a couple of slow claps which quickly gained in numbers and volume. Josh discretely nodded and quickly rushed to Kim and grabbed her hand. He timidly said, "Let's get out of here."

Kim held Josh's arm and rushed away. When they got a block away Kim squeezed his hand and said, "Its ok. Your actions were appropriate."

Josh looked into her caring eyes and escorted her into Dave's Restaurant. A smiling greeter stood with two menus and asked, "Welcome to Dave's. Will that be for two?" Both Kim and Josh smiled and nodded.

The couple followed the greeter to a large table where her friendly voice said, "I'm sorry to put you at this large table but our booths are all taken. Your waitress will be right with you."

Josh replied, "This will be fine." He pulled out a chair for Kim to sit and positioned himself close beside her.

Josh regained his composure but felt that he had crossed the line. He feared that his adjustment to civilian life was taking him too far to the point of breaking the law. He started to feel embarrassed.

Kim hugged his arm, softly kissed his cheek, and said, "I saw it all Josh. They escalated the fight and forced you to hurt them. They'll survive and maybe next time they will think before they brutalize anyone else."

Josh smiled in relief and said, "You're a mind reader sweet princess." He then kissed her.

The waitress approached and began to speak but was interrupted by Josh, "Young lady, the princess here would like a glass of red wine and I'd like some Crown Royal on the rocks. If you have no Crown Royal any kind of rocket fuel will do."

The waitress nodded and quickly rushed away.

Kim directly said, "Just so you know, the mother said it all started when the big guy slapped her butt as they walked by. The seventeen-year-old son told him off and got backhanded across the mouth. The dad and the daughter were window shopping next door and missed the whole thing. When dad came over to inquire about the commotion the big guy threatened him."

Josh nodded, "Good. They had it coming then." Before Kim could comment she was interrupted.

"Excuse me sir. Would you allow me the honor of buying your dinner?"

Josh and Kim turned to find the family involved in the disturbance was now timidly standing behind them. Josh started to decline the generous offer but thought that it would be rude and inconsiderate. Josh replied, "Mr. that would be very kind of you but if you insist then we must insist that you join us."

The man smiled proudly, turned to his eager family, and responded, "We would be honored to join you."

As the family sat down the group introduced themselves. Josh looked at the teenage boy and said, "My lovely wife here told me that you suffered your injury when you came to the aide of your mother."

The teenager, named Matt, nodded and shyly said, "Yes, sir."

Josh smiled, extended his hand, and said, "I admire a man with courage. Standing up to a monster like him took guts. You did well." Josh then turned to his father and said, "You've raised him well."

The father extended his hand and said, "My name is Paul Cole, this is my wife Betty, son Matt, and daughter Sara."

Josh shook his hand and the group exchanged greetings. As the family sat down the mother spoke, "Mr. Stark. I am generally a peaceful person who detests violence but as God is my witness, I must confess that I admired what you did back there. I think God sent you to help us. If you would not have made the scene that animal would have hurt Paul. That monster had evil in his eyes."

Matt asked in a relaxed voice, "Mr. Stark. How did you learn to fight like that?"

The waitress arrived with the drinks for Josh and Kim. Josh said, "Our friends here have decided to join us. Is that acceptable?"

The waitress smiled and replied, "Oh certainly. Would you like something to drink?"

Paul spoke up, "I'll take what he's drinking, my wife will have what she's drinking, and bring us a Dr. Pepper and a Sprite for the kids please." The waitress delivered a friendly smile and walked away.

Josh poured water in his drink and answered Matt, "I've learned a lot of techniques and have picked up moves that fit well with me that are effective. I work hard to tune my body in preparation of the unexpected. I practice, practice, and practice. After a while I got pretty good at it. Just remember the saying that there is always someone tougher and stronger than you are. But on a comforting note, there is another old saying that goes something like, old age and treachery shall overcome youth and strength."

Matt replied, "It was like watching a Steven Segal movie."

The group laughed. Betty asked, "Where are you two from?"

Kim proudly replied, "My husband and I are on our honeymoon and we're from Timber Creek Oklahoma."

Betty opened her mouth and said, "Oh goodness. We're intruding on your honeymoon."

Kim reached out and patted her hand, "No, don't be silly."

Josh spoke up, "All I was going to do was sit here and tell her how beautiful she is and how much I love her. She'll hear that stuff the next forty years or so anyway."

The group burst out in laughter.

Paul said, "We're down here from Nebraska. What kind of work are you in Josh?"

Josh replied, "I've just completed a career change and just started teaching part time at the university outside Meadville. Kim here runs a diner in Timber Creek."

Betty said, "How nice. What did you used to do?"

Josh replied, "I was a law enforcement officer in Kansas."

Matt's eyebrows rose, "That's what I want to be."

Paul replied, "No offense Josh, but I've tried to talk him out of it. What would you say if he was your son?"

Josh took a drink, leaned back, put his arm around Kim, and replied, "I'd tell him to go to college first and get a business degree. It will help him in both law enforcement and perhaps later on out in the civilian world. Then I'd warn him about the side effects of the job such as working holidays, doing shift work, and sacrificing yourself and the welfare of your family. Then I'd tell him to be prepared for conflict and disappointment."

Paul half smiled, "It sounds a little grim Josh."

Josh leaned forward, "Yea, but the upside is it's the last frontier and once you get it in your blood your hooked."

The waitress arrived, took everyone's order, and soon returned with some appetizers.

Kim noticed ten-year-old Sara watch every move she made.

Kim asked, "So, what do you want to be when you get older Sara?"

Sara smiled, "I want to be a singer."

Kim replied, "Well, that sounds challenging. What kind of music will you sing?"

Sara excitedly said, "Mostly country like Shania Twain and some modern stuff like Hanna Montana."

As the women conversed Betty explained that she was a third-grade school teacher.

Josh asked Paul what kind of work he did. Paul said that he was a manager of an office equipment company in Lincoln.

The waitress arrived with the food and the group continued in conversation. Paul announced, "Well, we have one thing in common. We have an excellent taste for restaurants."

Everyone nodded. The waitress came around and asked if anyone would like another drink. Josh looked at Kim who nodded and replied, "It's our honeymoon, and I'm not holding anything back." Everyone chuckled and nodded in agreement.

When the waitress returned with the drinks Josh delicately poured water over his Crown Royal. He found Paul watching and discretely said, "Do you Nebraskans find this offensive like those Oklahomans?"

Paul laughed and replied, "Nope. It's your whisky and you can drink it however you like. Besides, I've seen what you do to people who are disagreeable with you."

The couples later walked outside into the early evening air. Soft country music was flowing and harmonized by the changing-colored streetlights. Betty pulled Kim aside, "I haven't seen Paul take to someone as quickly as he did with Josh."

Kim whispered, "Yea. He's got that something about him that captures your attention. Doesn't he?"

Betty whispered in her ear, "Lucky girl."

As the couples walked toward the river front Paul waved for the children to join them.

The group slowly turned their attention to the beautiful flowing river with the lights reflecting and glittering. They paused with their hands resting upon the railing. Kim put her arm around Josh who eagerly held her tight. The river wind gently blew her long blonde hair to the side and brightened her smiling lips.
Little Sara stepped upon the lower railing and stretched her arms upward with a heavy breath and said, "It is so beautiful here. I wish we could just stay here forever?"

The group smiled as Betty replied, "I wish we could too honey."

Kim leaned closer and molded to Josh's side. He brought his cheek down to the part in her hair and gently inhaled the refreshing fragrance that filled the air. He felt her heart beating and her gentle breaths massaging his side.

There's something about a slow flowing river that opens one's heart and mind to a dimension of peacefulness. Your worries and thoughts fade away to somewhere that cleanses and untangles them. The feeling of contentment radiates in your blood and circulates peace and quiet throughout. The body energizes and transmits endorphins that cure the ills and impurities. It is as if a sea of solitude enters your body and brings you closer to God and goodness. A song of quiet is played and shared with others to hear. Matt broke the silence with, "It would be so cool to ride a boat out there."

Josh spoke out, "What a wonderful idea. But I think we're going to mosey on back to the hotel room and jump in the Jacuzzi."

Kim smiled as the group pulled away from the peaceful moment and walked on. They passed the water fountain that sprayed high up into the air in an aqua aerobic spectacle performed for everyone to see. Excited sight seers pointed and reached out to feel the cool mist. The colored lights enhanced the beauty and made the water glow with enthusiasm. The friendly shop keepers waved and spoke to passing visitors. The trolley passed by with the bright red paint shinning from the colored lights.

Children's arms waved from the open trolley and filled the air with laughter. Couples walked hand in hand and brought forth a romantic aura to the scene. Josh and Kim led the way like a prince and princess. Kim's soft blonde hair waved in the flashing lights and her snug fit dress emphasized her tight and attractive figure. Her tan and muscular legs were perfectly proportioned and complimented her feminine features as her curved hips slightly swung from side to side.

Chapter 18

"Surprising Visitors"

The beautiful Branson evening soon found Kim and Josh in their hotel room overlooking the waterfront from their balcony. The moonlight peaked upon Kim's bright blue eyes and illuminated them like heavenly stars. A knock came upon the door and Josh cautiously opened.

One of the men said, "Don't be alarmed Mr. Stark I'm agent Wells with the FBI. May we come inside and visit with you and your misses? No one is in trouble."

Josh reached out for Kim's hand and said, "Its ok honey."

The group sat down and Josh calmly said, "What can we do for you gentlemen? We're on our honeymoon and we have a bottle of Champaign chilled and waiting for us."

The talkative agent said, "This is agent Cochran and Brooks. You're not a difficult person to follow Mr. Stark. All we have to do is look for the ambulance."

Josh replied, "You gentlemen won't need one, will you?"

Wells smiled and said, "Hopefully not and neither will you. We're here to offer you an employment position."

Josh replied, "I've already got a job."

Cochran stepped forward and said, "Mr. Stark your portfolio is quite impressive and unique. Your country needs your services once again."

Josh said, "I am honored for your consideration but I have other responsibilities and obligations. She is number one in my life and I intend to keep it that way."

Kim's concerned expression turned to a smile as she inconspicuously squeezed his hand.

Josh stood up and said, "I'll hold on to your card and will think over your offer should I reconsider."

Kim stood up and spoke, "Thank you for your visit gentlemen. My husband and I have plans for the rest of the evening."

Wells stood up, placed his business card on the table, and said, "We'll keep in touch just in case you would like additional information or should decide to change your mind."

Agent Brooks lagged behind with his jet-black hair and matching dark eyes. He definitely carried the traits of an American Indian.

Brooks paused while the others walked out the door and said, "Mr. Stark I like the job you did on that second guy at the pub. I may suggest however that you tone down your enthusiasm just a tad. You almost put a little too much effort in that neck strike and nearly killed him. That would make it more difficult for us to cover for you." He then handed Josh his business card, looked deep in his eyes, and just before closing the door said, "Later Lighthorsemen."

Kim put her arms around Josh. Josh said, "It's all right honey. They're just doing their job trying to recruit people. You can forget about them for tonight and concentrate on your husband who is desperately craving to get you in that Jacuzzi."

Kim laughed and said, "Ok let's go but you better prepare yourself for a long and restless night."

Josh picked her up and said, "I can't wait."

As the Jacuzzi filled with water the couple took a shower and poured the chilled Champaign. Kim seductively slid into the Jacuzzi and gently laid her head back and draped her leg along the top. Josh slowly climbed in beside her and handed her a glass of Champaign. He kissed her forehead and said, "To us, beautiful."
He then pulled her into his arms and the couple relaxed in contented silence. The jets of the Jacuzzi swirled and bubbled the water that massaged their romantic intensions. The dim lights from the mirror reflected off the Jacuzzi tile and illuminated the wet bodies with a shine. The Champaign glasses sat dormant as the couple embraced with caresses and kisses.

Outside the honeymoon suite the sidewalk laid empty with only the streetlight shadows and mystic fountain. The dusty footprints from earlier were now like ghosts that blew into the evening darkness. The moon above shined upon the gently flowing river. Stars sparked above among the clouds and the moonlight. It was as if a summer holiday was blessing the Branson visitors.

As the evening drifted away midnight welcomed the early morning and enticed the couple from the warm water of the Jacuzzi into the awaiting covers upon the bed. Their emotions once again romantically exploded and found their bodies tightly intertwined. The moments turned into hours and when the sun came up over the horizon a light peaked through the balcony window to reveal the couple in complete stillness. Kim lay in Josh's arms with only her breaths gently moving her chest slightly up and down to manifest life. The quiet breaths from Josh gently waved Kim's soft majestic hair. The blanket and sheet were upon the floor in disarray along with damp towels.

Josh opened his eyes that closely followed Kim's tan and trim body that lie snuggled close to him. Her gentle snores were more of a kitten's purr that gently sounded from her tender lips. As Josh carefully kissed her head her lips widened and created a beautiful smile. She slowly rolled over on top of him and laid her long blonde hair upon his face. Her warm smooth body then flattened upon his and gently pressed down to blend with him. Josh's hands then gently rested upon her lower legs and slowly brushed upward to her shoulder blades. He repeated the caressing and felt her breathing increase and heartbeat become more pronounced. Her blue eyes opened and became alert with awareness. The couple then passionately made love while the morning was breaking.

Nine o'clock arrived and found the couple laughing in the shower once again. Kim's feminine giggles amused Josh. He laughed and held her close. The happiness he felt was beyond his expectations and left him with euphoric joy.

.   Kim buried her face in his chest and smiled a happy tear. The couple exerted more energy than a couple of high school students pursuing puppy love. Josh often held back his expression of emotion as tears of joy struggled to break out. He was overwhelmed with happiness and in a place where he had never known had existed. He felt he was in heaven and blessed by God. There was no other explanation for this fulfillment of desire. He felt a level of devotion and everlasting commitment that he never knew could exist.

Kim stepped out of the shower and wiped the water from her body. As she started to walk away Josh pulled her back and passionately kissed her neck. She arched her back and giggled. Kim asked, "So, what are we doing today?"

Josh replied, "I suggest that we grab some breakfast, come back, and hit the fitness room."

Kim said, "You're on. Then let's do some miniature golf, and later can we see a show?"

Josh pulled her close and said, "Whatever your precious heart desires."

The streets of Branson were bright and exciting even in the day light hours. The friendly family atmosphere exploded with intensity. People walked along the sidewalk with bouncing children. Couples walked hand in hand and pointed to the shops and show signs. The 4-runner climbed and descended the hilly roadway then curved the busy route. Kim pointed to a restaurant up a head several blocks. As she lowered her arm, she pointed to a white cat sitting on the curb. Josh looked over and said, "If he steps off that curb, he's libel to become a flat cat."

In the mist of all the warmth and emotional viewing suddenly the cat bolted off the curb and in front of the traveling 4-runner. Kim gasped as Josh abruptly braked and slid the tires. As the tires cried and the rubber slid the cat just barely made it safely across the street. Josh straightened the vehicle out and proceeded down the street toward an intersection. Just as they approached the intersection Kim removed her hand from her shaking chest and shouted, "Josh!"

A vehicle entered the intersection against a red light at a high rate of speed in front of them. Before Josh could brake, the vehicle passed and disappeared as quickly as it came. Bystanders on the corner could be seen holding their hands over their mouths and shaking their heads.

Josh crossed the intersection and pulled into the parking lot of the restaurant. Shakily he said, "Wow. We almost squashed a cat and got crashed by a car all within seconds."

Kim reached out for his hand and said, "Josh, if you wouldn't have slowed for the cat we would have been in that intersection."

Josh looked up at the sky and replied, "Oh God. You are indeed mysterious, first shadows, and now cats. What's next?"

The couple entered the restaurant hand in hand and rested inside a booth. An energetic waitress appeared and explained the menu. The couple elected to have the buffet where they encountered a short but slow-moving group of patrons.

One elderly man sarcastically said, "Jack, grab some grub and quit your sniffin'. What are ya a damn hound dog?" The man ahead of him turned and answered, "Hold your britches Mr. Garbage Disposal. Unlike you I like to know what I'm eatin'. I'm not like a hog at the trough." People ahead turned around and smiled.

A group of college students huddled around a large circular table. One of them got up with his loose pants fitted below his butt with blue checkered boxer type shorts showing. Kim couldn't help but stare until she turned and quietly asked, "Josh, look at his pants. Why does he wear them that way?" The man ahead leaned his head back to listen to the response.

Josh answered in a normal tone of voice, "Well dear, an ingenious designer created them for the inner-city crooks as a means of deterring crime. The idiots bought into them because they thought they made them look different and cool. When the crooks committed a crime and tried to run from the cops, they'd get all tripped up and fall on their faces."

Kim asked, "Are you serious?"

Josh kissed her head and replied, "Well, who really knows for sure, but it works." The man head leaned back forward and chuckled.

Old folks waddled about with their straw cowboy hats which reminded Kim of back home. Josh saw her staring in solemn and asked, "Do you miss home?"

She smiled and said, "Maybe a little but my place is with you."

Josh held her hand and said, "Kim, sometimes a person just fits in at a place they call their home. Their presence enhances other people's lives and brings fulfillment to theirs. When that happens, a special connection is created. Perhaps those hearts come together in God's will. I won't really have the answer. But I do know that I will never ask you to leave your hometown."

Kim turned her head and returned with watery eyes, "Thank you. You certainly know how to get to a woman's heart."

Josh took a sip of orange juice and replied, "Well, I'm only after one special person's heart." He then reached out and caressed Kim's soft face.

As the couple began dishing food onto their plates, they noticed two state troopers quietly sitting alone eating their breakfast. Kim whispered, "Should we tell them about that car?"

Josh replied, "No honey. The last thing those guys want is someone interrupting their meal to tell them about a traffic complaint."

Kim nodded in agreement when over one of their portable radios they heard, "All units be advised of an armed robbery just occurred at the Buy Rite Liquor Store on Collier. The suspect is described as a white male with blonde hair, a go-tee, wearing a blue t-shirt, left on foot in an unknown direction."

Josh approached the troopers and said, "Excuse me gentlemen but I just saw the suspect as the front seat passenger three minutes ago Northbound at the East intersection in a blue colored older model Plymouth Fury type vehicle. The vehicle had no hub caps on the right side and a large dent in the right rear fender."

The troopers looked at each other and one asked, "Are you sure?"

Josh pulled out his wallet, displayed his badge, and said, "Yes. I'm sure alright. We'll be staying at the hotel by the landing if you have any questions."

The radio then announced, "Further information on the armed robbery was the suspect may have left the area in an older model blue colored vehicle." Both the troopers stood up, grabbed their hats, and thanked Josh.

As they began to walk toward the door they heard, "Units be advised of an injury accident at the corner of Southwest Highway and oak involving a white colored van and an older colored blue vehicle." Both the troopers ran out the door.

Josh sat down his plate, grabbed Kim by the hand and said, "Come on. Those two may need help if the crooks are heavily armed."

Josh and Kim ran out the door and got into the 4-runner at a much faster pace than the troopers. Josh said, "Now we're just going to respond to the area and stay back out of the way. Remember that in the console is a spare .45." Kim nodded and looked both ways as Josh started the engine and mashed the accelerator part way to the floor. The rear tires squealed as the 4-runner quickly jumped over the parking block, across the sidewalk, and down the curb.

The troopers had just exited the driveway with their lights flashing and sirens blaring. Josh first fought to maintain control of the 4-runner that slid from side to side burning rubber. He then slowed to create more distance behind the troopers. As he scanned from side to side watching for traffic he said, "Honey, stay with the car and keep the gun down. We don't want other responding officers to mistake us for bad guys."

Kim removed the spare .45 from the console and nodded.

The 4-runner took turns and curves sliding sideways in companionship with the trooper cars. After about three minutes they topped a hill and saw the debris of mangled metal up ahead in the intersection. The troopers quickly and strategically positioned their patrol cars to protect the scene and rushed out with their guns drawn toward the blue vehicle. They quickly holstered their weapons and began talking with the injured.

Josh pulled onto the sidewalk and stopped. The younger trooper shouted toward the more seasoned one and pointed toward the east. The trooper then looked at Josh.

The steam of antifreeze was spraying into the air. The Branson sun was shining and reflecting upon the shattered glass on the street. Pieces of plastic and metal was scattered about. Josh looked in the direction where the trooper had been pointing and saw a shadow figure appear in the tree line. He accelerated and drove off in that direction.

Josh reached under his seat and came up with the stainless steel .45. He then said, "Let's keep our eyes open and hope that the local police show up soon." He then drove down a side street and slowly crept in anticipation. Off in the distance he heard sirens.

The road took them into a residential section where children were out playing and a woman was watering her plants as she conversed with another. Josh pulled up to them and said, "There are two armed suspects out here somewhere on the loose. You better gather your kids, go inside, and lock your doors. If anyone comes to your door or you see anyone suspicious call 911." The adults quickly scattered and gathered the children. Josh shouted, "Telephone all your neighbors and tell them!"

As Josh slowly drove through the neighborhood, he saw a state patrol car quickly come up on his rear. The patrol car rushed up to his side and Josh pulled over to the side and stopped. The young trooper said, "We got a report that a citizen saw them climb into a window just down the street. The local police should be here any minute." Josh nodded and followed.

The trooper drove about a block, blocked the roadway, and exited with a rifle. Josh pulled off to the side, reached down below the rear seat, and came up with a bushmaster .223 rifle. He told Kim, "Stay here honey, hold on to that pistol, and keep the cell phone handy." Kim nodded.

As Josh started to climb out of the 4-runner Kim grabbed his hand. With a worried look on her face she said, "Please be careful." Josh smiled and patted her hand.

Josh ran up to the rear of the trooper's car and took up position beside him. The trooper looked at his rife, smiled, and said, "Let's slowly move to that gray house and listen. They should be right next door."

Judging by the landscape and construction of the homes the neighborhood appeared to be upper middle class. Josh was concerned that there would be many stay at home moms. This posed a problem as becoming a possible hostage situation. Their vehicles were parked far enough away and around the corner where the suspects would not know they were there.

Josh followed the trooper where both men were able to use bushes as concealment to take up position on the side of the target house. The trooper took off his hat, laid it on the ground, and peeked in through the kitchen window. They stood there about two minutes when the trooper suddenly ducked down. He turned to Josh and motioned with his lips that they were inside.

The trooper and Josh stepped back out of view and conversed. They decided that they should back off and wait for the local police to coordinate negotiations with the SWAT team. As the trooper was about to talk over the radio, they heard screaming from inside. Josh said, "Oh hell. Here we go again."

Josh followed the trooper into the house through the back door where they moved fast enough and quiet enough to be unnoticed. The crying from the woman drowned out their attempted stealth like entry. As they entered the dining room, they came to face with two sobbing women and two suspects. The trooper pointed his rife in the face of one suspect who stood frozen like a deer in the headlights. The second man was close to Josh whom Josh ran full speed toward and side kicked into the wall.

As the trooper ordered the first man to the ground Josh grabbed the second by the shirt with his left hand as he held his rifle to the side with the other. Josh stomped the man's foot which caused him to buckle down in pain. Josh then pulled the man down while he fired his right knee upward and into the man's twisted face. The impact echoed throughout the room and splattered blood upon the hard wood floor. Josh released the man who fell to the ground and lay silent.

The trooper handcuffed the first man and stood up to console the hysterical crying woman. The handcuffed man got to his knees and began cursing at Josh for beating his friend. Josh approached and fired a powerful front kick into the man's stomach. The man flew against the wall and laid upon the ground gasping for air. The trooper turned and looked at Josh who said, "I thought you could use a little help." The trooper looked at the gasping man, smiled, and directed his attention back to the crying woman.

Two police officers stormed through the door with pistols displayed. The trooper greeted them and motioned toward the two men. One of the officers handcuffed the second man and dragged him to his feet and out the door. The second officer approached the still gagging and gasping man and said, "Shut up your wining you big baby." He then pulled him to his feet and dragged him outside.

The trooper shook Josh's hand and thanked him. Josh said, "If it's all right I'd like to get back to my wife. It's our honeymoon and I don't want to keep her waiting."

The trooper said, "Go ahead. I'll look you up if I need to." Josh walked back to his car and was met halfway by Kim who ran to meet him. She wrapped her arms around him, squeezed him tight, and asked, "Is everyone all right?"

Josh patted her back and replied, "Yep, we didn't have to shoot anyone this time. Let's get that breakfast."

The couple returned to the restaurant and enjoyed their meal. Kim took a drink of orange juice and said, "You know hanging out with you is anything but boring."

Josh smiled and replied, "I think Lou referred to it as being no picnic."

Kim said, "We should call him and see how they're doing."

Josh nodded, took out his cell phone, and scrolled down for his number. A couple of seconds later he was laughing at the voice on the other line. He replied, "Well, the criminals down here are tamer than the ones up that way. We didn't have to shoot these."

After a couple of minutes, he handed the phone to Kim who laughed and replied, "Yes. He sure knows how to entertain a lady." After breakfast the couple made their way back to the hotel where they planned for an evening show. They then visited the fitness room where they ran on the tread mills and the elliptical machines that overlooked the pool viewed through a window.
Two of the four walls were lined with windows which allowed not only the view to the pool but also to the hallway. People would walk by and glance in through the windows. Occasionally they would stop and take notice. Josh said, "I might just have to come over there and run behind you on that tread mill. You're gathering up quite an audience."

Kim just smiled and continued at her pace. Josh finished the workout with a series of kicks and punches. Kim asked, "How is your leg healing up?"

Josh replied, "It's as good as new."

Kim nodded as she jumped off to begin stomach crunches then replied, "I guess the guys at the Irish Pub found that out."
Josh strained and said, "I recon so."

Kim asked, "Were you surprised that the one agent called you Lighthorsemen?"

Josh replied, "Yes. I wonder where he got his information."

Kim said, "Perhaps we should visit the old Indian when we get back."

Josh replied, "Good idea. There are many questions I would like answered."

The couple stretched out and walked out of the fitness room to run face to face with the Johnson's. Betty said, "Hi there love birds! What ya up to?"

Kim said, "We thought we'd work off that Champaign from last night."

Paul put his arm around Josh and said, "Hey buddy. We've got a deal on Kirby's Magic Show tonight at six o'clock. Twenty buck tickets each!"

Josh turned to Kim and said, "Hey, how about Kirby at six o'clock?" Kim nodded. Josh said, "Cover me and give us a call in a few hours." Josh grabbed a pen and a piece of paper from the courtesy desk and wrote down his cell number.

Paul patted him on the back and said, "You got it."

After a few minutes of conversation, the group split and went their separate ways. Josh said, "You know I might just have to persuade you into a different style of running shorts."

Kim said, "Really, why?

Josh said, "Your butt is getting everyone's attention and I'm getting jealous."

Kim stopped, covered her mouth, and laughed, "Oh my gosh. Not this forty-one-year-old butt?"

Josh stood with his hands on her hips and replied, "It looks more like a thirty-one-year-old and the entire package is gaining attention."

Kim smiled, leaned into his welcomed arms, and said, "Well, as long as they look but don't touch!"

The couple slowly walked through the lobby upon the soft plush carpet. Bell hops dressed in suits scurried by bringing nods and friendly gestures. Guests entered and departed the establishment displaying friendly notions with excited smiling children at their side. The elevator bell went off and the doors opened. Enthusiastic bodies rushed out and politely moved around the couple. As the elevator door closed Kim stood in quiet as Josh looked at her. She lowered her head slowly and smiled in anticipation of a romantic attack. Josh jumped and wrapped his arms around her as she pretended to pull away with laughter. He then buried his lips in her soft blonde hair and gently kissed her ear as she squealed in delight. The elevator stopped and the door opened to reveal a surprised family. Josh picked her up and as he exited the elevator said, "It's our honeymoon and we're just warming up." Kim burst out into laughter as the two adults looked at each other and then smiled.

As Josh carried Kim through the woolly western hallway Kim squeezed his large muscular arm and said, "You know I really like these."

Josh replied, "Well, they're pretty much fond of you too."

The couple entered the hotel room and later found themselves out on the balcony overlooking the friendly street below with the smooth flowing river in the near distance. The wind gently blew and the bright Branson sunlight brought soothing comfort to their faces. Josh said a silent prayer and thanked God for all that He had given him. Kim moved slowly to his side and inhaled the morning splendor.

As the hours passed the couple found them once again sightseeing along the busy Branson roadway. They stopped at a building with the sign *Miniature Golf* posted out front. As they eagerly rushed for the door Kim said, "You're going to be in trouble here buddy. Up until you came into my life, I spent every Saturday evening at our putt-putt."

Josh said, "By the talented swing in your little hips it wouldn't surprise me if I get creamed."

Josh was correct in his prediction. Kim tried to take risky shots and hold back but still managed to beat him badly. She would laugh until she lined up with the ball, slowly strike it down the carpet, and into the hole on the first or second shot every time. Josh continued to shake his head which was continuously greeted by a warm and sympathetic kiss from Kim. The holding of her hips and the kisses in her ears caused only minor distractions and still landed the ball in the hole.

The couple slowly walked along the green carpeted course among the artificial plants and flowers. The sound of running water further mellowed the atmosphere. Miniature water mills twinkled from colored lights and splashed the sparkled water down into the tiny pools below. The outer walls were painted country scenes with trees and colorful mountains. Then Josh placed their clubs on the front counter and escorted Kim out the door into the tiled arena of gift stands and information booths. The heavy doors led outside into the Missouri sun light smiling upon the Branson board walk.

Kim walked closely to Josh as they proceeded to the 4-runner. Josh asked, "What is your desire now since you've humiliated my manhood back there?"

Kim laughed, "Don't be so hard on yourself. We Oklahomans have a special gene that provides us with superior golfing talents. Kind of like how perhaps you Kansas guys have talents in, you know other areas."

Josh kissed her neck and replied, "I actually prefer those other areas."

Kim whispered in his ear, "Yea, me too."

As they got in the 4-runner Josh looked at the clock and said, "You know, I would sure like to take the boat ride for lunch."

Kim smiled, "That's a splendid idea. Let's go!"

The couple drove to the east into the old part of town and parked at the river boat dock. Several other cars were arriving and struggling to find a place to park. Josh and Kim quickly walked toward the pier and hurried up to the ticket booth where they purchased their tickets from a robust jolly woman dressed in a bright white blouse and black tie. The woman smiled and explained that the boat would board in twenty minutes.

Josh and Kim stepped off to the side and leaned against the railing overlooking the smooth-running water. The other side of the bank had roots and tree limbs reaching out into the water. Occasionally a squirrel or bird could be seen approaching the river for a visit or perhaps a drink. The rustic peer created an old-time atmosphere and took the visitors a hundred years back in time. The soothing setting enticed the on lookers to imagine what it was like when Mark Twain wrote about Tom Sawyer. The gray colored wood and green stained peer posts accented the ancient decor.

Kim closely cradled Josh's arm and both faces discretely displayed smiles. Kim's gentle breaths trumpeted romantic tones not by intensions but by emotional expression. Her feminine features pulled Josh's attention like a magnet. He looked deeply into her sapphire resembling blue eyes and became frozen in admiration. Her lips gently opened as her head tilted back with her eyes closed. Kim's movement was quickly answered by Josh's responsive lips which quickly met with Kim. His free hand braced her neck and pulled her close. For a moment the couple forgot they were not alone and primitively pursued their passion.

During their encounter, in unsuccessfully taming their urge, the boat approached the dock. They broke free and returned to reality. A voice shouted, "All aboard!"

A line formed and patrons walked the plank and onto the boat where they found a friendly captain standing at parade rest. Josh had a flashback to when he was in the military several years ago and used to stand at attention, salute, and ask, "Sir. Sgt. Stark request permission to come aboard." A Naval officer would return his salute and reply, "Permission granted." Josh would then complete his salute and walk onto the ship.

The couple boarded the boat and quickly took their seats at a table near the side of the boat. A friendly waiter asked if they would like something to drink. The boat naturally had no green tea on board but the couple settled for black tea. As the couple sat quietly experiencing the beauty of the river their minds drifted into a pleasant trance. The waiter returned with their beverages and brought them back into the present.

As Kim slowly removed the tea bag from her cup, she artistically added sweetener and with a serious tone said, "Thank you for being my husband."

Josh was caught off guard and replied, "Well darling, thank you for allowing me to be your husband."

Kim asked, "Did you ever imagine you'd be here like this?"

Josh quickly replied, "I never imagined a woman like you existed."

Kim squeezed his hand and looked to the side as she wiped her watery eyes.

The boat quickly got under way and drifted out into the welcomed water. Waiters bought large silver trays of food to the tables and catered to their guests like kings and queens. Soft Ozark music sang out from the multitude of speakers on the boat and echoed off the banks and the surface of the river. Baked Cornish hens were brought out with mashed potatoes and gravy. Several servings of vegetables were also offered. Both Josh and Kim slowly indulged and exchanged friendly smiles and conversation. Their attention was so extremely magnified within their own world to which they forgot they were in the company of others.

Entertainers appeared and sang songs. A magician later came out and mesmerized the audience. People clapped and shouted at the magnificent performance. Kim and Josh sat quietly holding hands with smiles and occasional claps. As a couple of hours passed by the boat slowly returned to the dock. The patrons filed off with smiles and expressions of gratitude. Josh and Kim waited until the end then slowly walked off where they were greeted by the captain.

Kim said, "I feel like I have just taken a ride in a time machine."

Josh placed his arm around her and said, "Yea, can you imagine how life was back then?"

Kim replied, "My relatives used to talk about the time before cars. When they used to place delivered ice in a cabinet to keep food cool. When wash boards were used to clean clothes. And the Bible was read by candlelight."

Josh held Kim close while they stood upon the rustic peer and said, "There is a lot to be said about the family values and close devotion shared by those people who had to rely upon their family for support and comfort. They had no television to distract them and no internet to pull them away. They worked hard and then spent all their time together at night. When the day would come to an end, they would huddle around the fireplace and be comforted in each other's company."

Kim said, "Let's never get too busy to not appreciate our time together."

Josh replied, "That won't be hard. If other men had wives as beautiful and charming as mine the world would be quite a different place."

Kim smiled, kissed him on the cheek, and said, "You're so kind Mr. Stark. Can we have some of that entertainment tonight?"

Josh said, "Yes, Mrs. Stark. I would be honored to bring pleasure to you."

Kim covered her mouth and laughed as they proceeded toward the 4-runner.

Josh telephoned Paul and arranged to meet at the show. The 4-runner exited the parking lot and left the river boat and the peer reflecting in the distance through the rear-view mirror. The frontier feeling created by the boat ride left the couple happy and contented. They felt they had become closer through the experience even though it was simply a two-hour trip. Every moment Josh and Kim spent together they deeply engrained their devotion together.

They arrived at the show and quickly found the Johnson's waiting enthusiastically out front. Josh slipped forty dollars in Paul's pocket and thanked him. The group entered the theatre and quickly settled into their seats.

Velvet drapes covered the walls and overhead colored lights systematically illuminated the desired mode. An announcer came upon the stage and explained about gifts and souvenirs being available up front. Josh whispered to Kim, "Conrad." As he grabbed Paul by the hand and coaxed him out of his seat and toward the stage. Josh purchased a magic book and monitored Paul's purchase for Sara then returned to his seat.

Kim smiled in delight at Josh's remembrance and thoughtfulness about Conrad. As they settled into their seats the lights dimmed and out walked Kirby and his wife Bambi. The presentation was nothing short of magnificent. The illusions were amazing and left the audience breathless. Both Josh and Kim were mesmerized at the realism and brilliance of the show. The illusions truly appeared real and brought splendor to the set. The audience applauded and projected their appreciation to the cast.

The show further had a unique Christian perspective at the end. Kirby sat quietly on stage with the lights down dim and performed a philosophical skit with the theme relating to God. The generality was so well done that the message appeared to be non-intrusive to all. The crowd's hearts were touched and joy radiated throughout. Kirby finished by reminding us that there is no such thing as magic, only illusions, the only real magic comes from God. Josh caught Kim looking at him several times throughout the presentation. Eventually he leaned over to her and asked, "What dear?"

As the audience applauded Kim leaned over to Josh and whispered, "Thank you for making me your wife." Kim then smiled and cradled his arm close.

As eight o'clock came around the end of the show did too. The crowd poured out the doors and into the parking lot. Betty approached Kim and discretely whispered in her ear. Kim nodded and pulled Josh close, "Honey. Today Paul got a disturbing telephone call from his boss. Why don't you accompany him to the Irish Pub for some conversation while Betty and I do some shopping?"

Josh replied, "All right. But don't forget about our Jacuzzi appointment later."

Kim laughed and replied, "You bet mister!"

Josh reached out and pulled Paul toward him and said, "Hey old man. Why don't you and I down a few beers while the ladies engage in some shopping?"

Paul proudly smiled and replied, "You're on."

The couple met at the hotel and coordinated the events. The children stayed in the hotel room occupied by video games and movies. Josh and Paul walked down the block to the Irish Pub while the ladies shopped.

The men entered the pub and took up residence at the bar. A red-haired burley bartender with red cheeks and a friendly tone appeared from around the bar and asked with an Irish accent, "What would you gentlemen fancy?" The two men ordered beers and watched the bartender fill the mugs using his large muscular arms. He looked more like a lumberjack than a bartender. The bar was made of oak with a shiny brass foot bar across the bottom. Old time ceiling fans gently spun for mainly decoration. An array of whisky bottles was displayed behind the counter along with stained glass and lighted signs to bring the Irish heritage to the Branson landing. A large mirror reflected the scene from behind which consisted of a couple of pool tables in the background, a shuffle board, and two colorful dart boards.

After a few minutes Paul said, "I'm about to lose my job and I feel defeated."

Josh was stunned but sincerely replied, "What are you going to do?"

Paul replied, "Come up with a game plan before we leave here."

Josh took a drink of his beer and said, "Well, let's see now. Pretend that not you but some else is in your predicament. What would you say to them?"

Paul said, "Well, I guess I'd have him to list all his options in consideration with his qualifications. Then pray."

Josh asked, "Have you ever left a job before?"

Paul replied, "Oh sure."

Josh said, "And you've survived and carried on right?"

Paul replied, "Yea."

Josh said, "That's what life's all about. It's like the glass half empty concept. You can busy yourself with worry or look forward to improving your life with the change. Think about it. Every time a door closes another one opens. Take this change as an opportunity not a defeat. A positive attitude is like fuel for success. It energizes one's soul and brightens the path ahead. I wouldn't worry about it if I were you. You're a smart guy and you will be successful."

Paul looked at Josh and smiled, "Thanks. That was a good speech."

Josh replied, "Yep. Nothing like a cold beer and Irish inspiration to open one's mind." Both men laughed.

As time passed Kim and Betty paraded through several shops and found themselves a couple of blocks into the old downtown area. They came across a club with outside tables and several middle-aged women laughing and drinking wine. Betty said, "Hey, let's go in and have a drink."

Kim said, "Well, I don't know."

Betty quickly interrupted, "Those guys are going to be busy for a while. They won't miss us."

Kim said, "Okay. I guess so." She then took her cell phone off her belt and began to telephone Josh."

Betty teased, "Does this new husband require that you check in with him?"

Kim felt slightly irritated and replied, "No. I just choose to be courteous and let him know where I am in case, he needs to get in touch with me." Betty smiled.

Kim quickly phoned Josh and told him of their plans. He thanked her for being thoughtful.

The women entered the club and found themselves outside on the patio with the sun ducking down behind the horizon and a colorful fire in the center fire pit. A large group of women were apparently celebrating a bachelorette party. Kim and Betty sat a distance across from them and became amused at their drunken dialog. Betty whispered, "I hope none of them will be driving."

Kim replied, "Yea. We're staying really close to the buildings on our way back to the hotel."

One of the women from the party staggered over to Kim and Betty then said, "Hey ladies. Why are you sitting alone all the way over here?"

Betty answered, "Well, we really should be joining you by the sound of all the fun you're having."

The woman grabbed Betty's hand and said, "Come on sweetie, the maids of honor all got delayed and won't be here until in the early morning. Until them we have all this wine and Champaign that will be going to waste if we don't get some help."

Kim and Betty felt a little strange but the persistency of the woman was such that they didn't want to appear rude and discourteous. The waiter went to the empty table and was shouted to by the woman, "These two are with us honey." The waiter smiled and nodded.

The group quickly began to mingle and before long all behaved as if they were neighbors at a block party. All the women were around the same age at or near forty. As the evening progressed husbands lingered in and out to retrieve their celebrated and intoxicated wives. The occasion was so enjoyable that ten o'clock rolled around and found Kim and Betty sitting alone. Betty phoned to check on the kids and then leaned back in the chair with her head back, "Wow. I haven't drunk this much since I don't know when."

Kim replied, "Yea. Usually, two glasses are enough for me. I think I'm at double my capacity." Betty leaned forward in laughter.

As the women talked and laughed two men came up and stood at their table. One of them asked if they could join them. Before Betty could answer Kim replied, "Thank you for your interest gentlemen, but we'd like to be alone."

Betty looked to see that there were two other men sitting in the back at a table watching as if they had been with the others. The two men sat down against Kim's wishes and began to talk. Betty said, "We're married guys and not interested."

The two became persistent as they held their mugs of beer in front of them taking small sips. Kim said, "Harassing women can be hazardous to your health."

One of the men became agitated. Kim pulled out her cell phone and began to make a call.

Josh and Paul were now laughing with the bartender telling jokes. Several patrons had joined them and were laughing loudly. As Josh took a drink he glanced in the mirror and saw a shadow in the window. He quickly turned and saw the shadow move away. Josh turned back to the bartender and changed his tone, "Sir, what do we owe you? I'm sorry but I have an emergency."

Paul looked at Josh with a puzzled look. Josh stood up and said, "Paul, I can't explain right now but we've got to get to the women, now."

The bartender pulled out his pad and Josh took out two twenties, "Will this cover us buddy?"

The bartender surprisingly replied, "Yes sir, but that's too much."

Josh said, "You were fine company sir, thank you." He then headed toward the door with Paul close behind.

As they exited the building Josh began to jog and heard his cell phone ring. He answered it in concern, "Are you all right?"

Kim replied, "There are a couple of obnoxious guys here who do not understand the word no."

Josh said, "Stay where you're at and I'll be right there."

As Josh increased his pace Paul ran up behind him, "Is everything all right?"

Josh replied, "A couple of guys are begging for counseling."
Back on the patio the two men began to use vulgarity toward the
stubborn women. As one of the men touched Kim's leg, she grabbed
his mug of beer, stood up, and poured it over his head, as she said,
"Here, maybe this will cool you off, jerk."

The two men at the other table laughed out loud, clapped,
and whistled. The man with the beer hair-do angrily stood up face to
face with Kim and grabbed her by her left arm. Kim's other arm
quickly slung the empty mug of beer against the side of his face. As
the man fell into the table behind him, he slid to the ground, and laid
still.

Josh entered the scene and was met by Kim who ran into his
arms. "Well, it looks like he now understands the word no" as Josh
looked upon the guy laying on the ground. His friend went to
comfort the dizzy headed guy on the ground and said to Kim, "you
didn't have to smash his head with the mug!" Josh stepped forward
and angerly replied, "don't give a disrespectful tone toward my wife
minster. You won't find me as gentle as her."

The guy stood up and looked into Josh's intense and ready
eyes, took a calm timid breath, and said, "I don't want no trouble
mister. Just let us collect our friend and be gone." Josh nodded and
walked away with Kim under his arm. Paul entered the bar out of
breath and asked, "what did I miss?!" The couple walked out the bar
with Betty eagerly describing Kim's performance with the beer and
beer mug.

Paul and Betty stepped back as Josh and Kim slowly walked
on. As they reached the hotel they stopped and looked up at the

smiling Branson moon. Betty said, "This is the most interesting vacation."

Josh said, "Yea, quite a memorable one."

Paul extended his hand out to Josh, "Thank you for this good time and the experience to have known you."

Josh shook his hand and said, "And thanks for your company and friendship."

The couples entered the hotel, walked across the vacant lobby, and into the elevator. When the door slowly opened the couples parted way and nodded in separation.
Josh used the entry card to open the hotel room door. He walked in first and said, "Its safe, no FBI agents." Kim followed with a giggle. Josh escorted Kim toward the balcony where he opened the sliding glass door and walked her outside into the soft evening breeze. As he stood with his arms wrapped around her waist, he gently kissed her neck. Her head slowly eased back and her eyes closed. Her mouth gently opened and inhaled the Branson night and the delight within. As he rested his cheek against her ear he asked, "What will tomorrow bring us my little princess?"

Kim smiled and replied, "Another day of wonder and excitement my gentle warrior."

The couple soon found themselves tenderly caressing in the shower and later wrapped in passion once again upon the bed. Several hours passed and soon welcomed the morning light to break over the smooth flowing river. Kim woke up and glanced through the curtains at the sunlight that began to peek over the treetops that moved with the morning breeze and pasted friendly shadows upon the wall. Josh sat up and stared at the beautiful spectacle. She turned around and momentarily froze for his admirable inspection. The sun rays peeked through the curtains to reveal her unclothed body. A smile came across her happy face. Every part of her tailored body was curved in all the right places. Her long soft hair accented her stature and brought a stunning magnificence to her feminine beauty. Josh crawled his muscular body across the bed and paraded his dominant presence to meet her. His aggressive approach quickly diminished to a passive touch upon Kim's embrace. Josh's muscles cradled Kim and displayed the strength of love, protection, and devotion to her submission. She melted into his arms and was carried to silk sheeted podium of pleasure.

Two hours passed and found the couple lying in relaxation. Josh whispered to Kim, "I think I better get this lazy butt of mine on the treadmill."

Kim touched his nose and replied, "I'll bring mine with you." The couple found the fitness room empty to their delight once again. After running a couple of miles on the treadmills they moved to the ellipticals where they were able to watch the news on the screen and talk.

Josh said, "Last night was the first time I saw you get mad. You cracked that guy's noggin pretty good with that beer mug."

Kim replied, "I think a wise man once used the word diversity to describe it. Sometimes it's appropriate and necessary to crack a guy over the noggin with a beer mug."

Josh said, "Yep. I thought he was going to hit you as I cleared that fence."

Kim replied, "I was about to kick him in the joystick when you arrived with the intent to finish him off."

Josh laughed, "Joystick."

Kim looked over at him with perspiration showing a gentle smile. A family was beyond the window jumping and splashing in the swimming pool. Kim directed her attention toward the blissful sight and looked over at Josh. She asked, "Josh. Do you ever think about your son?"

Josh was somewhat taken back and replied, "Several times every day."

Kim said, "Do you want to look him up sometime?"

Josh nodded, "Yes. The time is coming when it will be right."

Kim smiled, looked over at his display, and said, "I'm going to beat you."

Josh replied, "How about the first one to reach four miles gets to choose what we do today."

Kim said, "You're on. Wait a minute. I bet I know what you'll want to do."

Josh replied, "What?"

Kim smiled, "Go back to the hotel room, take a shower together, and make love."

Josh laughed and said, "And what will you want to do."
In unison the couple laughed and said, "Go back to the hotel room, take a shower, and make love."

In their course of laughter, the door opened and in walked the Johnsons. Betty said, "Well now, here's a couple matched in heaven. These silly people love exerting pain so much to themselves they almost fall off the machine in laughter!"

The group broke out in laughter. Little Sara approached Kim and said, "Wow Ms. Kim, you're all sweaty. But you still sure look pretty." Laughter again filled the room.

The group engaged in small talk as the kids slowly walked upon the treadmills. Sara was next to Kim and said, "I heard you kicked someone's ass last night."

Josh slipped and almost fell off the machine. Betty quickly snapped, "Sara, that's not a nice word."

Sara looked down and replied, "Sorry momma. I just wanted to be accurate in what I heard daddy say to Matt."

Betty looked over at Paul who was sitting on a bench covering his face. Matt replied in laughter, "Yep. She's accurate all right." Laughter again filled the room.

Josh jumped off the elliptical put his hands on his knees, breathed heavily, and patted Sara on the head. He then said to Kim, "I won."

Kim jumped off, looked at his display as she wiped tears of laughter, and replied, "Sorry honey. My times faster."

Paul said, "So, what does the winner get?"

Kim looked over at Paul and smiled. Paul returned the smile and said, "God, what a lucky guy!" Betty playfully slapped him on the shoulder. Paul then said, "Well, when you guys decide to come up for air we'll be going to Dave's Restaurant for lunch around noon and playing some miniature golf around two if you're interested."

Kim said, "Sure, gals against the guys."

Before Josh could respond Paul said, "Great."

Josh said, "Buddy if you think some butt kicking happened last night then hold on to your shorts. Kim plays the golf club like Roy Clark plays the banjo. Leave your male ego back at the room because we're going to get creamed."

After Kim and Josh stretched out, they all paraded out the door and down the hallway. Betty whispered to Kim about not letting the newlyweds be alone. Kim told Betty that she and Josh both enjoyed their company and they were not intruding. Betty smiled and said, "The way that I figure it is we drank last night for free so we can splurge today if we like."

Kim nodded, "Yea. I wish we could find the bride and express our appreciation for the hospitality with a gift."

The Johnson's said goodbye and walked out of the hotel while Kim and Josh entered the elevator. Once inside Kim shyly looked down again with a suppressed grin. Josh jumped at her, kissed her neck, and lifted her off the ground. The elevator opened at the fifth floor to reveal the same family as before waiting with a smile.

Josh said, "I'm taking her to the room to check her for ticks." Kim covered her mouth and shook with laughter as the family froze with puzzled smiles.

As they exited the elevator and preceded down the hallway Kim's joyful laughter echoed and soon became contagious. A cleaning person exited a room and also found humor in her laugh. Josh couldn't resist staggering and laughing as he tripped and rested against the door holding his laughing wife.

The couple nearly crawled into the room and began preparation for their day. After some intimate interactions they visited the balcony where they wrapped their arms around each other and watched the shoppers below. Behind the shops was the familiar soothing river sparkling in the background. A canoe floated by with an adventurous couple dressed in orange life vests wearing friendly expressions. Two ragged mutts ran along the riverbank in search of excitement with dangling tongues and matted fur.

Josh whispered, "Would you like to shop around for a little while this morning?"

Kim replied, "Sure. There are plenty of shops at the South end I haven't been in. Would you really like to go?"

Josh replied, "Yep. Honestly I'd just enjoy walking and watching behind you." Kim pinched him and laughed.

The couple left the room and stood waiting at the elevator. The door opened and there stood the family from earlier. Josh nodded friendly, kissed Kim's head, and said, "No ticks." The family walked widely around them as Josh entered with Kim and pushed the first-floor button. As the door closed Kim leaned over with both hands covering her face. Josh got down on one knee, pulled her close, and together the couple burst out in laughter. Josh said, "Those poor people will never stay in this hotel again!"

The elevator arrived on the first floor and eagerly opened the door for the couple to exit. Kim swallowed hard, wiped her eyes, and exclaimed, "Oh, Lord." Josh shook his head, put his hand in her rear pocket, and pulled her closely into him.

Josh escorted her down the walkway, out the door, and toward a jewelry store. He asked her, "How come you rarely wear earrings?"

Kim cleared her voice with a slight tone of embarrassment and replied, "I don't have very many that match what I wear." Josh said, "Diamond's match anything princess."

Kim replied, "Yes. I'm sure they do. Maybe someday we'll look into them."

Before Kim could pull away Josh spun her around and said, "Let's see what they have in here."

Josh entered the store with Kim in respectful protest. A smiling attractive older lady sat down a pair of large chrome scissors on the glass display she was using, quickly came to Josh's rescue, and said, "What can I show you lovely couple today?"

Josh put his arm around Kim and said, "My wife and I would like to look at your diamond ear rings." The jewelry store was brightened by white colored chandeliers enhanced by tiny recessed spotlights mounted in the ceiling. The exquisite jewelry sparkled in the shiny glass cases.

The lady gently extended her hand and said, "My name is Katherine. It's a pleasure to meet you." As Josh and Kim introduced themselves Josh saw a shadow in the back room.

Josh quickly surveyed the store with his keen eyes and found no one else present. He then walked around Kim in the direction of the door where he feared the threat could enter. Kim and Katherine walked toward the side and slowed as Josh separated from their company. As he discretely pretended to look in the displays Kim said, "Honey. The earrings are over here."

The beating of Josh's heart drowned out her plea. His deep breaths forced oxygen to his blood and caused his muscles to swell in preparation. His awareness sharpened and targeted the door although his head pointed down toward the display case.

Kim stood still and said, "Honey. We're over here." Katherine looked puzzled and also stopped. Then the door opened. In walked a young man in his twenties with a loose fitted t-shirt. His eyes were dark and wide with dilated pupils dressed in evil. He appeared unsteady and glared into Josh's eyes with distinct intent. Out of his crazed mouth came the order, "Everyone get their hands up and get to the back room now!" A black barreled pistol came from his under his t-shirt and pointed at Josh.

Time appeared to momentarily stand still. The evil one became puzzled and alarmed as he looked into Josh's eyes that changed in temperament to ice cold expressions like a shark in the ocean.

Katherine began to move toward the back as ordered and noticed that the scissors were no longer on the glass counter. Kim remained still in anticipation of obedience by her husband.

As the evil one began to give a second order, he was quickly interrupted by the store window that was impacted by a large bird. He flinched and turned to see the glass buckle and feathers explode. When he turned around the pair of scissors shot like an arrow from Josh's hand and impaled into the center of his chest. He stood silently in shock gasping for breath as Josh quickly covered the ten feet distance between them and fired a horrendous side kick into his abdomen. The power forced his extremities forward and sent his body backward like a cannon through the glass and onto the sidewalk where he slid to a stop. His eyes remained open in disbelief as his heart beat its last evil beat.

The pistol spun around on the store floor like a bottle at a party and gradually came to rest. Katherine's eyes filled with moisture as her shaking body leaned against the counter. Kim reached out and cradled her with her warm soothing arms. Josh slowly walked to the women, stopped in front of Kim, pushed her hair aside and tenderly kissed her quivering cheek. Before a word could be spoken two police officers rushed inside holding pistols and asked, "Is everyone all right?"

A third officer arrived with his pistol pointed down at the evil one. He felt the side of the evil one's neck and quickly holstered his weapon. He stood up and shook his head to the officers inside. One of the officers inside holstered his weapon also, looked at the window, and then back at Josh to ask, "What in the hell happened?" Katherine rushed to the police officers and began to quickly explain the circumstances.

Josh softly stroked Kim's face, kissed her, and replied, "I guess he came to the wrong store at the wrong time to do the wrong thing."

Josh looked down in the display case and asked, "Let's see. These full karat ones look pretty. Don't you think honey?"

Kim was still shaken by the incident, took a deep breath, and shyly said, "Yes dear. But we can't afford them."

Katherine picked up the cordless telephone and said, "Sam. You need to get here right away."

Josh spoke with the police officers and motioned with his hands about how the events had transpired. One of the officers looked at the window that showed a distinct impact with slight blood and feathers. He curiously said, "Whatever it was it sure was big. It must have just flown off."

Several professionals arrived including the owner of the jewelry store who immediately approached Josh and shook his hand. Josh said, "Sorry about your window but he left me no choice."

The owner said, "The hell with the window. Thank God you did what you did. That's my wife back there whose life you just saved!" He rushed to his wife who wrapped her arms around him and broke down into tears. For several minutes Katherine and the owner huddled and spoke in quiet tone.

The owner retrieved the full karat diamond earrings, approached Kim, and said, "Young lady try these on."

Kim blushed and said, "Thank you. They are beautiful but I'm afraid that they are outside our price range regardless of what my loving husband says."

The owner said, "I insist. Try them on."

In fear of being discourteous and rude Kim tried them on. As Katherine held up a portable mirror, she smiled in delight as Kim's face glowed with joy. Her eyes sparkled and her lips parted open. She searched desperately for the words and finally said, "Oh God. They are so beautiful."

Josh walked over and said, "Yes. Just what a princess needs."

The owner pulled Josh aside and argued with him. Kim stood staring in the mirror and lost track of everything around her. Katherine smiled as she wiped a tear of joy from her eyes. She stared at Kim as if Kim was a little girl with a new doll. Kim's expression was sincere and childlike. Her moment of joy was such that she forgot about everything else in the world including the team of police officers that took photos and collected evidence around her.

Josh handed the owner his credit card and continued to exchange words of negotiation. The owner walked away and returned with a receipt for Josh to sign. As Josh smiled and shook the owners hand the owner pulled him forward and hugged him. The owner's back slightly shook as they slowly pulled apart. Josh took a deep breath and motioned with his body what appeared to be joy and gratitude. He gently patted the owner's back and walked toward Kim.

Josh said, "The police said they are through with me for now. We can continue on our way and they'll call if they have anything additional."

Josh and Kim walked past the covered body and officials studying the scene. Josh looked over his shoulder to the store owners, motioned with his lips, "thank you" as they faded into the crowd down the street.

The store owner hugged his wife with intensity, reached over to the credit card machine, and pressed 'delete transaction' on Josh's credit card purchase.

Kim slowly walked in silence in a state of joyful surprise. She paused by a store window and stared in the reflection, "Josh. Aren't they beautiful?!"

Josh smiled, tenderly kissed her soft ear, and replied, "Yes they are. They were meant for you."

Kim grabbed his cheeks with both hands and aggressively kissed him with quivering lips. She then pulled away and choked out the words, "I've never had anything as exquisite as this." The trolley passed by with a cheerful crowd packed tightly with arms waving.

Josh cradled her close and replied, "You already thanked me my darling princess by becoming my wife."

The couple slowly walked past the stores toward Dave's Restaurant. Josh looked back at the crowd surrounding the jewelry store. Yellow barrier tape was being placed around the store with portable stands. A blanket covered the body still lying on the ground with glass scattered around. People walked by with stares. Some bystanders stood off to the side watching and whispering.

Josh opened the front door for Kim to enter. A waitress recited the friendly greeting and escorted them toward a booth. Josh looked at his clock and said, "Perhaps we should sit at a larger table. There are some guests we may be meeting."

Josh caught Kim hesitating again looking in a mirror at her earrings. He stopped, looked squarely at her face and said, "Yep. They are beautiful all right. They're not as beautiful as the one wearing them, but still beautiful."

Kim smiled and proudly saw the waitress staring at the sparkling diamonds.

They both ordered water and were looking at the menus when the Johnson's appeared. Kim motioned for them to join them. Betty began to sit down and loudly said, "Oh my gosh! You got some diamond ear rings!"

Kim proudly smiled as Betty continued, "This must be some kind of honeymoon for you to earn those." The group laughed.

Paul whispered something in Josh's ear. Josh replied, "Actually I had to darn near fight the jewelry store owner to pay what I did for them."

Kim excitedly explained what had happened at the jewelry store. The Johnson's sat attentively and listened to the story. The waitress came around and Paul said, "Give us a few more minutes please." As Kim continued the Johnson's sat back with their mouths open.

Paul said, "Scissors! How the heck did you do that with scissors? And where did the hawk come from?"

Josh took a drink of water and replied, "We're assuming it was a hawk. The impact was loud and shook the entire glass."

Paul sat back and said, "You're a one-man rescue team buddy."

Josh smiled and replied, "Hey, I just mind my own business and excitement comes my way."

Sara spoke up, "Daddy, did Mr. Spark kick someone's ass again?"

The table of patrons burst out laughing and Paul said, "Well honey. I guess those are the correct words all right." The crowd at a neighboring table looked over and chuckled.

The waitress returned and took everyone's order. Kim continued to discretely feel her diamond ear rings and glance over at Josh. She had for some odd reason always secretly cherished diamond earrings as both a young child and as an adult. She sat quietly and became further overwhelmed with a feeling of gratitude and appreciation. She realized that she had found a man who truly loved her with immeasurable dedication and passion. The evidence was not just in the diamonds but his desire to bring her joy. He had looked deep inside her heart and saw that this material pleasure was important to her although she tried to hide it. He discovered the want and vigorously pursued it. She fought hard to conceal her desire but he refused to accept her denial. She sat reassured that this person is the one whom she has waited for her whole life. Forty-one years on this earth and God had graciously blessed her with this treasure. She bowed her head in silent prayer.

Josh noticed her solitude and gently placed his arm around her as he continued in conversation with the Johnsons. Her timid smiling response sent his heart the message. He leaned over and softly kissed her in discrete recognition. His message radiated from his soft stare and deeply into her receptive heart. Kim lost connectedness and concern with the rest of the world. She honorably stared into his loving eyes which penetrated his warrior way toward his soft side.

Josh had indeed proven himself to be a hardened man with a soften heart. He carried courageous concern for the innocent and distain for the evil. He could embrace a call from an innocent victim and immediately take battle to the perpetrator without hesitation. Kim felt this presence and passion and thus liked it. She yearned to share the excitement Josh created and translated to others. His strange gift to protect the right from the wrong was mystic and exciting to this seemingly timid country girl.

As the group consumed their meal in friendly conversation Josh announced that he and Kim would be checking out today. Kim explained that they had decided they would travel at night for a change and enjoy the evening air and desolate roadway. The couples sadly exchanged farewells and promised to meet again someday down the road. As Josh and Kim departed the table Sara jumped from her chair and threw her arms around Kim sobbing. Kim got down on one knee and gently hugged Sara who eventually leaned back with tearing eyes and said, "Does this mean Mr. Stark won't be here kicking anyone's…?"

Betty quickly interrupted and said, "Yes Sara. He'll have to do it somewhere else now." The group burst out in laughter.

Kim asked Sara to call her when she records her first song. They then exchanged farewells and departed the restaurant. As Josh and Kim walked past the spraying fountain they stopped and watched the splendor. Kim said, "I'm going to miss this place." She then wrapped her arms around Josh and said, "This has been the best time of my life."

Josh tenderly embraced her and replied, "Mine too. Maybe we should look into buying a little vacation place around here."

Kim nodded and replied, "I'd like that."

The couple entered the hotel for the last time and began packing their belongings. Kim sadly stood looking at the Jacuzzi. Josh walked up, placed his arm around her, and said, "Is everything all right?"

Kim dropped her head, frowned, and replied, "I'm going to miss that Jacuzzi."

Josh hugged her and said, "We can get you a Jacuzzi."

She then whispered in his ear, "Actually, I liked the activity that went on in that Jacuzzi better."

Josh brushed her soft hair aside with his cheek, slowly kissed her ear, and said, "There's a lot more of that I can get you also."

Kim said, "You better stop that or we're going to be delayed."

Josh gently picked her up, repeatedly blew kisses in her ear, and carried her to the bed. As Josh romantically undressed Kim he said, "Why don't we relax here for the evening and leave out sometime after midnight."

Kim lay back on the soft covers with her eyes closed and replied, "Yea. I've got a craving for relaxing right about now."

The couple romantically engaged for a couple of hours and then fell fast asleep. The sun drifted down over the horizon and sleepy birds cuddled upon branches in the nearby trees. A blanket of quiet gently fell over the landing with glaring stars that winked in the sky above.

Josh wakened to find Kim sitting on top of him kissing his cheek. As his eyes opened, she softly said, "Hey sleepy head. It's one o'clock."

Josh stood up with one strapping arm cradling her and said, "Wow. We better hit the shower and get out of here."

At two o'clock the 4-Runner traveled through the downtown area of Branson and headed for the highway. The place looked like a ghost town and the sound of silence echoed between the empty shops and desolate country air. The Indian Chief outside the five and dime stood in stature guarding its territory. The heated exhaust cloud was all that was left behind from the departing 4-Runner. Josh landed upon the country highway and set the cruise control to sixty-five, leaned back in his seat, and placed his arm around his contented Kim. Kim discretely flipped down the lighted visor to admire her diamond ear rings. She then smiled and leaned over against Josh's arm.

The highway was vacant with the exception of an occasional car. The moon light slightly illuminated the long twisty roadway up ahead that was beautified by cut out rocky canyon along the sides. Rustic brown trees waved naturally as travelers passed by with their headlights smiling. Wild oaks and pine trees intermingled in vast patches of forest along the way. Pine trees emitted their soothing fragrance and gently swayed in the early morning breeze. An occasional owl could be seen gliding across the sky searching to perch for a perfect view.

Josh opened the sunroof then cracked the rear window to eliminate the pressure noise. The beautiful Branson night blew solitude and comfort into the 4-Runner. Kim poured a cup of tea out of their prepared thermos and handed it to Josh. He took a drink, placed the cup in the center console, and returned his arm around Kim. Kim's bare left foot was tucked under her other leg which stretched her feminine shorts upward. The moon light shined in through the sunroof and displayed her tanned and toned legs. Josh could not resist the temptation to reach down and gently caress her soft skin. A smile came across Kim's lips as she looked out the window. Her arm rested up the back of Josh's seat and tenderly stroked his hair.

Kim turned to Josh and delicately asked, "So, what's this Eureka Springs bed and breakfast like?"

Josh said, "I guess it's a romantic get-away where you relax, indulge in fine food, and spend a lot of time in bed."

Kim smiled, "It sounds like heaven to me – as long as there is an exercise room or a jogging trail."

Josh took a sip of tea, sat down the cup, and caressed her leg as he replied, "I'm sure we'll get plenty of jogging up and down hills. That place is hilly and full of trees."

Kim smiled and closed her eyes. The soothing sound of the wind singing in through the sunroof was immensely relaxing and soon carried Kim off to sleep. Josh smiled at his sleeping beauty and began reflecting back upon the last several months. It was truly a whole new life that berthed before him. The burden of past discontent simply became lifted when he drifted into that small town of Timber Creek.

The 4-Runner easily climbed up the high grade but struggled to keep from running away on the decent. Josh applied the brakes to reduce the chance of meeting up with an eager deer or a grumpy state trooper. He imagined what it was like only a hundred years ago when horses and wagons dominated this area. He dreamed of black kettles on a wood burning stove with busy women pacing across dusty wooden floors. Men coming up out of the woods carrying rabbits or whatever they could find for the stove.

As he took another sip of tea, he imagined the smoke coming out of the top of cabins, chickens wondering freely on the front porch, and dogs chasing each other's tail. With all our modern technology he wondered if it was all worth it. He felt we have somewhat evolved to become slaves to our advancement. Technology was causing us to run ourselves into the grave in order to keep up with changes. People back then simply took life as it came to them. He thought that dads held their kids in their laps and rocked as they told them stories. Did mothers possess hearts filled with contentment? Did they feel fulfilled and happy with their simple place in that wilderness world?

Josh looked out the window at the passing trees and concluded that perhaps times have always been rough in one way or the other. The good old days were perhaps only as good as one's heart believed they were. For people have always struggled and dealt with troubles and disappointments. He came to the conclusion that the best time in one's life is right now. Contentment is actually a choice not based upon circumstances.

Josh looked over at Kim and fought the temptation to caress her soft innocent face. She had truly been a miracle in his life. He wished he could accurately express his gratitude and love for her. He looked up through the sun roof toward heaven and thanked God for all that He had given him. He then looked away and blinked as his eyes became full and reflected his emotion. Josh prayed that he would always treat Kim with honor and respect as a measure of his appreciation for her heart. Then as the 4-Runner topped another hill and began the decent he found a flash of flares and flashing lights in the roadway ahead.

Chapter 19
"The Detour"

Josh slowed and came upon a state trooper who motioned for him to stop. The trooper told him, "Sir, the roadway is closed up ahead. Take this exit west about three miles toward the next town. You'll find a diner open and catering to other stranded motorists. I'll let everyone know when the road is back open."
Josh thanked him and asked, "Is there any idea how long it might be?"

The trooper replied, "We've got a big rig on the side. You can count on a few hours."

Josh asked, "Is there another main road we can take into Eureka Springs?"

The trooper shook his head, "Nope. The bridge is out to the east. You'll just have to give us a few hours to clean this up."

Josh thanked the trooper and drove off. He took the exit as Kim woke up, "What's happened?"

Josh explained about the accident and said that they would need to relax at a diner for probably a few hours. The roadway twisted and turned as dancing tree branches waved overhead as if to calmly cradle the visiting motorists. Eventually the journey brought the 4-Runner into the town of Auburn. Josh stopped in front of the restaurant and asked, "Well, how about some eggs and toast."

Kim stretched, "Sure. How long had I been asleep?"

Josh replied, "Not too long my sleeping beauty."

As Kim climbed out the passenger side Josh discretely removed a five shot .38 revolver from the side panel and stuffed it in his waist band held in position by a soft holster. He then paused and slowly breathed the early morning air. Kim asked, "Is something wrong?"

Josh shook his head and said, "Nope. But the air feels light or something and it sounds unusually quiet."

Kim paused and replied, "Yes. I feel it too. It's really weird. You haven't seen a shadow, have you?"

Josh said, "No. But if I do, you'll be the first to know."

The couple found several cars parked in the gravel parking lot. It appeared that they were not the only ones delayed by the accident. As they opened the door a friendly waitress immediately greeted them and escorted them to a booth. She quickly sat down two cups and with a welcomed smile asked, "Coffee?"

Both Josh and Kim nodded as the waitress poured the cups full and rushed away. Kim said, "Wow. I need her back at the diner."

Josh stirred in some sweetener and replied, "Yea, she's good but nowhere near as pretty as the one I have."

Kim smiled, looked around, and said, "My goodness, this place is busy for four o'clock in the morning."

A couple of families were huddled in booths with sleeping children in their arms. Various couples sat talking. Some were more energetic and awake than others. Four men were seated at the counter with no apparent relationship between themselves. Several regulars dressed in farmer attire were also congregated at the counter dominating the atmosphere with their jokes and occasional comments to the waitress. The waitress would pause with her hands on her hips and throw quick humorous words right back at them. The diner was of old back woods construction with large glass windows and bright lights that shined upon the glossy tabletops. The front counter was long and trimmed in chrome with comfortable revolving chairs. Paintings filled the walls with artificial flowers and electric candles.

As Josh and Kim conversed over the menu the door opened and in walked three young marines dressed in uniform. The waitress quickly rushed to their assistance. As she escorted them to a table an older bearded man climbed off his stool and began to slowly clap. Others followed and joined in. Within a few seconds the entire restaurant was standing and applauding. The marines proudly nodded, motioned with their mouths a thank you, and sat down near Josh and Kim.

As Kim sat back down Josh walked over to the marines and said, "Semper Fi gentlemen. Are you on your way to Iraq?"

One of the marines replied, "Sir, we've just returned from Iraq." He then stared at Josh and said, "You sure look familiar sir." Josh replied, "Well, you probably saw my picture at Kaneohe Marine Corps Air Station in Hawaii. I carried the battalion colors for the change of command back in '79."

One of the other marines replied, "Excuse me sir, but you look familiar to me also and I've never been to Hawaii." Josh spoke to the waitress who was standing patiently still, "Give these men anything they want and put it on my bill please."

The marines all smiled in surprise and thanked Josh. As Josh walked back toward his booth he turned and replied, "I expect you men to order some steak with those eggs." The marines smiled in appreciation.

Out from the back room shuffled an older man who asked, "What's all the commotion about?" He then spotted the men in uniform and stood frozen in silence. The waitress paused and filled her face with concern as she approached the old man to comfort him. The old man ignored the waitresses' presence and walked toward the marines.

He stood at their table and said, "Are you boys coming back from that damn war?"

One of the marines stood up and replied, "Yes sir. We've spent a year there and have come home on leave."

The old man said, "That damn president of ours won't be satisfied until all you boys are dead."

The still standing marine replied, "Sir, we want to fight for our country. We've all requested to return to Iraq as soon as we've been approved."

The old man stood in surprise and tilted his head and asked, "What'd you say?"

One of the marines sitting explained that the media was not telling the truth about what is happing over there. He said that most of the people there love us and do not want to see us leave. He explained that there are a lot of appreciative innocent people there who desperately want to have a future which only our fighting force can provide for them by removing the insurgents. As the marine continued to speak the entire restaurant listened.

Kim reached over and held Josh's hand. Josh looked at her and smiled.

An irritated yet distinguished man seated with his family spoke up, "Young man the politicians are only using you."

One of the marines stood up and said with a strong Tennessee accent, "We're fighting for America's freedom and for those innocent people over there, not politicians. We don't have all the answers, but we do know that we cannot desert those people and our comrades who are still there."

The seated marine spoke out, "We signed up to fight and protect our country. When we go into battle, we also fight to protect our buddies and we never leave anyone behind."

The black marine nodded, "We're all green marines. There are no Whites, Blacks, Mexicans, Indians, or anything else."

The old man angrily shouted, "My son died over there! For what?! Those people have been killing themselves for hundreds of years! Nothing has changed!"

The seated marine calmly replied, "When they attacked us then they changed things. Now they are paying the price."

The black marine said, "We're sorry you lost your son, sir. But freedom is not free and in war people sometimes die."

The old man slowly sat down and with trembling lips spoke, "I never got to tell him I was sorry. I never got to tell him how proud of him I was. I - I, never took the time to tell him I loved him. Now he's gone and he'll never know."

The black marine walked closer to the old man, placed his hand upon his shoulder and said, "You know we have a lot of time to think over there. We sit up at night and think about all kinds of things. Most of those things we think about involve our families back home."

The old man had shivering lips and watery eyes and said, "Not my boy. He was too damn stubborn like his father. Sgt. John Collins never gave a thought about us back here."

The other standing marine looked at the others in surprise and said, "Did you say Sgt. John Collins?"

The old man wiped his nose and said, "Yes."

All the marines stood up in silence and surprise. One of them said, "John Collins was our sergeant. He died only last month!"

The old man slowly leaned against the chair and said, "They came to our door, two of them dressed in uniform, and handed me the telegram."

One of the marines said, "He used to talk about home all the time."

The old man looked up in surprise and replied, "The devil he did?"

The marine continued, "He talked about a fishing pond that he and his dad used to fish at on Sundays. His often said that he wished he was back at that fishing hole with his dad now listening to him tell old WWII stories."

The old man leaned forward and said, "My Johnny said that?"

The marine continued, "Yep. He said that the best days of his life were back there sitting on that old wooden pier with his dad. He laughed as he talked about how you would sneak Red Man chewing tobacco and spit at the spiders in the water."

Another marine chuckled, "Yea. He said it was like in the movie *Josey Wales* when Clint Eastwood would spit on that hound." Everyone in the restaurant was intensely listening as quiet and discrete chuckles echoed.

The marine then cleared his throat and said, "He also said that someday he was going to introduce us to his dad who was the best man he ever knew."

The old man turned his head to hide the tears that flowed from his eyes.

The black marine said, "I was there the day he died." The old man looked up with a shaking jaw. "We were clearing a large building and came across a family hiding in a closet. As we lowered our rifles a grenade came in from the hallway and landed beside me. I paused and before I could jump Sgt. Collins flew past me and landed on top of it. It exploded. I sometimes hear it when I close my eyes at night. That awful sound shook the floor and left him motionless." As the marine slowly sat down he said, "Sgt. Collins died that day for his men and his country. He was a hero. We have to win this damn war so men like him didn't die for nothing."

The old man stood to his feet, rested his hand upon the marine's shoulder, then slowly walked back toward the back room and was met halfway by a frail old woman who tightly held a handkerchief to her face.

The waitress came close and said, "John was my brother. Did he ever talk about me?"

The Black marine smiled and said, "Yep. Oh, him and this crazy Sergeant from headquarters would always grapple, you know wrestle, to see who was the toughest. Sgt. Collins was big and strong but had his hands full with the other who was a martial arts expert."

The marines had now shifted their tones to where they were laughing. One of them reached out gently for her arm and said, "One day they really got into it and had each other in choke holds. Neither one would tap out and they ended up both going unconscious!" Sgt. Collins woke up first and argued that since he came to first, he was the winner. The headquarters sergeant argued that since Collins woke up first, he must have gone out first."

The restaurant was listening intensely to the story and laughing along with them. The marine continued, "They ended up standing up and punching it out. They damn near broke each other's noses and still had to call it a draw!"

As they laughed one of them said, "Sergeant Clint Stark. He was sure a crazy one."

Kim turned to Josh in surprise. Josh asked, "What did you say?"

One of the marines said, "He said Sergeant Stark was sure a crazy one." He then looked at Josh and then back at his friends. "Stark! I knew he looked familiar!"

Josh stood up, grabbed the marine's arm, and anxiously asked, "Tell me about this Sergeant Stark."

One of the marines said, "He's in his middle twenties, from back West somewhere, but didn't talk about his family much."

The black marine said, "He once mentioned that he had a father that was a cop in somewhere like Kansas I believe."

Kim quickly rushed to her husband's side and directly asked, "Is he alive?"

The group laughed, "Alive! Sgt. Stark can't be killed." One of the marines added, "He can smell danger and track like an Indian."

Quiet came upon the restaurant when a voice from the back booth said, "He is a Choctaw Indian Lighthorsemen." Josh couldn't see where the voice came from but he recognized it.

The tone of the marine quickly changed as he sat down and explained. The day that Sgt. Collins got killed he was right around the corner. He arrived out of nowhere, picked up Collins body, held him in his arms, gently sat him down, then went crazy. Tommy was there."

The black Marine said, "Hell yes I was there! He ran out in the hallway of that building shouting for us to 'clear this building now!' He fired that M-16 from the hip and commenced to kicking down doors and shooting everyone except women and children. Fortunately, they all turned out to be insurgents."

One of the marines had sat down and seriously exclaimed, "He was like a crazed tornado going through that building. I couldn't keep up with him. God certainly was with him then because when it was all over, he stood there with an empty rifle hanging from the slung, an empty .45 pistol with the slide back, and a bloody knife in his hand.”

The restaurant sat in silence with the exception of the waitress that scurried past the crowd with a cup and coffee pot. She paused, looked around, and in a troubled tone asked, “Where’d he go?”

The customers looked around confused. “He was right there. The Indian, with the tan hat and plaid shirt. Where did he go?”

The ghostly silence of the restaurant held voices still. Josh cleared his voice and gasped to ask, “How can I reach this Sgt. Stark?”

One of the marines took out a pen and wrote on a napkin an address. As he handed the napkin to Josh he asked, “You’re his father from Kansas, aren’t you?”

Josh wiped his eyes and softly said, “That I am young man.” Kim put her arms around Josh, told the marines thank you, and escorted him back to their booth.

The waitress quickly returned to Josh and Kim then said with watery eyes, “I am so sorry I forgot to take your order.” As she looked around, she said, “Oh, and that poor Indian fellow must have thought I had ignored him and somehow he slipped out.”

Josh said, “You’re fine. Actually, if it’s all right I would like to just sit here for a while and drink some coffee. In a little while I’ll order something.”

Kim politely nodded and asked, “Do you sell any greeting cards here?”

The waitress nodded, "Sure up front. We also have a stamp machine at the counter."

Kim thanked her and said to Josh, "I'll be right back." Kim smiled her bright blue eyes at Josh and like a prescribed medication soothed his heart. His hand slightly shook as he stirred his coffee. He looked over at the marines who appeared so impressive and young. He wondered where all the years had gone. He began to feel uncomfortable and embarrassed at his negligence in finding his son. He had not explained to Kim that his attorney had told him to discontinue looking for him due to false allegations made from his ex-wife. He felt ashamed of the investigation of harassment charges placed upon him during his search.

As Josh filled his head with thoughts, regrets, and confusion Kim returned with her beautiful smiling face that glowed like the sun coming up over the horizon. She handed him a card and a pen. She then said, "Write him a note and be sure to include your cell phone number."

Josh's hand shook as he slowly wrote down the words he had kept trapped in his heart for years. He then sat the pen down and struggled to hold back his emotion. After taking several deep breaths he picked up the pen and continued to write. When he had finished, he handed the note to Kim who wiped tears as she read.

Kim placed the card in the envelope and said, "Well done my gentle warrior."

Josh addressed the card and set it aside then said, "Well, I'm ready for some breakfast after all that excitement."

Kim smiled with delight, "Yes, me too."

The waitress returned and was taking their order when the door opened and in walked a deputy carrying a box. The deputy took off his hat and said, "Ladies and gentlemen, may I have your attention please. The roadway is now open. Thank you for your patience."

One of the local farmers spoke up, "Did Chuck lose another truck load of chickens?" The deputy replied, "Naw, this time it was a shipment of stationary. There are boxes and boxes of old Indian Chief Writing Tablets." He sat the box on the counter and said, "Here, help yourselves. The driver said the entire shipment was a lost due to the spill and to just give them out to people."

The deputy sat down and cradled a warm cup of coffee which the smiling waitress had waiting for him. The deputy then quickly stood up and announced, "Be alert when you go outside. When I pulled up, I saw a large dog sitting on the ridge looking toward the diner. My eyes must be playing tricks on me, but I'd swear if I didn't know better, it was a wolf." Josh and Kim stared at each other. People began to scurry out the door and quickly climb into their vehicles. When the dust from the gravel parking lot cleared only a handful of people remained in the picturesque diner.

The sun quickly came up over the horizon and filled brightness and warmth through the windows. Kim turned to Josh and said, "Honey, I think we should reschedule Eureka Springs and head back home." Josh stood up and said, "I agree."

As the 4-Runner headed back home Kim called her mother and explained they had decided to come back home. The two ladies spoke for several minutes and Kim appeared somewhat puzzled.

When she disconnected, Josh asked if everything was alright. Kim said, "Yes. Mom said that Aunt Maggie wanted us to come visit her the minute we got home." Josh turned on some country music, rubbed Kim's leg, and said, "It's off to Maggie's house we go."

Chapter 20
"AUNT MAGGIE"
Saved

Aunt Maggie was Kim's mother's older sister. She had been a widow for as long as Kim could remember. Maggie was a jewel of a lady and was always found either on the front porch holding her dog Lady and reading her King James Bible or sitting in the living room holding her dog Lady - and reading her King James Bible. Maggie knew her Bible.

As the 4-Runner pulled up in front of Maggie's, Kim bolted from the front seat and ran to embrace her Aunt Maggie with a hug and a kiss upon her cheek. Secretly, Kim was Maggie's favorite but she always tried not to show favoritism around her other nieces and nephews. Kim spent a lot of time with Maggie and also held a great deal of knowledge about the Bible.

Josh walked up with a smile, leaned over to hug Maggie, and petted Lady. Maggie told the couple to sit down and relax. Josh sat in the porch swing and Kim squirmed up upon his lap with giggles. Maggie said, "Joshua Spark, you disappoint me young man." The couple looked wide eyed and puzzled." Maggie continued, "I would expect you to return home here with your wife so exhausted from kissing that she would have to communicate with sign language!" The group broke out in laughter.

Josh replied, "Yes mam, I promise to work on that tonight." Kim giggled, looked down, and slightly blushed.

Maggie said, "Joshua, I'm too old to beat around the bush. Sometimes one must just come out with it. Are you a born-again Christian?"

Josh looked slightly startled and replied, "Yes mam. I think I am."

Maggie said, "Joshua Stark, come sit here beside me. Maggie, you sit yourself beside your husband." The couple obeyed Maggie's order. Maggie then said, "If a man says he thinks so to an answer such as that, one of the most important factors in his life, then that means he's not sure. We're going to make sure that you are sure."

Maggie placed her Bible in Josh's lap and instructed Kim to assist him in finding scriptures. She then took Josh on a tour that she described as down Roman's Road. She said, "Turn to and read Roman's 3:23." Kim quickly turned to the page.
Josh read, "For all have sinned, and come short of the glory of God." Maggie explained, "We have all inherited sin from our first father Adam. Adam died 'spiritually' when he sinned, which means he became separated spiritually from God. Now stay in the book of Roman's and read 6:23. Josh read, "For the wages of sin are death; but the gift of God is eternal life through Jesus Christ."

Maggie spoke, "We have all earned death but God sent his only begotten Son Jesus Christ to pay the ransom for our eternal lives. It is a gift. It cannot be earned. Now, read 10:9 thru 10."

Josh read, "That if thou shall confess with thy mouth the Lord Jesus, and shalt believe in thine heart that God hath raised him from the dead, thou shalt be saved. For with the heart man believeth unto righteousness; and with the mouth confession is made unto salvation."

Maggie said, "Joshua, you need to confess with your mouth and believe in your heart. Many people believe in their heads, but that is not enough. It must come sincerely from your heart. Then when you confess it is made unto salvation. You are thus saved. Do you believe Joshua?"

Joshua recited after Maggie, "I believe that Jesus Christ died on the cross for my sins, was buried, and after three days and three nights He was resurrected and left my sins dead and buried in the ground so that I may have eternal life."

Maggie said, "Do you feel any different young man?"

Immediately Josh felt a deep feeling of peace and contentment. Maggie gently patted his knee and Kim hugged him in tears.

Maggie instructed Josh to turn to the book of John 1:12-13. Kim quickly turned the old wrinkled pages backward where Josh read, "But as many has received him, to them gave he power to become the sons of God, even to them that believe in his name: which were born, not of blood, nor of the will of the flesh, nor of the will of man, but of God."

Maggie looked deeply into Josh's eyes and softly said, "You have become born again, spiritually of God, you are now a son of God. When we compare scripture to scripture, how the Bible says, spiritual things with spiritual things, we find that the Apostol Paul, who wrote Romans, wrote to Timothy in 2 Timothy 2:2." Kim turned the pages toward the end of the Bible.

Josh read, "And the things that thou hast heard of me among many witnesses, the same commit thou to faithful men, who shall be able to teach others also."

Maggie explained, "There is much you have to learn about the word of God. A son of God has responsibility to learn and share the word with others. The Lord does not desire that any shall perish. So, it is up to us to bring others to the Lord as he had Paul command to Timothy. All 66 books in the Bible have the same author, the Holy Spirit."

Josh sat quietly renewed in his new position in life. Maggie said to Kim, "Sweetie, go get that package on the living room table along with a pen and give it to Joshua." Kim got up and returned with a box containing a book. She sat down and handed it to Josh. He opened the box and found a brand-new shiny black leather King James Bible. At the bottom right corner was stamped in gold print, "Joshua Stark."

Josh's eyes got wide and watery. As Kim hugged him, Maggie said, "Kim, take the pen and fill out who the book belongs to and that it was given by you on this date." Kim followed Maggie's instructions.

Josh and Kim explained to Maggie about the "shadow" Josh would continue to see just before a troubled incident. Maggie said, "Turn to Exodus 7 and read verses 10 through 12." Josh read, "And Moses and Aaron went unto Pharaoh, and they did so as the Lord had commanded: and Aaron cast down his rod before Pharaoh, and before his servants, and it became a serpent. Then Pharaoh also called the wise men and the sorcerers: now the magicians of Egypt, they also did in the manner with their enchantments. For they cast down every man his rod, and they became serpents: but Arron's rod swallowed up their rods."

Maggie leaned forward and explained, "this passage signifies that Arron's rod, the rod of our Almighty Lord, swallowed up or consumed the others. There are examples of other 'gods', little 'g', in the Bible. And the Bible reminds us that our God is the all-powerful. You must remember to keep your eyes upon our God because all others are of the Prince of Darkness, or the god of this world, Satan."

The three continued to converse and ended with Josh promising for him and Kim to regularly visit their Aunt Maggie.

Chapter 21
"Back Home"

Josh and Kim drove to her mothers to say hello, gathered up some boxes, and Arrow, to take to their house. After providing an update on all the interesting events they drove home. Kim opened the front door and said, "come on girl, this is your new home." Arrow walked from room to room sniffing and inspecting. Josh closed the door and stared at Kim in a pretending sinister way. Kim slowly backed up then ran as fast as she could upstairs with Josh in fresh pursuit.

Kim dove onto the bed with Josh crawling and growling on the bed toward her. He pulled her toward him as she laughed and squirmed. He then began giving quick peck like kisses to every exposed part of her skin from her neck to her stomach when she'd twist and roll. After a few minutes they hugged in warm embrace both breathing heavily. Kim moaned and smiled then said, "I'm glad we didn't go to Eureka Springs. I miss our home." Josh gazed into her warm soft eyes and replied, "me too."

Out of nowhere here came Arrow who jumped on the bed and crawled in between them with her tail wagging like an airplane propeller. They laughed, petted her, and reminisced about their honeymoon.

The phone rang and it was Lou. "Hey buddy. How was the honeymoon? Rumor has it you are back. Can we meet?"

Josh leaned over, kissed Kim's ear, and whispered, "Lou wants to meet with me." Kim said, "tell him to head over. I'm going for a run. I've missed Timber Creek."
Josh told Lou to head on over as Kim changed and headed out the door.

Kim ran down the blacktop and then took the dirt road that curved around town to avoid any traffic and to sight see scenes of her younger days when everything was dirt roads. White picket fences glowed in the soft Oklahoma sun light and red rusty barns brought back memories of hayrides and the drinking of sun tea that Aunt Maggie had perfected to an art. Stray dogs ran with their tails waggin' and tongues floppin' in the wind. An occasional farmer plowing his field on his tractor waved.

As Lou and Josh conversed, Arrow sat at the rear sliding glass door and began to wine. Josh asked, "What's up little girl?" Josh glanced out the window and saw what appeared to be a wolf sitting in the field looking toward the house. A glimpse of a shadow appeared out of the corner of his eye.

Josh jumped up and shouted, "Come on!" Both men scrambled to Lou's car and headed toward Kim's running route.

Kim came to the wooded part of the roadway where trees were close to the road and branches touched in the middle. Up ahead dust was dragging behind a truck moving at high rate of speed. Kim moved over to the right side of the road and the truck slowed and then skidded to a stop. The door opened and out stepped a young man from behind the wheel followed by another on the passenger side holding a bottle of beer. They stared at Kim and smiled in an evil tone. The passenger said, "Well, hello there little lady. How about a ride? You can even sit on my lap."

Kim stood still breathing heavily and thinking of the best move here. Her right hand slowly moved behind her back where Josh had fitted a ten-inch bowie knife for her protection. As the driver started to approach, he stopped fast in his tracks. Both he and his companion froze with fear in their eyes. They quickly jumped back in the truck as the driver fumbled to put the truck into gear to speed off.

As the truck accelerated and spun a cloud of dirt a patrol car came from behind and turned on its emergency lights. Another patrol car quickly arrived to assist from the other direction. Both officers approached and spoke with the occupants of the truck. The officers then ordered them out. The police arrested the men and placed them in the patrol cars.

Officer Billy Brisco respectfully approached Kim, took off his hat, and said, "Good mornin' Miss. Kim – or ah, Mrs. Kim."

Kim smiled and replied, "Good morning Officer Brisco. What brings you out this way?"

Officer Brisco explained that the occupants of the truck had been at the Casey's and the clerk called that they looked suspicious. Ever since the Thompson place ordeal everyone has been on edge and watching out. When Ellie relayed the license plate number, dispatch said there was a pick-up order out on the registered owner. I was checking the area for them when I saw the commotion. Billy then asked, "Where's the wolf?"

Kim said, "I beg your pardon?' Billy said, "The wolf. Both those two varmints also claimed that as they started to approach you a giant wolf came out of the brush with snarling teeth from directly behind you. It scared the crap, well they used another word, out of them and they jumped in the truck to get out of here."

Kim paused in thought then said, "Oh, it must have been that big dog back there is all."

Billy smiled and replied, "Yea, you're probably right. But as big as it was and all, I mistook it for a wolf myself. Do you need anything Miss. or Mrs. Kim?"

Kim smiled and said, "No Billy, thank you."

Lou's car approached and skidded to a stop with the passenger door open as Josh sprinted to embrace Kim. Lou spoke with the backup officer, Jake Johnson, who stood outside his car keeping a visual on the prisoner in his and also the one in Billy's back seat.

Josh intensely glared at the prisoner seated in Billy's car. Lou nodded at Josh and walked over the Billy's car and opened the rear door. As Billy approached, Lou said, "Go speak with Officer Johnson, Billy. I'm going to have conversation with this guy."

Lou leaned close to the criminal's face and with the veins swelling in Lou's face he intensely and forcefully spoke. The criminal leaned away with his head down in a submissive manner. Lou spoke for a few minutes in a loud voice as he grasped and squeezed the headrest in extreme expression. His eyes were wide and scary.

Lou then stared at the criminal in silence. He closed the door and said, "He's all yours Billy."

Billy quickly approached and asked, "Do we have any charges for what happened here?"

Lou replied, "Nope. Make sure Jake conducts an intensive inventory search of that truck with a fine-tooth comb. Then tow it for safe keeping per policy. Good job Billy. Oh, who called you on this?"

Billy explained the tip of the suspicious persons and how he was checking the area when he saw the wolf. "Lou asked, a wolf?"

Billy replied, "Yea, it's crazy, but I know dogs, especially the ones around here, and that sucker was a wolf!"

Lou looked over to Josh, and then to Kim in puzzlement.

Lou drove Josh and Kim back home and then departed in deep thought.

Chapter 22
"The Chief Visits Lou"

The kids were getting ready for school when Lou's phone rang. He answered, "yes, sir. Okay. Yes, that would be fine." Lou disconnected and Darla asked, "Who was that dear?" Lou replied, "it was the chief. He's coming by to pick me up for some coffee and conversation." Darla asked, "Is that a good thing?" Lou paused and said, "I hope so. God is in charge so whatever will be is in his hands." Darla threw her arms around his neck and replied, "That's my man. Wise and reasonable."

The Chief arrived and drove them to Sandy's Diner where they sat in the rear booth. The waitress quickly sat down coffee cups and filled them about the time their butts came to rest. The Chief smiled, "Thank you kindly Tiffany. Coffee is all for now."

The Chief said, "Before we get started let me tell you that all is well. No worries or concerns. You and your buddy Josh are in the clear. You guys did an amazing job."
Lou relaxed in the booth and breathed a sigh of relief.

The Chief took a sip of coffee, looked up with his eyes only, and continued, "I just got a call from the Branson Police Chief. He wanted to alert me to the fact that I had some kind of ninja living in my city. It seems some meth head waltzes into a jewelry store, pulls out a revolver, points it at the store owner and two customers. Guess who the customers were?" Lou replies, "Ah, Josh and Kim?"

The Chief nodded, "Yep. So, the crook orders everyone into the back room then all of a sudden, some giant eagle crashes into the front store window and causes the crook to turn around startled. When the crook turns back around a pair of scissors, launched by our ninja friend Josh, sticks right in the crook's heart. He drops with a thud. Lights out for good."

"He sent me the store surveillance video. This eagle is shown approaching the window with its claws extended outward and crashing at full speed. It hit so hard that it bounced back and then rammed the window again! The window mounted tube light, "OPEN" shook and shorted out. The damnest thing was, the eagle hovered in front of the window with its claws open protruding forward!"

The Chief took another sip. Lou sat quietly with his mouth open. The Chief continued, "That's not the end of the story. It turns out the crook matches the description of a varmint that did the same thing in Arkansas but shot the store clerk in the head, a twenty-nine-year-old mother of two, two days ago. She was a magistrate's daughter, and he wants to give Josh an award! Josh Stark is becoming so popular that he should run for congress!"

The Chief paused, looked inquisitive, and continued, "What's the deal with that Josh Stark? He comes to town bustin' jaws and shooting people every time he turns the corner! I can't figure. Can you? And the crazy thing that's been going through my mind is, the only pattern is that they come here first and typically confront him. It's like some protecting spirit has brought him here. I'm not complaining mind you. Since most of the bad guys are dead it makes prosecution and court room testimony easy! Do you believe that most everyone still alive is working with the feds to cooperate or plea out?! And these varmints were sitting up shot to manufacture heroin! What's the story here Lou? Level with me. Who and what is this Josh Stark?!"

Lou explained that Josh was indeed a stand-up guy in ever since. He said, "Look. He even married the queen of the county! The guys got some powerful mojo, that's for sure. But there is one thing." The Chief leaned forward in full attention. "He's been out to see the Indian."

The Chief's eyes got wide, he leaned back, and said, "Lou, that Indian died years and years ago. There's nothing out there but snakes and a damn haze that never fades away."

Lou rubbed the back of his head, "Yea. But Josh told me some things. Things that are not consistent with imagination or deception. He showed me a knife the Indian apparently put in the front seat of his truck! It's an authentic hand-made early 1800's hand carved piece of art!"

The Chief spoke, "I know you're close and that's why we are here. I like his results. He's run off or killed most all our problem people. Hell, even Cliff has become a saint! It's just weird with all these happenings is all. Keep an eye out will you?" Then the Chief leaned forward and whispered, "Because if there is something supernatural going on here, and nothing else makes sense, then we want to be prepared when evil comes to town to visit Mr. Ninja!" Lou looked into his coffee cup and nodded.

The Chief then took a breath and spoke with a different tone, "One final thing. You are one of our senior officers and one of the few with a college degree. I trust you Lou and I hold you dear as a son. The sheriff's department is going to be in turmoil dealing with this incident. I don't know how it's going to end up but I envision changes blowing in. We need leaders to embrace and guide these changes, whatever they may be. I want you submitting your application for sergeant tomorrow morning. Begin working on your application letter tonight. Do you hear?" Lou's mouth dropped, "Sergeant application letter tomorrow?"

The Chief slid out of the booth, "Yes. You come back to work first thing in the morning." The Chief threw some dollar bills on the table and they left the diner with Lou dazed in surprise.

Chapter 23
"Josh Revisits the Indian"

The 4-Runner sped out of town onto the dirt road then off into the wilderness. Josh followed the road to the end and left on foot to visit the Indian. This time Josh was more comfortable in his pursuit. He followed the trail and came once again to the rustic shack with smoke coming out the stack of the fireplace. There sat the Indian upon the porch with his wolf by his side.

Josh slowly and respectfully approached. The Indian spoke, "Sit with me gentle warrior."

Josh sat and asked, "Much has happened since I have arrived in Timber Creek. Many evil doers are dead. I now have a wife and a life. Will I have peace?"

The Indian spoke, "You have done well gentle warrior. The white part of you contains the gentle and the Indian part contains the warrior. These forces are within you and will guide you through life. The bonds with your woman are as your Bible says you are together one. The spirits recognize your bond and your heart. They will protect her because she is part of you. And that other part within you of the Lighthorsemen also remains. Whichever spirt you feed will emerge. It is a great honor what you carry. Take heed to share your gift with your son. For he also carries the blood of a Lighhorsemen. Take care gentle warrior. Walk in the Light." The Indian stood, looked deeply into Josh's eyes, turned and walked inside.

Josh sat in quiet in deep thought while the warm Oklahoma wind blew upon the treetops. Gentle waves of wind comforted his heart. He wondered what the Indian had meant by sharing his gift with his son whom he did not know. He stood up, nodded a friendly gesture to the wolf, then disappeared back into the wilderness.

<h1 style="text-align:center">Chapter 24</h1>
<h2 style="text-align:center">"Getting Settled"</h2>

As the days passed Josh and Kim settled into their new life together. Arrow added contentment and protection to the home. She was always there displaying her dedication and loyalty. Josh loved dogs and easily bonded with Arrow. Although they became engrained in a daily routine, Josh and Kim retained a connectedness at heart. They continued their romantic and loving behavior toward each other. Since they had both suffered loss and heart break one might say they appreciated each other even more.

Every moment found them expressing gratitude and soft embrace. Even Arrow received an abundance of praises and pettings. Love was indeed prevalent at the Stark residence. Weekends were exceedingly intimate – almost fairy-tail. Kim and Josh chased each other around and curled up together as forever newlyweds. Somehow, they never argued or took each other for granted. An aura of love and respect encompassed the home.

Lou and Darla routinely came to visit every weekend. He and Josh became closer as Darla and Kim became as sisters. The Powel kids knew Kim and Josh as Aunt and Uncle Spark. Campfires out back brought childhood stories with memories of kindness found in days long past. Kim often spoke of hayrides and uncles with no teeth. Darla reminisced about wooden shacks, fireplaces, and outhouses. Laughing was always to be heard coming from the Spark residence on those weekend nights. The neighbors didn't mind though. They often invited themselves over carrying popcorn, corndogs, and coolers when the campfire lit the sky.

Lou became known as Sergeant Powel within the community. His participation with Josh on the meth raid gained him much respect and popularity. Josh strived to take a back seat to the recognition.   He always pointed to Lou for the credit.

The days, weeks, and months passed. But their hearts never changed. They remained close and loyal to one in other.

Josh and Kim's love grew stronger and stronger. They were always together and warm welcoming to all. Hugs and kisses flourished in the Stark home. And mentions of God was always present.

They always gathered together for family dinners on Sunday afternoon. Kim's relatives quickly bonded with Josh and never missed a gathering. Included in the festivities was the Powel family. Josh and Lou were inseparable as was Kim and Darla. Josh had finally found love and peace. Kim also received the answer to her prayers – a loyal godly man who truly loved her.

Although Kim and Josh knew they would never have children, they were at peace with it. Josh had long accepted that his son had carved his own trail through life and it did not travel toward him.

Timber Creek quieted down and slowly faded back into the mellow Norman Rockwell setting. The cows across the road from the diner got used to seeing Kim and Josh jog by together. Occasionally folks would see Josh pausing from the parking lot shouting comments to the inquisitive horned beasts. The curious cows would naturally stop their chewing and turn their ears toward him. The large bull in the pasture would occasionally snort and stomp a front leg. Josh would politely speak to him upon occasion, such as, "Nope Brutus, I don't want to play today." Josh didn't know his name but thought that Brutus was appropriate.

Kim took classes toward completing her college degree to fulfill her dream to become a college teacher, but her focus remained upon her marriage. She occasionally filled in at the diner and trained the younger motivated waitresses to learn how to run things. Since the foundation of the diner was poured from a portion of her heart, she could not abandon it. When Kim would work an occasional shift Josh would always be there with her roosted in a back booth correcting papers and pausing occasionally to glance up to admire his wife. Kim loved it and smiled during every moment.

Strangely enough the summertime visits from the biker gangs ceased. Perhaps word got around that a respected presence was there and it was best to leave it be. That didn't stop Josh from being prepared though. He turned their walkout basement into a gym equipped with weight machines, mirrored walls, and punching bags. He even had a large area with mats for ju-jitsu training. He and Kim wrestled around down there several times a week. Kim got proficient enough to throw Josh to the ground and quickly apply an arm bar or a choke hold with precise precision. Naturally, every session ended with the couple embraced with locked lips.

Josh even trained Lou in ju-jitsu who used it on duty when dealing with rowdy drunks and angry fighters. Friday nights would find Lou boldly laughing and telling stories about the week's encounters. Lou bragged that the beauty of it all was to shut someone down without causing harm to them.

Many times, Josh wanted to revisit the Indian. But deep inside something told him to leave well enough alone. He thought he didn't really want to stir up anything, still, the mystery intrigued him. Besides, all accounts were that no one lived out there in that wilderness. And strong rumor was that all of those who used to live there were dead and buried. Still, he and Kim often spoke about it.

Lou occasionally asked for Josh to reenter law enforcement as a part-time officer. Josh declined the offer. He knew his season was over regardless of his desire to jump back in. Kim could be seen attentively monitoring their conversation on the topic with her head down and eloquent eyes peeking up with nodding in agreement to Josh's refusal. Kim's kindness and patience did not extend to the concept of Josh dodging bullets.

The little boy down the street, Conrad, was a regular visitor at the Stark residence. They could be seen playing catch out in the front yard. Since Conrad was small for his age, Josh taught him some self-defense moves. Conrad took to the instruction and became a natural. He quickly made a reputation of himself with the bullies and became a protector of others. His abusive father had left the family and headed back east somewhere. Josh and Kim became surrogate parents to him when his mother had to work long hours. Kim made sure Conrad always had cloths to wear and food to eat. She would often tell him, "Conrad, I've always wanted a little boy, and if I had one, I'd want him to have a pair of black cargo jeans just like these. Do you think he'd like them?"

Conrad would have an excited expression and with big blue eyes reply, "Yes, Mrs. Kim. He'd sure love 'em!" Kim would say, "Well, since I don't have a son, could I give them to you?" Conrad would get watery eyes, nod his head, and say, "Yes! Thank you, Mrs. Kim." Conrad knew Kim had bought those jeans especially for him out of sincere kindness. He played along with the dialogue out of respect and appreciation. Conrad loved Kim as a second mother.

Early one morning on the way to the university Josh and Kim came upon a commotion on the highway up ahead. A group of motorcycles were collected, some on the shoulder, and three or four in the roadway laying down. There was a crowd of bikers down upon their knees tending to the ones in the roadway. Josh slowed, activated his four-way flashers, and said to Kim, "Remember what's in the glove box." He then exited the 4-Runner and approached the crowd.

Kim reached into the glove box and stuck the .45 pistol into her waist band. When Josh bent down over the injured biker, he was surprised to see that it was the leader he had conversed with a while back in the diner. Several of the bikers stared at him but out of fear held their notions. Josh saw that the biker had a critical injury involving a broken leg with a shattered bone protruding out of his blue jeans. Blood was running out like a faucet upon the road.

Josh said, "Hurry, give me a belt or rope!" One of the bikers handed him his belt. Josh then tightened it around the top of the injured leg and installed a tourniquet. He then ordered, "Quickly, we need to get him to the hospital before he bleeds out! Three of you pick him up and carry him back to my 4-Runner! Another one of you hold up that leg so it stays straight and parallel to the other one.

The group did as ordered and Josh hurried northbound. Kim looked back and found a woman held the injured leg in her lap while she sat on the floor. Her other hand softly stroked the biker's head as she sobbed. The biker glanced past the woman into Kim's eyes and motioned with his head and eyes in appreciation. Kim smiled and nodded back.

Josh slowly pressed the accelerator to the floor and the 4-Runner's modified engine groaned in compliance. The passengers were held back tightly against the seat as the speedometer reached 90 m.p.h. with still room to climb.

The 4-Runner pulled up in front of the hospital as the group carefully pulled the leader from the vehicle. Nurses and a doctor rushed out with a gurney. As the group placed the leader on the gurney the doctor asked what had happened. One of the bikers explained that a deer had ran out in front of the group. Everyone braked and moved right onto the shoulder but the ones up front and to the left were unable to move in time before the collusion. The leader got the worst of the impact and tumbled down the highway.

Josh instructed Kim to drive to the university and he would contact her later. She kissed his cheek, slightly lifted her shirt to display the shiny pistol, and said, "Will you be needing this?" Josh answered, "No honey. I've already got one, but I doubt I'll be needing it."

A deputy showed up at the hospital and questioned everyone. The leader briefly gave an account and as a nurse was about to cart him off to surgery he said, "Wait!" He looked at Josh who stood up and walked over to him. The leader smiled and said, "Well, old man, I guess I owe you another one. Thanks brother." The nurse said, "had that tourniquet not been put on quickly as it was you wouldn't be here." Josh gently patted the leader on the shoulder and said, "You take care, and get healed up. Someday maybe we'll have a cup of coffee or even a beer." The leader smiled and nodded.

A large group of bikers was now in the waiting room. One of them was massively large with giant arms and fists. Josh recognized him as the one he had smashed in the face with the butt of his pistol back at the diner that day. The large man reached out to shake Josh's hand. Josh complied and heard the man growl, "Thank you for helping us." He then smiled. Josh stared at the man's glaring smile to see his front teeth were all shiny metal. Josh said, "You're welcome gentlemen. Sorry about your teeth. Actually, that's a good look for you. You'll look like the grill of a Mac Truck riding down the road." The crowd laughed and nodded as Josh walked out the front door.

The deputy was now seated in his patrol car filling out the report when he glanced at Josh and said, "Hey Josh. Get in and I'll give you a ride." Josh climbed in and shook the deputy's hand. The deputy said, "I did a records check on you and I need to say that I am honored and proud to meet you." Josh replied, "Well thank you. I think it's only appropriate to give all the credit to Sergeant Lou Powel for the fame."

As the deputy drove off, he looked over and said, "That's not the way I heard it." Both men made small talk as they headed toward the university. When the patrol car came to a stop Josh got out. He reached over and shook hands with the deputy who held his hand and said, "Thanks for helping out back there. Those bikers have been causing a lot of trouble in our area. You had won their fear but now you have won their respect. I have a feeling your connection to this area will tame them up a bit." Josh smiled and replied, "Yea. Sometimes we need a kick in the butt and sometimes we simply need a pat on the shoulder." The deputy smiled big and drove off.

Josh texted Kim and went about his duties at the university then later met up with her to drive home. During the ride Josh filled her in with all the details. Kim smiled, kissed him on his cheek, and whispered, "I'm proud of you gentle warrior. You communicated with a gang of rough bikers and broke no bones or knocked out any teeth." She then giggled.

Josh shared in the laughter and explained how the large biker would look like a Mac Truck riding down the road with his shiny new teeth. They went back and forth with jokes and laughter when Josh came upon the dirt road leading up toward the Indian. He slowed the 4-Runner, pulled onto the road, and stopped.

Josh asked, "You think we should try to speak with the Indian?" Kim paused and answered, "Sure. Once we reach the end of the road, we might want to jog up there to save time." Josh proceeded forward but just before the road ended Kim started breathing heavy and appearing anxious. He desperately asked, "Honey! Are you alright?!"

Kim's eyes were opened wide and with deep breaths she gasped, "We need to leave! We need to leave now!" Josh accelerated hard, turned the wheel, and spun the 4-Runner back out of there. When they reached the blacktop road Kim was calmed down and breathing normal. Josh asked, "Are you alright? What happened?"

Kim explained the heaviness in the air was choking her, and all the black snakes slithering along the side of the road didn't help either. Josh hugged Kim and kissed her forehead. As the 4-Runner cruised back toward Timber Creek Josh was puzzled. He had not seen any snakes.

When the couple arrived home, Arrow was eagerly jumping and playfully rolling on her back as Kim and Josh rubbed her tummy. Kim kissed her cheek and asked, "How was your day baby?" Kim's cell phone rang and it was Aunt Maggie. She then asked Josh, "Aunt Maggie wants to know if you could come move a couch for her." Josh nodded and Kim said that he would be right over. Kim disconnected and said, "By the time you get back I'll have some supper ready." Josh replied, "Outstanding." He then tilted his head down and looked up with sinister eyes. Kim giggled and started to run away as Arrow barked and chased after with a wagging tail. Josh caught Kim in the living room and commenced to quick peck like kisses to her neck. Kim wiggled, laughed, and struggled to escape. Then she stopped and both couples' lips met as they gently kissed and caressed each other. Kim separated her lips from Josh and with heavy breaths said, "You better get going mister, or Aunt Maggie's couch isn't going to get moved." Josh smiled and ran out the door.

Josh pulled up in front of Aunt Maggie's and found her sitting outside on the porch. He approached with a friendly greeting and Maggie said, "Good afternoon Joshua. Please, sit with me." Josh sat down as Maggie poured them a cup of tea from the vintage tea pot resting on the table. She then said, "So, Joshua. Entertain this inquisitive old woman about what is new in your and Kim's life. I am much pleased that you purchased the Miller residence and have remained close to our family."

Josh filled in Maggie although he was doubtful that he had told her anything new. She spoke with Kim often on the telephone and during routine visits. He had a feeling something else was on her mind. After several minutes of nodding and sharing kind responses Aunt Maggie cleared her throat and began to explain.

Maggie took a sip of tea and said, "Many generations ago a distinguished white man named William Dougan entered the land and began trading with the Indians. He developed a long-standing relationship with them and was regarded as an honorable and honest man. A Blackfoot Indian Chief gave his daughter, Dyani, to William to be his wife. William later moved with Dyani back toward his people to a nearby homestead and the couple had a daughter they named Dawna. Shortly thereafter once Dawna was weened Dyani died. William was devastated beyond relief. He took Dyani back to her people to be given a proper Indian burial. He then traveled about with baby Dawna who was at that time able to walk.

Indian uproars spiked up everywhere between the Indians and the whites. The couple happened upon an abandoned homestead where everyone had just been slaughtered, well, nearly everyone. As William and Dawna took shelter in a cabin an eighteen-year-old woman appeared out of a camouflaged hole in the ground. The woman's name was Elizabeth.

As Maggie filled their tea cups she continued. "William and Elizabeth instantly fell in love, quickly married, then settled in the Timber Creek area. Elizabeth raised Dawna as her own and professed that she had birthed her. Dawna had more of an appearance of a white than that of an Indian, so nobody questioned. The truth was forever kept a secret, even to Dawna."

Dawna grew up to be a beautiful charming woman with a spotless reputation. She was an amazing artist and competitive athlete. She could run like a deer as her biological mother. Her biological mother's name Dyani means deer. William and Elizabeth went on to have several more children but Dawna stood out as the leader. Since she was the eldest the others naturally yielded to her positional power.

A local family, the Coopers, had a son named James who went by Jim. Jim met Dawna, fell head over heels in love with her, and asked her to marry him. Jim was a fine strong man also of integrity who happened to be a young aspiring attorney. Dawna was charmed off her feet and the couple quickly became husband and wife. That's how the Coopers started."

Josh's mouth stayed opened as he spoke, "So, Kim, well all of you, are descendants of the Blackfoot Indians?" Maggie chuckled at his surprised response and said, "Yes." Josh asked, "Well, how does Kim, and the rest of you ladies, come up with soft silky blonde hair and bright blue eyes?"

Maggie said, "You get blonde men and blonde women mixed in there then the colors begin to change. Dawna herself had her father's blue eyes. That's how you ended up with your beautiful princess." Maggie laughed and patted Josh's knee.

Josh then asked, "Does anyone else know this?"

Maggie replied, "Only the Indian in the wilderness and me. But I suppose he's long since dead. He'd have to be nearly a hundred and fifty years old by now. I met him when I was a young teenager while horseback riding out there. I got turned around and lost in the thicket. There he appeared upon a majestic white spotted

horse being accompanied by a wolf. I was tired, scared, and thirsty.
He led me to his cabin and gave me water."

Maggie accurately described the Indian, the wolf, and the
cabin as he himself had remembered them. Maggie continued, "The
Indian was old and intriguing. He captivated my attention and told
me many things about my family. He even described Dawna whom
he said was breathtakingly beautiful and the granddaughter of a
brave and powerful Blackfoot Chief. The Indian said he himself was
a member of the Choctaw Tribe and a descendent of the
Lighthorsemen.

He then said something strange." Josh leaned forward. "He
said, someday his people and my people will join together as one
and it will be strong medicine."

Maggie sipped her tea and said, "No one goes near that
wilderness anymore. It's rumored that only a Lighthorsemen is
allowed up there because it is sacred ground. I guess I was allowed
as a guest that day. Many people have disappeared out there in those
woods."

Maggie leaned back and said, "You better get home young
man before your charming wife becomes worried. The couch can
wait for another day." Josh nodded, stood up, thanked Maggie for
the conversation and the tea, then started to leave. Maggie spoke up,
"Joshua, some day when you and Kim are out jogging entice her to
run fast with you. A couple of blocks out increase your run to a
sprint then tell her to run all out. When she starts to lean forward

and leave you behind shout to her, "run girl run!" Then come tell me what happens.

Josh nodded and drove back home and into the arms of Kim who questioned what had taken him so long. As the couple sat down, they prayed and feasted upon a wonderful dinner. Kim was magical with creating fast and healthy meals. She was always kind and open minded except she was very picky about what she and even Josh ate.

When they would dine out and the waitress would ask if they wanted dessert Kim would quickly reply, "No thank you. I need to keep him looking like this for when we get old, he doesn't slow down." Waitresses would always chuckle.

Josh would lean forward and whisper some like, "That's right. You've got dessert ready for me when we get home." Kim would wink and nod with a gentle giggle.

Kim inquired from Josh what all he and Aunt Maggie had to talk about. Josh told her everything Maggie had said with the exception of the bit about challenging Kim to run. He thought he would find that out for himself.

Kim was unaware of most of what Josh had been told by Maggie. She had heard rumor that way back in the generations there was some Indian in their blood line, but Elizabeth was not Indian. The story about adopted Dawna was possible because although all the women were pretty, none had the exceptional beauty of Dawna.

She said she wished someone could have taken a picture but cameras weren't around back them.

That evening found the Starks retiring early as usual. They were always in the bed around 8:30 because they were up at 3:30 to work out five days a week. They would always have what Kim referred to as "play time" before going to sleep. Their newlywed behavior never left them. The weekend mornings were set for their stay in bed and rest, well – actually lengthy romance time. Josh had installed a doggie door for Arrow to go out in the morning so they would not be disturbed.

A couple of weeks went by and found the couple jogging one Saturday morning. They ran by the diner to confirm that all appeared well. Josh led Kim across the road as he shouted out into the field, "Hey Brutus! Let's race!" The massive bull stomped his front hoof and snorted. Kim laughed.

As they came toward the end of their jog and was about two blocks from home Josh asked, "Hey honey. Let's step it up a little and do some sprinting."

Kim smiled, "Okay. Let's do it." The couple took off and as hard and fast as Josh ran it appeared Kim was simply pacing beside him.

He reached full speed and shouted, "Faster! Faster! Faster!"

Kim took off like lightening. She leaned forward and breathed through her mouth and squinted her eyes. Her ponytail stretched completely backward parallel to the ground as she heard

Josh shout, "Run girl run!" Kim's long muscular legs swelled with power and rapidly fired back and forth. Her shapely bottom tightened and mustered her thighs as a finely tuned precision machine. Her feet tapped on the blacktop like a drummer quickly tapping a snare drum. Her hands flattened and fingers extended as her speed got faster and faster. Josh looked like he was standing still as she pulled farther away and left him in the dust. Kim was in total focus with complete concentration on speed. She reached home then turned around to slowly jog back. She not only found Josh nearly a block away trying to catch up but several neighbors standing out on their porches with open mouths in awe.

Little Conrad rode his bike over toward Kim and intently asked, "Mrs. Kim. Are you Wonder Woman?"

Kim laughed and replied, "No sweetie. I used to run fast when I was young. I guess I hadn't forgotten how." Several neighbors walked out to the curb and asked, "What was that?!"

Josh eventually arrived, nearly collapsed in Kim's waiting arms, and with an open mouth and heavy breathing growled, "Wow!!!"

Josh walked by Conrad and gently placed his hand on his head while panting out of breath. Conrad said, "Josh, Mrs. Kim is Wonder Woman, isn't she?"

Josh paused, looked to the side, and answered, "Well, Conrad. She's always been a Wonder Woman to me." Josh and

Kim chuckled then went inside to cool off, drink some water, and talked about the performance.

That Saturday night found Josh, Kim, and Arrow all curled up on the living room couch. The lights were off and several candles danced flames gently back and forth which formed romantic shadows. The seasons at Timber Creek were changing and the evening brought forth a cool breeze. A fire in the fireplace brightened solitude and peacefulness to their living room. A half full wine bottle sparkled upon the table. Josh sat with his back against the side of the couch with his left leg bent against the back with his right foot rested upon the carpeted floor. Kim was softly cuddled between his legs with her back resting gently against his chest as she cradled a glass of wine. A drink of wine, a kiss, a drink of wine, a kiss was the rhythmic motion.

Arrow began to snore and the couple smiled with closed eyes. Josh sat his glass of wine down and gently guided Kim's face toward his. He softly kissed her quivering lips and romantically caressed her cheek. He then felt a tear drop creep upon his hand. He leaned forward as Kim looked with watery eyes and he asked, "Is everything alright honey?"

Kim wiped her eyes and replied, "Things couldn't be better. I'm so happy and content that I am full of tears of joy."

Josh tenderly kissed her, carefully picked up his wife in a cradled manner, carried her slowly up the stairway, and gently placed her upon their bed with the Oklahoma moon smiling above.

Kim's bright blue eyes sparkled in the moon light and gently dripped droplets of joy which slowly streamed down her cheeks. She pulled Josh to her chest and held him close with one hand softly stroking his hair. She looked up to heaven and thanked God for the treasure He had brought her.

Chapter 25

"Conrad"

The next morning when Josh awoke, he found Kim tightly intertwined in his arms. They were both still fully clothed.

The days and weeks turned by like the pages in a beautiful artistic picture book. One day Josh and Kim were returning home from a run and noticed an ambulance and unfamiliar cars at Conrad's house. Conrad sat outside on the front steps with his face in his hands. Occasionally he would wipe away tears as his body partook in a rhythmic pout. Josh and Kim approached and leaned down with Conrad, Josh asked, "What's wrong little buddy?"

Conrad sobbed, "They said they gotta take momma away and put her in the hospital where I can't come. I don't wanna to go to a forester home place.   I can stay home and take care of myself. I've done it lots of times." He then looked up at Kim and sobbed, "Mrs. Kim. Can you beg them to not take momma? I promise not to fuss anymore and I promise not to cry ever again. Mrs. Kim. Can you ask God?"

Kim turned her head, took a breath, and replied, "Conrad. Sometimes people have to go to the hospital so the doctors can make them well."

Conrad looked down at the ground and said, "Momma told me she needs to go to heaven soon. She's real bad sick. But she said she will save a place for me in heaven for when I get really old and come to join her." Conrad's heart then broken open and out flowed a river of tears. Josh pulled him close and leaned his cheek against Conrad. Kim got up and walked inside the house.

Kim entered the house with her head tilted down, her glaring eyes squinted, and her hands tightened on her hips. Everyone inside froze and looked at her. Kim slowly spoke, "There is a little boy sitting outside crying and saying his momma is going to die. Can one of you explain to me why he is sitting out there all alone?!" One of the women started to speak but Kim quickly turned toward Conrad's mom and said, "Marla. You and I have been friends ever since we were little girls. We used to have sleep overs, played soccer together, swam in the creek, we even learned how to drive together. Now I find out you are on your death bed and you don't reach out to me? I love you like a sister Marla. Why?"

The other woman started to speak again but the stern stare from Kim brought her to silence. Marla sobbed and replied, "I'm so, so sorry Kim. I was so ashamed for how I've failed horribly in life. I didn't want anyone to know. Please forgive me."

Kim stepped forward, bent down on her knees, and as she held Marla's hand said, "Marla, you don't need my forgiveness. You simply need to forgive yourself. If God can forgive you then you can forgive yourself of anything."

Kim stood up and asked the younger woman, who had remained silent, for a card and a pen. Kim wrote on the card and said to Marla, "Here is my, Josh's, and our home phone number. Please call us at any time if you need anything." She then handed the card to Marla.

Kim then looked into the faces of everyone present, took a breath, and said, "One last thing. I want Conrad."

The one anxious woman in the room was finally able to talk and began explaining to Kim that the Foster Care Program does not work that way.   As she barked about requirements and applications.

Kim cut her off and asked, "Lady, is Marla able to make decisions for herself or is she incapacitated?"

The younger woman spoke up, "Yes. Marla is legally able to make decisions." She then gave a nod of approval with a gentle smile.

Kim up spoke, "Good."

Kim looked straight into Marla's eyes and asked, "Can I have him?"

Marla reached her arms out to embrace Kim with crying eyes, shaking shoulders, and said, "Yes, yes, yes. Thank you!"

Kim had been in Conrad's life since he was born. Marla and Conrad's father had never been married. He skipped town when he found out Marla was pregnant. After a few years of struggling with being a single mom Marla met the beast, Sam, whom she married. Sam by default became Conrad's step-father. He didn't start out as a beast but quickly evolved into one once he lost his career to a D.U.I. and the dove full force into a bottle.

Sam would strike Marla with the palm of his hand on the side of her head to keep from leaving marks. Marla was afraid to call the police in fear that Sam would come after her and Conrad in retaliation. It became easier for her to hide inside herself and be quiet. And that's what she did day in and day out. She shut out the entire world except with occasional openings to Conrad. Now Marla has an inoperable brain tumor with little time left in this world.

Kim turned around and walked out the door as Josh stood up with a puzzled expression. She grabbed his hand, walked down the steps out of hearing range of Conrad, quickly turned to face Josh, and began explaining to Josh what had happened. She then held Josh's hands and with a begging plea asked, "Can we?"

Josh hugged her, kissed her on the cheek, and whispered into her ear. Kim jumped into his arms, wrapped her legs around his waist, and cried tears of joy. Conrad watched in surprise.

Kim and Josh approached Conrad and asked him if he wanted to come live with them. Conrad jumped up and tightly squeezed Josh's neck. After a round of sobs and kisses Kim took Conrad by the hand and escorted him into the house where they packed clothing and necessaries.

The three departed Conrad's house and shortly thereafter entered the Stark residence. Conrad's eyes bugged out, his mouth stayed open, and he stood in awe. He couldn't believe he had his own bathroom that even had a shower.

Then Josh got down on one knee and explained about house rules. Conrad intently nodded in agreement as Kim stood by in audience. At the end Josh said, "And the most important rule is, always knock before you enter a closed door." Kim turned her head and smiled.

Kim immediately made several phone calls to make the legal arrangements. Their attorney took care of everything and after just a few days Josh and Kim were the adopted parents of Conrad.

Marla was taken to the hospital that day and never returned home. She would pass away after two weeks. Kim and Josh saw to it that Conrad visited his mother every day, even the day she slipped into a coma and never awoke. The three kneeled down at the foot of the hospital bed and prayed until Marla took her last breath. Conrad was able to feel contentment that his mother's pain was all gone and she was in heaven with God.

Now Saturday nights included the Powell family and three members of the Starks, well, and Arrow too. Conrad got the home he had thought that only dreams were made of. Kim got her son whom she had secretly prayed for. She cherished him with all her heart and smothered him with kisses. Josh and Conrad had long man to son talks and even workouts together. By the way, Josh was by no means neglected because of Kim's motherly duties. Kim made sure their nightly "play time" was still on the schedule right after reading and praying with their son. Life was now complete and Timber Creek was peaceful

Chapter 26
"The Visit"

Josh and Kim were in the kitchen early the next Sunday morning looking out the sliding glass door at the sun coming up to shine a friendly greeting when Kim asked, "have you seen Arrow?" Josh stood up, looked out the back door and shouted Arrow's name.

Kim walked out of the kitchen and saw that Arrow was laying down in the hallway facing the front door with her head down. Kim walked over, bent down, and asked, "Arrow, are you okay baby?" There came a knock on the door.

Kim opened the door and there stood a Marine in uniform, holding a duffel bag in his left hand. He had a familiar face and carried a strong and majestic stature. Kim saw that he was wearing sergeant stripes upon his shoulders and several metals decorated his left breast. He spoke, "good morning ma'am. I'm Clint Stark." Kim's eyes filled with tears as she turned to shout, "Josh!"

Josh stood in the doorway with his hands on his hips. His eyes turned warm and his lips closed tight.

The Marine dropped the duffel bag, came to attention, rendered a reverent salute, and said, "hello dad."

The three embraced, naturally with Arrow's tail wagging in approval, and all stood in silence with only sobs and tears. In softness Josh cleared his voice to speak - but that is a whole other story.